With Grace

Samantha Wayland

Also by Samantha Wayland

Destiny Calls
Fair Play (Hat Trick #1)
Two Man Advantage (Hat Trick #2)
End Game (Hat Trick #3)
Crashing the Net (Crashing #1)
Home & Away
Out of Her League
Checking It Twice (Crashing #2)
Take a Shot
A Merry Little (Hat Trick) Christmas (Hat Trick #4)
Breaking Out
Traded Out
Poetry in Motion
Changing the Rules (Crashing #3)

With Grace

Published by Loch Awe Press
P.O. Box 5481
Wayland, MA 01778

ISBN 978-1-940839-17-2

Edited by Meghan Miller
Cover Art by Ben Ellis, Tall Story Design

Dedication

For two fabulous women whose humor, intelligence and friendship I will always cherish. Karen: You helped me return to writing after a long hiatus, for which I cannot express enough gratitude. I'm proud of and inspired by how you followed your heart, even if it was all the way to Oregon. And Kari: You had no idea what you started when you said, "I think you'll like this book." I wish my first signing could be at Muffins n' Cream. Thank you.

Acknowledgements

First, foremost and without exception I would like to thank The Quirky Ladies. This book, these characters, and this author wouldn't exist without their contributions and support.

Chapter One

Grace Anderson loved her job. Perched at the hostess stand, she surveyed Valentine's, one of the hottest bistros in Boston's South End, and smiled. Everything was exactly as it should be. Candles in cut glass and cleverly hidden light fixtures bathed the room in a warm glow. Ella Fitzgerald's sultry voice wove through the murmur of intimate conversations, while tempting scents from the kitchen stirred the appetite. It was decadent. Indulgent.

Perfect.

Settling back on her stool, Grace relaxed and let her eyes return to what she enjoyed watching most of all. While the job had a lot going for it, the single greatest benefit was that she had plenty of opportunity to ogle Mark Valentine, even if she often chastised herself for doing so.

Owner and head chef of Valentine's, Mark was her boss, her friend, and her favorite innocent flirtation. Well, maybe *innocent* wasn't exactly the right word. They were strictly friends, but the fantasies that ran through her mind were most certainly not friendly. Or, rather, they were *very* friendly. Who could resist those broad shoulders? He was tall and lean, and his shapeless chef's jacket couldn't disguise the muscle definition hidden beneath. His dark hair curled against his crisp white collar, begging for her to run her hands through it and let the ringlets wrap around her fingers.

Even ignoring his considerable physical assets, he was a joy to watch as he worked the room. He came out of the kitchen when he could, and by the time he finished visiting each table, every one of their customers would have a personal connection with Mark—and to Valentine's.

A pang of something shockingly like jealousy struck her when Mark turned his attention to the attractive woman at table nineteen. Under the glare of his full-wattage charm, the woman's eyes sparkled and a blush moved across her cheeks.

Lucky lady. Grace loved to be on the receiving end of that smile. Even seeing it from across the room, directed at someone else, it sent a shiver down her spine and forced her to clamp her knees together before tightly crossing her legs.

What was it about Mark?

He had an uncanny ability to attract people. Take the nice-looking man who wasn't bothered in the least by his date gazing at Mark like he was the best thing on the menu. Or the older woman at table ten who had giggled like a schoolgirl when he'd bent to kiss her hand. Not a wonder why *she* was a regular.

With few exceptions, women wanted him. It could be in truth or in their fantasies, but it was real. It would have been threatening to the men around him, perhaps, except that men wanted him just as much—as a friend to go to the game with, or for their own, more private, fantasies. Everybody felt some kind of attraction when they met Mark.

Grace was no exception, though their relationship was purely platonic. Recrossing her legs, she was forced to amend that thought. She wasn't immune to the sexuality that practically oozed out of him. She wasn't dead, after all.

Being the hostess at Valentine's was the perfect job for her. When she wasn't at work, she was finishing her PhD in nineteenth-century literature at Boston University. Someday, she'd teach, lecturing about the rampant and fiercely suppressed sexuality of the Victorian era and how it manifested in some of the most famous and romantic books ever written. But for now, she attended classes during the day and, since Valentine's served only dinner, worked in the evenings for Mark. When things got slow toward the end of the night, he'd often encourage her to work on her reading at the hostess stand.

Recently, though, there hadn't been as much time for that, as she'd accepted more and more of the responsibility of running the front of the house. She loved rising to the challenge of meeting Mark's standards. Valentine's was his baby. He lived and breathed it. Every ounce of its success was owed to his talent in the kitchen and his business acumen. It meant a lot that he trusted her to look after the bar, the floor, and the door while he focused on the kitchen. He obsessed about everything being right, and now he trusted her to do that for him. And she did, every night, without fail.

At table twenty-three, Mark whispered into the ear of a beautiful woman seated with her equally stunning friend. Her response made him throw his head back and laugh, the sound reaching across the room. It was impossible not to respond. To smile.

Shaking her head, Grace turned her back and focused on the reservation book. Her awareness of Mark diminished, but only so much. He was still behind her, the barest tickle at the base of her spine. She knew he'd end up at her side eventually. He'd claim he was checking on things, which might be true, but he wouldn't be able to resist making one of his outrageous comments. The man would flirt with furniture if he thought he could get a reaction. And god knew she couldn't stop herself from giving him one.

She should have been appalled by some of the things he'd said to her, the way he made it his mission to see her blush. Not that there was much challenge there, given her fair complexion. But the truth was, she loved it. The double entendres were sexy, sometimes suggestive, but never lewd. His teasing looks were hot, if harmless. He had no way of knowing how he filled her head with the most delicious images. Or how many times he'd sent her home with her panties damp from the daydreams he'd inspired.

It worried her a little that one of these days, her boyfriend, Philip, might figure out that her frequent state of arousal when she got home from work in the evenings wasn't all about him.

She shoved aside a pang of guilt. *Screw that.* Philip didn't believe he was the only sexy man on Earth, and he didn't expect her to believe he was, either. Why should she feel guilty? Mark had no idea what he did to her, how easily he worked her up, and she would *never* be unfaithful to Philip, so there was no harm. Mark was a fantasy, a tasty treat to dream about. Philip was her scrumptious reality.

Speaking of...she checked her watch to find it was eight thirty. Philip had called a half hour before to say he would soon be leaving his office at the small downtown law firm where he worked. His promise to stop in and kiss the woman of his dreams on the way home had made her stomach flutter. *The woman of his dreams.* Imagine that. Sometimes Grace couldn't believe she'd found him.

She loved Philip completely. She'd never felt this way about any man before. Never been more sure that she wanted to spend her life with someone. They'd started to do things that signaled a longer commitment, like planning next spring's vacation, even though it was only late summer now. Like last night, when Philip had hinted about how much easier life would be if she moved into his apartment.

She wanted to move in with Philip. And not because of convenience, though his place was four blocks from Valentine's and not far from school. She wanted to move in with Philip because she wanted to spend as much time with him as she could. Between her classes, his long hours at the office, and her working nights, there was never enough time.

She might bring up the whole moving-in thing tonight, after she'd unveiled her little surprise.

Just thinking about it made her heart pound. What if it didn't work? What if Philip was horrified? Her stomach roiled thinking about it. She reminded herself to be optimistic. It might just turn out as she hoped. Or better.

The image of Philip Marsten, attorney-at-law, abandoning control and tossing her on the bed burst unbidden into her mind. Oh god, *please.* That's what she wanted. Uninhibited passion. Their sex life was great, but she wanted more. And she had a plan to get it.

The possibilities made her nipples pebble until they hurt.

Holy smokes, she needed to get a grip. Hunching her shoulders, she leaned over the reservation book, hoping the long fall of her hair would disguise her flushed face.

Mark's laughter rang out, startling her, and for a moment she imagined *Mark* tossing her on the bed as Philip watched. Or, better yet, as Philip joined in. Sucking in a deep breath, she grasped the edge of the hostess desk until her knuckles turned white. The very idea was outrageous. And ridiculously hot. She could feel her body swelling. Begging.

The fantasy was delicious, but one that, regardless of how things went with Philip tonight, she highly doubted she would ever share with him. More the pity.

As if conjured from her thoughts, Philip strode through the door.

"Hi!" she said, sliding from the stool and standing, her heart doing the funny dance it always did when she first saw him. She'd almost gotten used to it, but was smart enough to cherish each flutter anyway. His eyes sparkled when he saw her. She loved the contrast of his mahogany skin against his starched white shirt. Admired how his chalk-striped wool suit flattered his build, emphasizing his broad shoulders, flat belly, and lean hips.

"Hello, beautiful." Philip's smooth, deep voice made her shiver, each and every hair on the back of her neck standing up.

She lifted her face, expecting his usual quick kiss on her cheek.

Her breath caught in her throat when his hand slid behind her neck, tilting her head back before capturing her mouth with his. She let her eyes drift closed when his lips brushed across hers softly, rubbing and enticing her, his tongue gently teasing her mouth open for a taste.

As quickly as he'd approached, he retreated. She opened her eyes slowly, savoring his touch, taking in his smile and heavy-lidded gaze, all of which spoke of the promise of more. She sucked in a lungful of brain-restoring air when he drew his hand from under her hair and brushed it down her arm.

"What was that for?" she asked.

Philips raised one brow. "What can I say? You look good enough to eat."

Her heart sped up. "I was just thinking about you, but the real thing is way better."

"Good. What time do you think you'll be home tonight?" His

voice was soft. Intimate. There was no mistaking the direction of his thoughts.

A burst of confidence rushed through her. Philip never put his needs on display, but tonight he seemed different. More aggressive. She knew without a doubt *this* Philip was going to love her surprise.

Arousal spread through her body like smoke filling a bottle. She pitched her voice low, so as not to be heard by the nearest tables. "I'm supposed to lock up tonight."

Philip moved closer, dropping his head so his cheek brushed along hers before pulling back. When his nostrils flared, she wondered if he could smell her arousal. He didn't say anything, just rocked his hips forward, pressing the full length of his erection against her hip. Words were not necessary.

"I'll come home as soon as I can." The words bursting from her unbidden.

Philip's laugh was the sexiest thing she'd ever heard.

"Good."

Jesus. Who was this Philip? And when could she rip his clothes off?

Grace and Philip were going to light the front of his restaurant on fire.

Mark studied the couple surreptitiously, filled with a mixture of desire and raw envy.

As was his habit, he'd been chatting up each table, slowly working his way to Grace. He didn't *need* to visit the front of the house every night—Grace could handle whatever needed handling and she wouldn't hesitate to call for him if it were ever needed. But he couldn't resist her. Her smile. Her face. He wanted to touch the silky strands of her dark chestnut hair where they lay against her back. To brush his hand down the soft curve of her cheek and over her delicate, pert nose. Her skin was like milk, a hint of pink roses warming her pale cheeks.

Well, pink roses—until he said something to make her blush,

and then she was all American Beauty. He would watch in fascination as the deep red stain moved across her skin. Not just on her cheeks, but up the long column of her neck and, if her blouse was unbuttoned just a little, sweeping across her chest, warming the lightly freckled skin above her breasts.

It drove him bat-shit crazy that she hid her lush body under tidy silk blouses and tailored slacks. Didn't she know they only served to emphasize her long legs and the glorious curves of her breasts and hips? And that ass...

As a rule, he wasn't usually such a complete idiot. But in this case, he really was. Anyone could see she was in love with Philip.

Of course, that was the other problem, Mark thought with something between a laugh and a grimace. Philip. Mark couldn't remember if he'd ever been this attracted to a man. There was something about Philip that just flipped his switch.

It had been years since he'd had a male lover—not for any particular reason, other than that starting a new business had pretty much killed his social life in general. The few women he'd found time for hadn't been serious or lasted long. Valentine's had become his job, his hobby, and his life partner all rolled into one.

Until a couple of months ago, it hadn't bothered him in the slightest. Still didn't much—he loved his work. His restaurant. He'd busted his ass to get it where it was and he was damn proud. He still had so many things he wanted to do, like opening for lunch and Sunday brunch. Once he'd conquered that, he might like to open another restaurant. But that was way off in the future. For now, Valentine's was more than enough.

Only, Mark thought as he rubbed his hand over the hollow ache beneath his sternum, *these days it wasn't enough at all.*

Sighing, he forced his attention back to table twenty-two.

He'd kept half an eye on Grace from the moment he'd come out of the kitchen. She always watched him work the room and he always wondered about her smile while she did. That look in her eye. He'd learned to tune it out after the third or fourth time a patron was forced to repeat a question because he'd been so zoned out of the conversation and zoned into Grace.

15

He'd seen Philip arrive. Had watched them kiss and wondered if something was up. Philip didn't usually go for public displays of affection while Grace was working. Or ever, from what Mark could tell.

Mark was only an arm's length away from where Grace and Philip stood, quietly murmuring to each other. He barely said a word to the couple at the last table, instead transfixed by Philip's cock tenting the front of his suit pants. When Philip pressed against Grace, Mark almost walked away from his guests mid-sentence. Thank god his chef's jacket covered a multitude of sins, including the biggest sin of all—his growing erection pressing against the front of his kitchen pants.

Philip and Grace were just so hot. So fucking beautiful. He couldn't decide who he wanted more. He could imagine himself sinking into Grace's welcoming wet heat just as easily as he could envision himself pounding into Philip's ass. Or his mouth. Or have Philip take his ass. Or...

Oooookay. Time to stop that line of thought before the nice lady sitting in front of him noticed what he hid not ten inches from her head.

He ended his chat as quickly and politely as possible, and moved to the hostess stand just as Grace and Philip pulled apart and Philip hid his gorgeous erection behind the tall desk. Neither of them seemed to notice Mark.

He took another moment just to look. To enjoy them. He respected them individually and as a couple. Counted them as friends. He admired their beauty and their commitment to each other.

And, goddamn it, it absolutely wasn't his style to interfere in something like that. It just wasn't cool and never would be. But even knowing this, he couldn't resist stealing a moment with them.

When had he become such a complete masochist? So stupid.

Easing up behind Grace, he noticed how her hands clenched the stool seat by her thighs, her arms locked to her sides. A rocket about to go off.

Philip was a lucky man.

Reaching out, Mark put his hand high on Grace's back, and let his thumb travel over the soft skin where her neck and shoulder met. He turned to Philip. "Am I going to have to get the kitchen fire extinguisher to put you two out?"

Touching Grace hadn't seemed to pull her from her daze, but his comment made her jump. He ducked his head, his lips to her ear. "Don't even try to deny it."

He hadn't meant for his voice to be that husky, but when his lips had brushed the shell of her ear, his throat had practically closed off. He was choking on temptation.

Grace snapped her head around, her mouth open with surprise and protest. They were so close their noses bumped, their lips only a breath apart, and for one electric second time stopped.

Oh boy.

Mark's need to taste her sent a spike of desire to his cock so powerful it was a wonder that it didn't buckle his knees. It took every ounce of willpower he possessed not to move the fraction of an inch it would take to bring their lips together. Instead, he clamped down on his almost uncontrollable urge to kiss this beautiful woman. The moment drew out, the possibility hanging in the air around them.

Slowly, reality returned to his arousal-soaked brain.

Blinking, he stared down at Grace's upturned face. Her eyes were half closed, her lips parted as if waiting for his kiss. Her long lashes threw shadows across the coveted wash of color staining her cheeks.

Mark thought he could have gazed at her like this for hours. He *wanted* to.

Which was not smart.

Then again, if he were smart, he'd be back in the kitchen minding his own business. Or, at the very least, in the employee bathroom, trying to relieve some of the pressure in his balls. Not rubbing noses and almost lips with his hostess—and right in front of her devoted boyfriend, to boot.

When Grace's eyes lifted to his, Mark hesitated to turn away. He didn't want to look at Philip. Dreaded it. His friend was going to be pissed. Philip might not go for public displays of affection, but public displays of possessiveness had never been lacking.

Mark told himself he'd have to accept the consequences of his impulsive actions. Swallowing hard, he met Philip's steady gaze.

Philip's dark eyes were unfocused under heavy lids, his skin warm with a hint of flush.

Mark blinked. That wasn't right. That couldn't be right.

Philip looked...*turned on.*

Mark had to be mistaken. He'd never asked, of course, but since Philip practically screamed *straight guy*, he'd never thought to. What if...

He turned to Grace. Her expression was thoughtful as she glanced between the two men, lingering on Philip's face. Goddamn, she saw it too. Mark didn't know if this was good news or bad, but at least he no longer believed wishful thinking had taken over his ability to reason.

For the first time in more years than he could count, he didn't have one fucking clue what to do or say. His tongue, his entire nervous system, was locked up in a twist of need and rampant arousal.

The explosion of twenty pounds of his beautiful and expensive china crashing to the floor of the kitchen snapped Mark from his paralysis.

Sweet Jesus, someone was getting a bonus!

Gratefully seizing the excuse, he barely managed to mumble "excuse me" before spinning on his heel and bolting for the kitchen, actively resisting the urge to run.

Someone very wise had once commented on the value of a well-timed and hasty retreat. Smart man.

When the dishes shattered in the kitchen, Philip jerked his gaze from Mark and back to Grace. The questions he saw in her eyes were not ones he could answer.

Philip didn't understand what had just happened. All he knew was that watching Mark and Grace together had sent a thunderbolt through his already highly aroused body.

Damn, he had so many desires. So many needs. *Too* many needs. Grace was a good girl, a gentle woman who couldn't possibly understand the fantasies floating through his brain. He didn't always understand them himself. All he knew was that watching Mark almost kiss Grace had turned him on. And not just a little. He hadn't been able to tear his eyes away.

Then when Mark had looked at him like that. Holy shit. His heart had rolled over in his chest while more blood had rushed to his already aching cock.

He was straight. He was sure of it. Well, pretty sure. Okay, he'd always been straight in the past. That much was definite fact.

But *damn*, there was something about Mark Valentine.

Philip knew and accepted that he had a strong voyeuristic bent. He had long fantasized about watching Grace fuck someone else. But he also knew he could be possessive. Not jealous, not mistrusting, just...possessive. He was smart enough to know the voyeur and the possessor wouldn't play nicely if they were to meet on any playground other than in his fertile imagination.

Since meeting Mark, he'd been the only one to costar with Grace in Philip's fantasies. More than once he'd discovered himself staring into space, imagining Grace's long legs wrapped around Mark's hard flanks, the muscles in Mark's ass bunching as he thrust into Grace over and over.

Okay, perhaps he shouldn't be dwelling on those images while Grace, the woman he loved and hoped to spend the rest of his life with, was staring at him like he was an alien being. *Shit.* After their promising greeting a few minutes before, he'd been so hopeful about what might happen tonight when she got home. Now she was probably wondering what the hell was wrong with him. God knew, he wondered the same.

Clearing his throat, he met her eyes again.

19

"You okay?" she asked, sounding concerned.

He tried for a reassuring smile. "Yeah, sure. I'm fine. Why do you ask?"

Grace shrugged a little. "I don't know. You spaced out for a second there. You're not mad at Mark, are you?"

"No. Why would I be?"

"Because he just...I don't know...nuzzled me?" Grace's mouth twisted with amusement. "He likes to tease me. Apparently, he likes to tease you, too."

Philip nodded. He supposed if he still lived on planet Earth, that might have been upsetting to him. But now he lived on the planet where Mark was sexy and Philip was confused. He didn't know the name of this planet.

He shook his head. He needed to get a grip. He needed to focus on Grace. Forget Mark.

He nodded again. Right. That was the plan. Focus on Grace. Ignore Mark. So what if Mark was...beautiful?

He shook his head. No. Not beautiful. Men weren't beautiful. What would make him think of such a word to describe a man?

Shit. This wasn't helping. *Focus on Grace. Focus on Grace.*

If Grace thought it strange that he stood there nodding and shaking his head without uttering a word, she was kind enough not to mention it. He needed to snap out of it. It was time to go.

Leaning over her desk, he kissed her gently. "I'll see you at home later?"

Grace touched his cheek. "Of course." She smiled. "I have a surprise for you."

His heart jerked in his chest. "You do?" He wondered at the flush creeping back across her cheeks. He also wondered if he would have to walk around with a full-blown erection for the next four hours until she came home.

"I do," she promised. "I'm guessing you haven't eaten yet. Are you hungry?"

He smiled. "More than you know."

Grace quirked one brow. "Oh really? And what are you in the mood for?"

Sexy banter was new ground for them. He was delighted, eager to continue. He leaned in for another kiss, but was interrupted by the arrival of Courtney, the bartender on duty. She stopped beside Grace, oblivious to the sparks flying around her.

"Hey, Grace. Hey, Philip." She held out a bag of take-out, which Philip accepted automatically, his gaze never leaving Grace's face. "That's your dinner. Grace ordered it for you earlier. I figured I'd bring it over, since I need to talk to Grace."

Grace turned to Courtney with her professional smile firmly in place. Philip was sure he was the only person who could see her impatience. She smoothed a hand down her hair, as if their teasing might have mussed it.

He smiled to himself. He'd get to that later.

"Thanks, Courtney. What's up?" Grace asked with remarkable composure.

"Some guy is on the phone about a flash drive he lost last night?"

"Oh...right. We found one. Can you get a number? I don't want him to come all the way here if it's not his. I'll find it and call him back."

"Sure. I'll let him know."

Grace nodded absently. Philip tried not to smile at her inability to stop darting him looks. She was distracted. He was delighted.

Courtney looked between them, realization dawning on her face. Without another word, she turned and hurried back to her customers at the bar.

The moment they were alone, he leaned in to kiss her again.

Grace laughed, pushing him back. "Oh, no you don't. Go. Before we make another scene."

He tried his best pout, but it didn't work and she ushered him out. Just the touch of her hands as she urged him across the entryway and through the door was enough to set his pulse pounding, all the blood headed south.

Yep, he thought as he hit the sidewalk. This hard-on wasn't going *anywhere*.

Damn.

Chapter Two

It was a beautiful night. The late summer heat had faded, and the sea air coming in off the harbor ran cool fingers down the back of Mark's neck. This was the kind of night he craved all winter, when it was so damn cold he had to run from Valentine's, dashing through the frozen South End streets all the way to his car or wherever he was going.

But not tonight. Tonight, he and his lovely companion were walking along at a leisurely pace, enjoying the night air and their own thoughts.

He snuck a peek at Grace. He didn't often escort her home after closing, since he rarely left Valentine's with the rest of the staff. Normally, he chose to stay in his office to prepare the deposit so he could swing by the bank on the way home. If no one was headed Grace's way, he would leave Valentine's just long enough to get her to the subway or Philip's door and then return. Tonight, though, he'd rushed everyone out, volunteering to walk with Grace before anyone else had a chance.

He knew it was stupid, but he'd been desperate for a few minutes with her. Five minutes, four short blocks to walk by her side, offering himself as protection and companionship. The breeze lifted her hair, the tips dancing across her shoulders as she turned her face to the wind, each strand a tendril of shiny silk in contrast to the creamy skin of her neck.

He imagined burying his face there. The taste of her beneath his lips. The dream was joy, the reality agony.

She caught him watching her before he could turn and stare down the street. The flash of awareness in her deep green eyes was like a song, calling him, his libido and his heart straining at the leash to answer.

He clutched the leash tighter. She was not his to have.

"I noticed you shut off the lights when we left. Are you not going back tonight?" she asked, her voice, like this walk, easy.

23

Mellow.

His eyes met hers briefly before he gazed down the street again, squinting as if he was searching for something in the far distance. "No. I'm headed home."

"Oh. You didn't have to escort me if you have your car back in the lot."

"I walked to work today. It was such a nice morning and I was hoping tonight would be exactly like this. It's the best kind of night, you know?"

She smiled. "I do know. I was just thinking the same thing."

He nodded, not surprised. He and Grace were often on the same page. Politics, life, friends. Philip.

In very little time, they arrived at the entrance to Philip's building. Grace pulled her key from her book-laden messenger bag and turned to lean back against the door. "Thanks for walking me home."

"You're welcome," he said quietly. His body blocked her from the street. He was struck how very like the end of a date this felt. Why was that? Oh. Probably because he wanted to kiss her good night.

Which wasn't good. She was standing on Philip's front stoop, for crying out loud, the security camera pointed right at his face. Not that it was really the issue.

"Good night." Her voice was low. The intimacy, the potential of the moment washed over him.

He didn't move, didn't look away. "Good night."

Forcing herself to turn away from Mark and put her key in the lock, Grace stepped back to let the door swing open. When her shoulders and butt came up against the hard wall of Mark's chest and hips, a thrill ran all the way down her body. She gave herself a moment to absorb the feel of him, the warmth and tension, before darting through the door and hauling ass for the stairs.

Don't look back. Don't look back. She shouldn't even think about checking if that had been a rather impressive erection nestled against her ass.

She made it up four steps before she gave in, stopping to look over her shoulder. He stood with his hand wrapped around the door, as if he'd reached for her and caught it instead. He didn't move. Didn't look away.

He was beautiful. The complete package. His scent, his wide shoulders, those deep blue eyes that could go from piercing to smoldering in a blink. He'd probably look hot in a burlap sack, but his faded jeans and white T-shirt clung to all the best parts of him in all the best ways. Something low in her body clenched when she dragged her eyes over his thighs and hips lovingly hugged in soft blue denim.

God, she wanted to run down those stairs and launch herself at him.

Which meant it was time to go.

When the security system began to beep, protesting how long the door had been held open, she turned and fled up the stairs. It was cowardly, but also smart. She shouldn't be so tempted by Mark, damn it.

Five flights later, she was done congratulating herself on her ability to resist temptation and was instead berating herself for not taking the elevator.

Letting herself into Philip's apartment, she stopped just inside the door to listen. She'd been so preoccupied with Mark, she'd forgotten about her surprise for Philip.

When she heard the shower running, she smiled. Perfect.

Dropping her bag next to the breakfast bar, she kicked off her low heels and hurried into the bedroom. Stocking footed, she padded around the room to turn on the small bedside lamp and shut off the rest of the lights.

A lot rode on this experiment. In so many ways, Philip was terrific. They never ran out of things to talk about, always found excuses to touch and be close. The sex was good—no one ever went to sleep disappointed.

But there was something missing.

Okay, maybe not missing. Lacking? *Ouch.* No. Not lacking. That sounded horrible and the sex was good. She had orgasms. On two occasions, she'd had more than one.

Well, *that* was just ridiculous. Counting orgasms? What was wrong with her? Why wasn't regular, decent, nice sex that resulted in good, solid orgasms enough? She should be content.

But she wasn't. Nice was nice, but she wanted mind-blowing. She wanted rough, wild, uninhibited bouts of fucking. She and Philip *made love* all the time. Every time. They had mastered expressing their love through the physical, which was wonderful. But what about expressing their lust? Their need? She craved something more carnal that would sate her body. She'd never been in love before, so maybe this was the price. A lifetime of regular, nice sex in exchange for her fantasies.

A lump of disappointment settled in her chest.

Consistent nights of one orgasm before bed in exchange for hours of exploration. Of needs met and exceeded. She was curious about so many things and she wanted Philip to be the one to appease her curiosity. What would it be like to have Philip fill her virgin ass, to stretch into her where no one had ever taken her? As far as she knew, Philip didn't even know it was an option. She hoped to enlighten him.

Stripping off her work clothes, she paused for a moment to study her reflection in the mirror over the dresser.

She'd bought the sapphire-blue satin merry widow on a whim weeks ago and stashed it under her bed, wondering if she would have the courage to wear it. She didn't doubt she looked sexy as hell—the corset was pulled tight so that her firm breasts were pushed up high and round, the tops of her areolas peeking out in pale contrast to the dark satin beneath. The garters were attached to sheer black stockings that matched the bits of black satin trim and the corset ribbons. She turned to make sure the seams up the back of the stockings were straight before sliding her thong down and off. She had a moment of total insecurity when she looked at herself.

She'd shaved so that only one tiny little strip of hair

remained. It looked kind of weird to her, but she'd been assured by people who claimed to know that *weird* wasn't going to be the word on Philip's mind when he saw it.

Okay, so what if the word is repulsive?

She shook herself, remembering how he'd pressed his erection against her, right in the middle of Valentine's. She had to believe he wanted this as much as she did.

They'd both been so turned on, in a room full of people. Brave, new, wonderful territory for them. It hadn't helped, or maybe it had helped a lot, that she'd given in to the impulse to wear the corset under her work clothes—an impulse that she'd been afraid she'd regret if the damn thing proved to be too uncomfortable. It hadn't. Instead, the anticipation had been building for hours.

Hurrying over to the closet, Grace dug to find the shoes she'd stashed there this morning. She almost never wore heels so high. How anyone could wear them for hours on end, day after day, was a mystery to her. But for her purposes tonight, they were perfect. She didn't plan to be on her feet for long.

She was just stepping into the shoes when the shower shut off. Dashing to the dresser one last time, she added a fresh brush of mascara and some eyeliner, but purposely left her mouth bare. She had plans to use her mouth in ways with which lipstick would only interfere.

A final bolt of nerves shot through her, but she forced them back and moved to the open carpet between the four-poster king-sized bed and the bathroom door. With one hand on her cocked hip and other tucked behind her, she waited for the bathroom door to open. Seconds seemed like hours.

She used those hours to chant her new mantra.

Please let him jump my bones. Please let him jump my bones. Please let him jump my bones.

Philip was tucking a tiny towel around his hips when he strode through the door. He looked up and stopped in his tracks.

How had she ever doubted he would go for this? Nothing could be more satisfying than the look on Philip's face. He was completely stunned, his mouth hanging open, his eyes wide.

She took advantage of his immobility to appreciate the view. His body was hard, tight. The drops of water running from his short hair slid over his rich dark skin, clinging to his smooth pecs and the hard ridges of his stomach.

His body made her mouth water. It fascinated her. There wasn't an inch of it she didn't want to touch. To lick.

Although at that precise moment, she was mostly focused on the erection blooming behind the little towel, tenting it outward at a rather flattering rate.

Nice.

With effort, she dragged her gaze back to Philip's face. Satisfaction purred through her while she waited for his eyes to finish their long trip back up over her body. She knew the moment he noticed the little strip of hair covering her mons, delighting in how his lips parted, as if in wonder. In awe. She took a deep breath and watched his eyes zoom upward to her breasts and her peek-a-boo nipples, everything in his expression begging them to pop free.

When his eyes finally met hers, another bolt of nervousness hit her, although now it was for an entirely different reason.

Her tongue poked out to wet her suddenly dry lips. He flinched in response.

"Surprise," she said, her lips quirking.

Surprise? *Surprise?* If the blood from his brain weren't dropping to his cock so damn fast he felt dizzy, he might have had the wherewithal to find that understatement funny.

Surprised? More like stunned. Fascinated. Rocked. So turned on, he couldn't understand why he hadn't fallen to his knees. Yet.

It might not be healthy for a man to become erect this fast. His cock ached, already leaking from the tip.

Mine. Mine. *Mine.* It replayed in his head as he dragged his eyes over her once more. When his gaze locked onto her bare pussy, a pulse of desire tightened his balls and he added another word to his mantra.

Now. Mine *now.*

He launched himself at Grace, his mind a muddle of needs. Demands. His hand fisted in the towel, ripping it from his hips and tossing it across the room. He never paused, not even when he reached her. Months of suppressing the urge to dominate, to *take*, boiled over in the space of a heartbeat. He had to have her. Fast.

Now.

Mine.

He caught her against his chest, propelling them both toward the bed as she squealed with surprised delight. When she would have stumbled, he grasped her waist and spun her around, steadying her for the last two steps before they came up against the bed.

The enormous old four-poster had never held so much potential. The high mattress pressed against Grace's thighs, pinning her against him. He couldn't contain the grunt of satisfaction when his cock jammed hard into the crease of her ass. Fuck. His body felt like a blast furnace, her silk and warmth pressed into him along his entire length, fanning the flames.

Grace lifted a knee to the bed's surface, trying to climb up and on.

No. Not this time. They'd get to that, he thought with soaring relief and desire.

His hand shot out and grabbed her hip, holding her still as he pressed his chest forward, so that she caught herself with her hands on the mattress. The angle allowed him to slide his cock down and over the tightly clenched entrance to her ass, before thrusting it forward along the folds of her damp heat.

Jesus. She was so fucking *wet.*

He slid his hand around the thigh still bent beneath her on the bed, dragging her knee across the soft duvet. He spread her legs as wide as they'd go. Farther than might be comfortable. He wanted her totally open to him.

The spike of her heel scraped along his thigh, sending his pulse higher. He ducked to press his face to her hair, biting down on the back of her neck. Her entire body stiffened.

Shit. Too far? Had he crossed a line?

In the blink of an eye, the fear that had held him in check for months came back, and with it loomed the return his self-imposed reserve. The prospect alone was terrible, but still he prepared to ease back, to give her some space.

Then Grace whimpered and dropped her head. His dire prediction instantly forgotten, his need soared as she offered him her complete submission. Like he'd dreamed of. Fantasized about. Her back arched, canting her hips against him, the head of his cock knocking hard against her clit, her arousal slicking his length.

He wanted to throw his head back and laugh. Roar. He'd been set free.

"You want this. You want this as much as I do," he said, astonished and elated.

Grace shivered beneath him. Her voice small. "Yes."

"Yes, what?" he demanded.

"Yes, please," she moaned, shifting to grind back against his aching cock.

"Please what? What do you want?"

She rolled her hips against him, running her swollen lips along his length, dropping her chest closer to the bed to change the angle. Begging him to enter her. To fuck her.

He almost gave in to the urge. To the demand in her every movement, the same demand that pounded in every fiber of his being. Instead he wrapped both his arms around her ribs, around the cool satin of her corset, and pulled her to stand up against his chest once more. "No, baby. Not yet."

His hands slid down, caressing hard bones, slick fabric, and soft skin until his fingers hovered over the tiny strip of fur she'd left. She squirmed, writhing in pleasure and impatience.

"Please." Her voice was soft and needy. It made his cock jerk.

Shit, he was going to lose it. She was panting as hard as he was.

His hands skated back up to the top of the corset, his palms running over her breasts as he traced his fingertips along the semicircles of her areolas where they peeked out above the black trim. With two small tugs at the tight satin, he freed her nipples from their confinement.

Grace moaned and arched her back, thrusting her lush, full breasts into his hands and grinding her ass against his hips.

"Does that feel good?" he asked, knowing it did but desperate to hear her answer.

"Oh god, yes. Please, I need..." Her voice trailed off as he plucked at her hard peaks, pulling them away from her body before soothing them with his rough palms.

"You need what?"

Her head rolled back on his shoulder, her hair falling over his arm. Her moan was long and low. A primal part of him that he'd long tried to suppress was quickly clawing its way to the surface.

He repeated his question. "What do you need, baby?"

"More. Please...*more.*"

He slid his hands down the front of the merry widow and stopped at her waist. "More what?"

"Please touch me."

He buried his face in her hair, against her neck. God, he'd wanted to do this since the minute he'd laid eyes on Grace.

"Touch yourself. You don't need me."

For a moment, Grace held herself still. He didn't know if she would do this, if she would touch herself for his pleasure. For her own. He felt how her heart thundered in her chest. Moisture coated her thighs and his erection. But still she hesitated.

She lifted her hands tentatively and he released the breath he'd been holding. "Yes. That's it."

When she cupped her breasts, lifting, his hips twitched against her ass. He sucked air into his lungs and made a desperate grab for control. He needed to stay sane long enough to make it good. To make it perfect for Grace. Steadied, he dragged his hands down her belly. He stopped just as his fingers brushed that strip of hair, waiting to see what she'd do next.

Grace rubbed her hands across her taut nipples. When she pinched one rosy peak and tugged, he couldn't suppress his moan. It mingled with hers.

He nibbled up her neck, adoring her, nipping and sucking as she tormented her own nipples. When she turned her face to his, their tongues met and his mouth moved over hers, trying to tell her what his raging heart and body couldn't put into words at that moment. She returned every thrust and parry of his tongue with her own, kissing him back with equal fervor.

His fingers moved lower and found her wet slit. He'd felt with his cock that she was ready for him, but still he reveled in the discovery of just how swollen and slick she was. He circled her clit with the tip of one finger, swallowing her moans, groaning into her mouth when her hands became frenzied, tugging and twisting her nipples.

He had never felt so totally out of control while being so totally in control. He didn't know how much longer he could last.

He broke the kiss, wrapped his arm around Grace's waist to steady them both, and plunged two fingers deep into her pussy. Her cry of pleasure was the sweetest sound, ringing in his ears. When he pumped his fingers, she reached back to anchor herself with one hand curled around his neck. Then she fucked his hand for all she was worth.

Her moans and whimpers were driving him over the edge. Her complete abandon in the search for climax filled him with awe. Drove him to take them further. Who was this sensual, sexual creature, and why the fuck hadn't he discovered her before now?

When the thrust of her hips became jerkier, he knew she was close and rejoiced. He wanted her like this always, wanted her to feel such pleasure that she would never forget this moment, as he never would. Holding her more firmly around her satin-cinched waist, he pressed his lips to her ear.

"Come for me. Now." He struck her clit with his thumb, rocking with the power unleashed from her body as she arched her back and drove herself down on his fingers one last time. Her shout of triumph and the clamp of her muscles around his fingers bespelled him, and confirmed that she, too, felt a newfound freedom.

There was no more waiting. The last shred of his control had left him.

He pitched her forward, her hands gripping the comforter for dear life as he pulled back and wrapped his hands around her hips. He braced himself, then his foot shoved hers across the floor and spread her farther. She opened to him, gave herself over to him. He thought his heart might explode.

Then he buried himself in her to the hilt.

For a moment, he could do no more than stand and absorb the feeling of her tight pussy wrapped around his aching cock. The vision of her bent over, her head thrown back and her hips tilted to take as much of him in as she could, waiting for him to fuck her, would be burned in his brain forever.

She was his. Forever.

Tightening his grip on her hips, he thrust forward, hard and fast. When she dropped her chest to the bed and shoved back, he reached new depths, his soul rocking with each impact. He moved his hands to her waist, hauling her back onto his cock as he slammed into her, over and over. The head of his cock brushed the end of her channel and his balls clenched up tight. Her hands fisted in the duvet and her hips canted even higher. Her moans and pleas urged him on. He loved it. Loved her. Had never been so deep. Felt so much.

The tingling at the base of his spine heralded his release. No way he was going to go without her. She was capable of multiple orgasms, and if what they'd done before could do it, this was not going to fail. He was not going to fail her.

He thought about reaching around to her clit, but his eyes dropped and focused on something else. Something new.

Without easing the speed or force of his thrusts, he pulled

one hand from her waist, the fingers of his other hand tangling with the corset strings for added purchase.

He traced a path down her spine. When he reached the edge of satin, he pressed one finger to the vertebra there before letting it glide down between the cheeks of her gorgeous ass. The thrill of what was once forbidden nipped at him, tightening his muscles until her ass trembled with the strength of his thrusts. Her pleas for pleasure escalated and with complete abandon she began shouting.

When the tip of his finger touched the tight pucker of her anus, just tickling the nerve-rich skin, she came undone. With a cry that would wake the dead, she threw herself back, the muscles of her pussy spasming, milking his cock. His head spun with agonizing pleasure. He clamped one hand on her shoulder for leverage and pounded into her, one, two, three more times before something deep inside him broke free of its tether and uncoiled. His shout rent the air and his climax shot like a bolt of lightning from his tight balls up his spine and back again. Grunts tore from him in time with the snap of his hips as he pumped every last drop into her welcoming depths.

Holy fuck.

It was all he could do to remember to breathe. Judging by the way he was panting, he wasn't doing a very good job of it. Consciousness returned, slowly, and he registered the tension draining out of Grace as she sank deeper into the bed.

With a herculean effort, he pulled himself from her heat, smiling when she whimpered a protest at his departure. Wrapping his arms around his wonderful, sexy woman, he hauled them up on the bed and managed to get their heads all the way to the pillows before collapsing. Holding her tight, he closed his eyes and thanked god for this miracle.

Mine.

Grace snuggled deeper against Philip's chest, listening to his heart beat in time with hers. She really did try not to be smug, but it was hard not to be pleased with herself. She tried to remember why she'd been nervous about unveiling her surprise.

No idea.

It was like their sex life hadn't existed before he'd charged at her, flung his towel across the room, spun her around and slammed her up against the side of the bed. And then, thank you, Jesus, just about fucked her brains out.

She had some vague recollection that doggie-style had been awkward for them before. Uncomfortable. But what had just happened had been spectacular, no-holds-barred hot, and she'd loved it.

Grace giggled. Ducking her head, she tried to suppress her mirth, but it proved impossible. She felt like jumping up and down on the bed and shouting her triumph to the entire world.

Philip's arms tightened around her. "You enjoying yourself?" he asked, sounding amused.

She looked into his face. He lifted an eyebrow in question and another giggle escaped. She was losing it.

"I'm sorry," she said quickly, still smiling.

His expression turned to one of genuine puzzlement. "For what?" His tone made it clear that he didn't think there was any reason to apologize.

"For laughing. I'm just so goddamn happy." And it was true. But there was so much more to it. The relief, the renewed surety that Philip was, after all, perfect for her.

He smiled widely before he leaned down and rubbed his nose along hers. "Me, too." He sighed, pressing a kiss to her lips. "I love you."

She wrapped her arms around his neck. "I love you, too. And I'm glad that you liked my surprise. I was afraid you'd be appalled." Saying it now, it seemed ridiculous.

"Appalled?" His huff of laughter shook the bed. "No, I was definitely not appalled." He tightened his grip around her, pulling her closer. "Fuck, Grace. That was amazing."

A thrill shot through her. Not just for the compliment, but for the language. Philip *never* dropped the f-bomb around her. Ever.

But something had changed. *They* had changed. Broken through some unknown barrier and found something a little more earthy. Sexy. Real.

Something where the f-bomb was *infinitely* appropriate, in so many ways.

She smiled at him. "That *was* amazing. *You* were amazing. When can we do it again?"

She could see by his face he hoped it would be soon. His eyes dilated, dropping to stare at her thighs, which shone with her arousal and his semen. She loved the way his lips parted, begging her to suck on them, to bite them, to pull his tongue into her mouth.

Just the thought got her mind racing toward some other fantasies she'd had over the months. Fantasies that she'd repressed in her failed attempt to be the nice girl she'd thought he wanted her to be.

But even those couldn't force back the yawn. It had been a long day and there wasn't a better sleep aid on Earth than a shattering orgasm, let alone two.

Philip smiled and tucked her head under his chin, an arm wrapped around her corseted waist pulling her into his body. Absorbing her. He grasped the side of the duvet and folded it over them, enveloping them in a warm post-coital cocoon.

She felt good. Really, really good. Loose limbed and well loved. She snuggled into Philip's chest, her nose and lips nuzzling the divot at the base of his throat. She made a mental note to spend some more time on that very spot when she next went exploring.

"I love you," she said quietly.

"I love you, too, baby," he replied, his voice thick with sleep, arms tightening around her again. "I love you so much."

Chapter Three

Grace was dead-to-the-world asleep, wrapped up in a little slice of heaven that involved only a merry widow, a naked Philip, and a duvet envelope she thought she might never want to leave.

That was, if she could get that goddamn ringing to stop.

It took Philip lifting his head, and thereby the covers, for her happy haze to dissipate enough for her to recognize the sound of her phone ringing out in the living room.

Screw it. She tried to snuggle back down and return to her sweet dreams. Philip's quiet laughter made her pop one eye open just as the noise stopped.

"What's so funny?"

His smile was soft in the light of the lamp they hadn't gotten around to turning off. "You. You look so cute and annoyed."

"Cute and annoyed," she repeated, rolling her eyes. "Great." Not the look she was going for.

Although Philip's smile made cute and annoyed seem pretty okay. Hmmm...there were a few ways to wipe that smile off his face that held some promise.

Then the phone started in again.

Philip looked out the door to the living room. "Baby, you should get that. It's two o'clock in the morning. It could be important."

Dang. He was right. Pushing herself up and to the foot of the bed, she stood on wobbly legs. She looked down.

How about that? She was still wearing four-inch heels. Whew. *What a night.*

With as much dignity as she could muster, and as much hip swing as she could reasonably get away with, she strode through the door to the living room, hoping the view would entice Philip into another bout of loving.

Too bad he couldn't see her when she bent down and

plucked her phone from its case.

She forgot all about seducing Philip when she saw the caller ID.

MARK VALENTINE

Shit. This couldn't be good.

She answered the phone, already striding back into the bedroom. "Mark? Are you okay?"

If her phone hadn't identified him, she wouldn't have known who the wild man babbling on the other end of the line was. He wasn't making any sense and the sounds of things crashing around in the background almost drowned out his voice. All she caught was, "...police...at Valentine's...your help."

"Mark!" she barked, putting a little mean into her voice to get him to stop rambling. Philip sat up in the bed, the duvet pooling in his lap.

Mark stopped talking. She could hear him gulping a great lungful of air and her heart dropped. He was shaken. Badly.

"Mark, tell me what's wrong. We can help you." As soon as she said it, Philip was out of bed and on his way through the bathroom door. A moment later she heard the shower turn on.

"Grace. Shit," Mark began, only slightly more coherent. "Something's happened at Valentine's. The police called, they're there. Someone broke in through the window, the alarm is going off, and I can't get my fucking car out of the fucking garage at this hour. You're so close. I trust you. Please, Grace. Please, can you go down there and shut off the alarm and stay with the police until I get there? I'm going to have to run there from fucking Back Bay." She yanked the phone from her ear when a particularly loud clang resonated in the earpiece. "And I can't find my fucking sneakers anywhere!"

"Okay, Mark. Slow down," she soothed, wincing when she heard another crash. "I'll send Philip to get you. He can bring you back."

"No! He should go with you. Please don't go down there alone at this hour." Another crash, then triumph. "Yes! I found them. My sweet Grace, I'm leaving now. I'll be there in fifteen minutes. Twenty, maybe."

His sweet Grace? She told herself to think about that later.

Fishing an old pair of jeans and a T-shirt from the closet, she tried to stay focused on what she needed to do. "Be careful, Mark. Take your time." Mark's apartment was a couple of miles away. She worried about him running through the streets at night and while upset. "Philip and I will be at Valentine's in five minutes and we'll look after everything until you get there. I promise."

"Thank you. Thank you so much."

The relief and panic in his voice made her heart hurt. She yearned to comfort him. "It's going to be okay. We'll be there. You just be careful."

She wasn't sure if he'd heard her before he hung up. Tossing her phone on the bed, she kicked off her heels and tugged on her jeans, shoving her breasts back down into the merry widow before pulling the shirt over top. She hesitated when she saw Philip standing in the bathroom door, his skin still damp, his mouth open as if to say something, but stopped mid-thought.

He shook his head and dragged his eyes away, moving quickly to his dresser. "Sorry. You're damn distracting in that thing under any circumstances, but watching you shove those gorgeous tits back into it short-circuited something in my brain."

She grinned. Nothing wrong with short-circuiting something in your man's brain. Nope. She was okay with that. God knew he could do the same to her. She admired his ass as he bent over to tie his running shoes. Before tonight, she'd never fully appreciated what a pair of really thin, old shorts could do.

It was her turn to shake her head. Now wasn't the time. Slipping her heels back on, she pocketed her phone and charged for the door, knowing she'd regret not taking the time to dig out more sensible shoes, but not wanting to delay.

They were in the stairwell, running down the stairs as fast as her shoes would permit, when Philip, still pulling on a tight white T-shirt, asked, "What in hell is going on?"

She faltered on the stairs. What a man, getting dressed and

hauling ass out the door at two in the morning before even asking. There was no better person. No better friend.

She told Philip what little she knew as they resumed their furious descent and blasted through the door to the street.

Two blocks later, they hit the brick and cobblestone crosswalks that heralded their arrival on Tremont Street. Philip didn't break stride as he looped an arm around her waist and hauled her up against him. Her feet barely touched the ground as they sailed over the uneven path.

"They call those things ankle breakers for a reason, you know," he said as he lowered her back down to the smooth concrete slab of the far sidewalk.

"Yeah, well, I didn't hear you complaining about them a few hours ago, did I?"

Philip's bark of laughter died as they swung around the corner to see Valentine's halfway down the block. Police cruisers clogged the one-way street, their lights blasting the neighborhood in stark strobes of blue and white. There were a remarkable number of people standing around watching the proceedings, given the hour.

Grace clutched Philip's arm around her waist, thankful he didn't let go until they reached the first officer they could find. After explaining who they were, the young patrolman pointed them toward Detective Patrick Brown before lifting the yellow tape holding the onlookers at bay.

She felt like she was on an episode of *CSI* as she passed under the tape, which was actually stamped with the words CRIME SCENE. That wasn't just for TV?

The entire sidewalk had been blocked off, not just in front of Valentine's, but for ten or twenty yards in both directions. She discovered why within three strides. The plate-glass window that had once been most of the front wall of Valentine's was shattered across the sidewalk and into the street beyond. The biggest pieces were the size of dinner plates, but the smallest were little more than dust glittering in the flashing police lights.

Her ankle wobbled dangerously when she crunched down

on the debris.

"Jesus Christ." Philip caught her close again, offering his support as they picked their way through the mess.

Her chest tightened, her worry soaring. If it was this bad out here, how bad was it going to be inside?

When they got to the door, they made quick introductions. Detective Patrick Brown was young and ridiculously handsome. He was also a giant of a man, towering a good two or three inches above Philip, who was well over six feet himself. The detective's smile was kind, his dimples boyish and disarming when they flashed in his cheeks. Not at all what she'd have expected, until she looked into his eyes. They were sharp, never still, taking in everything around him.

She hoped he knew what he was doing.

Because the door was locked and she didn't have a key, Philip boosted her through the window and onto the padded bench in the waiting area before climbing through and helping her back down to the floor. Detective Brown followed, explaining as he did that they'd already searched the premises once, but were waiting for someone who knew the property to arrive before they did anything else.

She anxiously scanned the room, not believing her eyes. Everything looked just as they'd left it a few short hours ago.

Shutting off the alarm, she found the key hidden beneath the bar and unlocked the door. She made a quick walk-through of the restaurant and kitchens with the detective and another officer, checking the register, the office, and the safe hidden under Mark's desk. Mark would need to open the safe to be certain, but everything appeared to be undisturbed.

She wished Mark would hurry up. He'd be so relieved when he saw for himself what little damage there was.

Except the window. The glass wasn't going to be cheap to replace.

Back at the bar, she eased herself onto a stool. As predicted, she had made truly the stupidest shoe choice in the long and painful history of stupid shoe choices.

She half listened to Philip speaking with someone about how the window ended up being blown *out* instead of *in*, as you'd expect in a burglary. It was an interesting question. And if she hadn't been nursing two sore feet and a truckload of worry, she might have joined in the conversation.

She heard Mark asking to be let through the police tape barrier and then the unmistakable crunch of glass under his feet. When he came into view through the empty window frame, Grace stood and moved forward, expecting him to come to her. Instead he stopped, bending down to pick up a platter-size piece of glass with a good portion of what was once the beautifully scripted "V" in Valentine's.

He looked heartbroken. Grace's own heart gave a painful twist and her eyes stung.

"Mark?"

He turned to her, his beautiful, laughing eyes sad. She held her hands out. "Come here."

Mark vaulted through the window and walked directly into her arms, wrapping his around her ribs, burying his face in the crook of her neck. He held on fiercely as she ran a comforting hand down the back of his neck, soothing him.

"Thank you for coming, Grace. Thank you for being here." With a slight shift of his head, she knew he was looking over her shoulder, trying to assess the damage.

"It's going to be okay, Mark. The window makes it look worse than it is."

Mark's breath shuddered. His voice was muffled and warm against her skin. "Promise?"

She eased back to look at him, but his arms tightened, pulling her flush against him.

It felt great.

Physical awareness stole through her. *Talk about not the right time.* But heck, it was pretty much impossible for someone with nerve endings and a single hormone not to notice the man was all hard muscle and warm skin. When it came to full-body hugs, he wasn't hiding anything, particularly in his running clothes.

Hadn't she just been appreciating the joys of thin shorts? How right she'd been.

Not that she could talk about wardrobe choices. He had to be wondering about the armor under her clothes. He was squeezing her tightly enough that there was no way he couldn't detect the corset bones caging her ribs, or the ridge of the ribbons threaded down her back.

Would it have the same effect on him that it had on Philip? The thought made her shiver but she shook it off, reminding herself now wasn't the time to think about it.

Running her hand through Mark's hair one last time, she stepped back. "It's going to be okay." She gave him an encouraging smile. "I'll stay with you."

"Thanks," Mark said, trying to return her smile and failing.

Together, they searched the entire restaurant, again, along with Detective Brown. Twenty minutes later, even Mark had to admit he was lucky.

The detective agreed. "Yeah, and it's because of the window. Best guess—they were actually trying to break in by cutting a hole in it. *Amateurs.*" His voice dripped with disdain. "That frame looks like it's decades old and was ready to let go. They must have shit themselves when the whole damn thing came out on top of them. The noise was enough to net three 9-1-1 calls, so they were smart to haul ass outta here." He surveyed the thick shards scattered across the sidewalk, shaking his head. "They were damn lucky they got out of the way. That window could have killed a person, no question."

Mark's face paled and Grace reached for his hand. She tried to move the conversation along before Detective Brown unwittingly made Mark puke. "Thank you, Detective, for all your help tonight."

"You're welcome, but we're not done yet. We need to take some fingerprints, just to see what we can find." He turned to Mark. "I can give you the name of someone who can board up your shop front and help you set a new piece of glass in here."

"Yeah, I guess I need to get that done before I go anywhere, huh?" Mark's hand made its thousandth trip through his hair, which now stood straight up on end.

"I'll get you his card. I think I have it in my glove box."

She and Mark watched the detective leave. Since Mark had arrived, Philip had kept to the side, chatting with a patrolman and trying to stay out of the way. When he saw they were available, he excused himself and came over. He grasped Mark's hand and conducted one of those manly handshake-shoulder-bump-hug things. Only once his arm had hooked around Mark's shoulders and neck, he held on.

Which was pretty damn interesting.

Mark's raised brows told her he also found it unexpected. Then he closed his eyes and wrapped an arm around Philip's waist, embracing Philip for a moment before letting go. Both men stepped back, Philip leaving his hand on Mark's shoulder.

Maybe her fantasies were getting the best of her, but that was twice in one day that it seemed like there was something going on between Philip and Mark.

Was Philip always this comfortable with physical affection? She tried to picture him with his friends, tried to remember him hugging them, offering comfort with a hand on their shoulder. But she couldn't. There were lots of physically affectionate men out there, but she'd never thought of Philip as one of them. Until now.

With Mark.

Mark looked between her and Philip, his words pulling her from her thoughts. "You two should go home. Get some sleep."

They responded in unison. "No."

She smiled at Philip. Of course he was on the same page. Then she turned back to Mark. "We're not leaving you to deal with this by yourself. I don't know what we can do to help, but we're seeing this through."

Mark shook his head. "You've already done enough. I can't tell you how much I appreciate you being here. I owe you a big bonus."

Ouch. Now he was starting to piss her off.

"Don't you dare," she said, pinning Mark with a look. "I'm not here because I work for you, Mark Valentine. Don't you dare say so."

When Mark opened his mouth to protest again, Philip cut him off. "Save it. You heard the lady. We aren't leaving. Get over it."

Mark sighed, his hands making yet another trip through his hair. "Thank you. You've done enough already, but thank you. It will be good to have you both here."

Three hours later, the horizon was shifting from black to indigo blue. Dawn was near. Not, Mark thought, that he could see it through his lovely plywood window, damn it.

The glass company had been kind enough to send someone out in the middle of the night with an estimate that made his knees weak, and not in a good way. They'd also, thankfully, brought several enormous sheets of plywood. Working together, he and Philip had managed to get the sheets secured, both inside and out. Short of a hurricane, Valentine's was protected from the elements.

Except, perhaps, the criminal element. Sighing, Mark stood facing the ugly plywood and tugged on his hair.

"You're going to snatch your head bald if you don't knock that off," Grace said from behind him.

His heart lurched and he took a moment to compose himself before looking over his shoulder. God, she was beautiful. Strong. What would he have done without her?

She walked over to him and it seemed like the most natural thing in the world to reach out and drape an arm around her waist. When he pulled her close, he felt the satin and bones underneath.

Fuck it. He could no longer talk himself out of asking the question that had been rattling around his brain for hours.

"What in the hell are you wearing?"

Grace's slow smile made his cock harden, flooding with the blood draining from his head. He'd never seen Grace smile like that. God, it made him ache.

"Wouldn't you like to know," she said, her voice husky. She didn't look at him, but continued to examine the plywood wall as if it were a masterpiece in a museum. Damn, could she be any sexier? At all?

"And what's with those heels?"

He felt more than heard Grace's chuckle, her only response other than to close her eyes and lean against him.

She might be sexy as hell, but she was also exhausted.

He knew he shouldn't, but he was tired and desperate for the comfort he knew he'd find, so for one moment, he allowed himself to pretend he had the right to rub his cheek across the top of her head. His eyes slid closed as her scent filled him. He gave into the weakness of enjoying her warm body against his side, her hip mere inches from his growing erection.

He sighed. Who was he kidding? Even if she *were* interested in doing something about his erection, he wouldn't be able to stay awake long enough to enjoy it. He was wrecked. She must have been too, since she didn't seem inclined to stop him from cuddling into her. It had been one hell of a night and nothing seemed real.

Philip stepped in front of them, looking between Grace's closed eyes and Mark's half-lidded ones. Mark watched, curious, as Philip's eyes roved over Grace's body possessively, lingering on her shoes. Foot fetish? Then Philip's gaze ran back up over Mark's body, stopping to lock onto his obvious erection.

Christ. *What was up with Philip?* For a straight guy, he was giving off some seriously interesting vibes. And Mark *so* wasn't immune. Wouldn't have been immune under the best of circumstances, but as tired and helpless as he felt, he was unable to hide even his most primitive response.

His cock twitched, offering itself up to Philip, breaking the other man's apparent trance. His eyes flew to Mark's face. Mark wondered if Grace could see the flush warming Philip's cheeks, and if she found it as completely fascinating and confusing as he did. He wondered if she felt the same squeeze around her heart because of it.

He peeked down and saw that Grace was indeed watching Philip closely, her eyes narrowed in the same thoughtful expression she'd had when he and Philip had locked eyes over her hostess desk. And later when they'd hugged.

Realization was slow to dawn in his sleep-deprived brain, but he was beginning to believe Philip had the hots for him.

Hot damn, he'd tempted Mr. Straight. God forgive him, but he wanted to laugh. He hadn't meant to do it, and in deference to Grace and Philip's commitment to each other, he wouldn't do anything about it. But boy-howdy, it was not helping him control his erection *at all* to think about the things he'd like to do to Philip. To teach Philip. To have Philip do to him.

Philip's eyes dropped to his cock again, no doubt noticing it was now at full mast, as if raising its hand to say *yes, please* to the ideas running through Mark's head.

Philip shifted uneasily, his eyes skimming over Mark's face, then scanning Grace's, before staring down at his shorts again. Mark almost pitied Philip. The poor guy was obviously having a hard time figuring out where he wanted to look.

When Grace began to straighten away from him, Mark tightened his hold, not wanting her to see the tent he'd pitched.

"You two should go home," he said, congratulating himself for sounding casual when he wanted to growl and pounce.

"What about you?" she asked, turned her head to look up at him.

He prayed her eyes stayed on his face and didn't dip south. His smile probably looked as strained as Philip's. "I'm fine. I'm going to stay here."

Frowning, she shook her head. "You need sleep. You can't stay here all weekend. The window won't be in until Monday morning."

It *was* going to be a long weekend. It was only Friday morning—barely that. But he couldn't go home. He'd built this restaurant from the ground up and he didn't feel right about being on the other side of town with the plywood up.

"I'll be fine. I'll just curl up on one of the banquettes when I can."

This time Philip shook his head. "Man, you can't be serious. You won't fit in one of those booths. Grace is right—you need to get some sleep."

Philip's gravelly voice was enough to stall Mark's progress toward erection withdrawal. God, he loved that voice. It took a moment to regain his focus and respond. "I can't go home. I have to keep an eye on the place."

Philip clasped his shoulder and squeezed. His touch wasn't going to help Mark's cock problems either. "Come home with us. We're just a couple of blocks away—you can come back and check anytime you want."

Damn it. Not even duct tape and cast-iron underwear were going to hide his erection after an offer like that. Jesus. Glancing at Grace to see what she thought, he found her smiling happily at Philip. Apparently, she approved.

A voice from the small part of his brain that was still functioning told him it wasn't a good idea. "Are you sure? I don't want to impose."

"I've got a fairly comfortable couch, and you can use my office to call your employees to tell them they have the weekend off."

Grace took his hand. "It's perfect, Mark, admit it. Come to Philip's."

His shoulders slumped as relief coursed through him. Being that close would be ideal. And it would be so nice to have Grace and Philip there to help. Screw the little voice. There wasn't anything wrong with staying nearby with friends.

"Okay, yeah. Thank you. That would be really great." He smiled, so pathetically grateful and tired his eyes began to sting.

Grace squeezed his fingers while Philip's hand gripped his shoulder tighter, both of them doing what they could to shore him up.

His voice was raspy. "I don't know what I would have done without you two tonight."

Grace touched his cheek with her fingers. "You don't have to worry about that. We're here. Now go get what you need. We'll wait for you out front."

He nodded before heading down the hall to his office. When he was out of sight, he reached down to rearrange his poor cock, tucking it back where it belonged. Jesus Christ. Having Grace and Philip to help him was a godsend, but how in hell was he going to get through a weekend with the two of them? If Philip kept looking at him like that, and Grace kept smiling at him, so innocent with her fuck-me heels and a corset—of all the mother-loving things—on under her tidy little outfit, he would have to take up permanent residence in the bathroom either jerking off or taking a wickedly cold shower.

Scooping up the night deposit bag, some paperwork, and his employee list, Mark made a mental note to run home at least long enough to get some tighter underwear and looser pants.

Chapter Four

Philip kicked himself for about the twentieth time since they'd left Valentine's. He couldn't believe he'd invited Mark home with them.

His hands planted on the edge of the sink, he leaned forward and looked at himself in the bathroom mirror. What the fuck was the matter with him? It had been quite a day. First there was the weird staring contest with Mark, when he'd been so shocked by his own arousal he hadn't been able to look away. Then he'd discovered his "good girl" Grace had a wild streak a mile wide, resulting in an orgasm that couldn't be described by adjectives that currently existed in the English language. Then the break-in at Valentine's and staying up all night, putting up plywood and dealing with the police.

And after all that, the only thing he could think about was the man about to go to sleep on his couch?

Well, okay, that wasn't exactly true. He couldn't wait to get back into bed with Grace. To pull her into his arms and snuggle down, drawing her body close and wrapping himself around her. He'd loved her for some time, but he'd never felt so connected to her as he did tonight.

Despite his raging hard-on for Mark.

For Mark. A man. A *man.* Philip had never been with a man. Never once. Never even kissed one. He couldn't lie to himself and say he hadn't found one or two attractive over the years, but he'd never even considered *being* with a man. But with Mark...

He shook himself. *Think about Grace, damn it.*

But that was just it. It felt right to have both Mark and Grace in his house. In his bed.

He jerked away from his reflection and stood up straight. No way was he going to take that whacked-out idea further than his fantasies the next time he jacked off.

No. He had to ignore this thing with Mark. Maybe if he'd met

Mark before Grace, he could have experimented a little. Could have found out what it would be like to be with him. But Grace was what mattered now. He was a grown-up. He could resist, no matter how much he didn't want to.

Squaring his shoulders, he opened the door to the bedroom. He'd expected to find Grace waiting for him, but the room was empty. Following the sound of her voice, he wandered toward the living room, stopping in the doorway to stare.

Grace and a shirtless Mark stood together in the wash of sunlight streaming through the plate-glass windows. They were wrapped in each other's arms, their heads resting on one another's shoulders as Grace offered Mark comfort, her hand small against Mark's broad back. Mark's biceps bulged as he squeezed Grace closer.

They looked peaceful. Intimate.

He thought he should probably be jealous. He was sure he would be normally. Only instead of the hot tide of possessiveness he would have expected, he felt a tidal wave of desire.

In the logical part of his mind, he knew it would usually upset him if a half-naked man were wrapped around the woman with whom he hoped to spend the rest of his life. Hell, those far less inclined to being possessive than he would have taken exception. But he didn't. He searched his mind and heart and all he felt was...hopeful.

Shit.

Clearing his throat, he tried to get a handle on himself and the situation. Mark jumped, dropping his arms and lifting his head. Grace, though, kept holding on, peering up at Philip, her cheek pressed to Mark's firm, bare chest. When he met her unblinking stare, a thrill raced from the top of his head to the tips of his toes before it settled into a steady pulse in his cock.

He had no idea what in hell *that* look meant. It was impossible to believe that Grace might be on the same page. That she could know what he was feeling, let alone be okay with it. One man couldn't possibly be anything remotely like that lucky. Could he?

He had to look away before he embarrassed himself. Staring out his living room windows, he squinted against the blast of sun coming straight in off the harbor and tried to rein in his scattered thoughts. Dropping his eyes, he took in the stack of pillows, sheets and the comforter piled on the couch.

The couch that was lit up like the beach at high noon.

Looking back into Grace's eyes, he tried to interpret whatever message was there. He doubted she could really be thinking what he was thinking. But god, he hoped. Maybe he could test the waters...

"Mark, there isn't any way you'll be able to sleep out here. I don't have blinds on these windows—the luxury of being on the top floor of the tallest building in the neighborhood."

Mark stood wide-eyed, perfectly still, staring at him. He was the picture of absolute disbelief. Grace, on the other hand, smiled, a slow, feline curve of her lips that made his stomach drop, even while his heart started a slow, steady knock against his ribs.

Damn. Excitement and fear warred in him. Encouraged, he jumped in with both feet.

"Come on. We'll all sleep in the bedroom. The bed is more than big enough for three." He managed to say it with a straight face, though he didn't know how.

Mark didn't move a single muscle.

"That's a wonderful idea, Philip," Grace said, taking Mark's hand and pulling him from his apparent stupor. "Come on, Mark. You'll get more rest in with us."

Then, as if it was the most natural thing in the world to bring another man into their bed, she led him around the couch and through the door to the bedroom.

Trailing behind them, Philip watched Grace carefully, looking for some sign that she wasn't just being naïve and generous while some of the most lascivious hopes he'd ever dared to dream were setting up residence in his rioting imagination.

She let go of Mark and left him standing in the middle of the floor, staring at the king-sized bed like it was the first time he'd ever seen such a thing. Philip felt so damn uncertain. He could only imagine how Mark felt.

Grace, on the other hand, was still behaving as though everything was perfectly normal.

"I'm just going to take a super-quick shower," she said, reaching into the dresser and pulling out a T-shirt and a pair of his shorts.

He loved it when she wore his clothes. Found it sexy and intimate. And she knew it. He had to fight back a hysterical laugh, instead remaining silent and watching her every move until she closed the bathroom door behind her, leaving Mark frozen in place.

Philip stared at the door for a moment. What the hell was he supposed to do now?

Fuck it. He'd just act like he wasn't on a high speed trip to Weirdsville.

Stripping his T-shirt over his head, he tossed it into the laundry hamper before sitting on the edge of the mattress to pull off his sneakers. He suppressed a shudder of excitement when he caught Mark staring at his chest, his eyes dark. He had the ridiculous urge to flex his abs, to present Mark with the full washboard effect, just to see the other man's reaction. He was pretty sure Mark would like it.

A lot.

When the bathroom door swung open a few minutes later, Grace smiled at both of them, not commenting on the fact that Mark hadn't moved an inch and Philip was just sitting on the edge of the bed staring at Mark. Brushing past their frozen companion, she stacked her carefully folded clothes on the dresser. The blue-and-black merry widow ended up right on top, the garter tapes hanging down over the light pine dresser in stark relief, the fasteners clicking against the hard wood.

Philip glanced at Mark and saw his jaw drop, his eyes wide and unblinking.

That little minx.

53

Love was like a fist in his chest, squeezing his heart, as he watched Grace move around the room, shutting off the lights. She grabbed Mark's hand on the way by, pulling him to the bed. She stopped to stand between Philip's thighs.

He grinned at her. "I love you."

She smiled back. "And I love you. Now, are you ready for bed?"

He had to force himself not to look at Mark. "Yeah. I am."

Lifting the comforter, he scooted back as Grace climbed in beside him, towing Mark in her wake. With remarkably little fuss, they all settled down before Philip leaned over to check on his bedmates.

"You both comfortable? Can I turn off the light?" It was hard not to laugh. Mark had his eyes squeezed shut and appeared to be barely breathing.

"Sure," Mark said, his voice higher than usual.

Turning off the light, Philip lay down and rolled to face Grace. He was excruciatingly aware of the sounds and movements coming from the far side of the bed. Of Mark. He tried to relax, to ease the tension from his hyper-aware system.

It was only a few minutes later he heard a soft snore from Mark. It *had* been a long night.

Ducking his head, Philip pressed his lips to Grace's hair. He'd never been more grateful to have found her. She was made for him. Sighing, he felt the curl of her smiling lips against his neck as they drifted off to sleep.

No! No! Not the ringing again. Wouldn't it ever stop?

Grace burrowed deeper under the covers, warm and content in her man-cocoon. She was exhausted, and determined to ignore the racket coming from the living room, come hell or high water.

Then Mark went and ruined it all by leaping out of bed. There was a painful thud when his leg slammed against the bedside table.

"Shit!" he exclaimed. "Where am I?"

Philip, no doubt wide awake since he was the morning person from hell, sat up. And as if forcing her out from under the covers wasn't bad enough, he turned on the light.

So much for that whole sleep thing.

With a resigned sigh, she opened her eyes to see Mark staring down at her and Philip. Safe to say he now remembered where he was. Then the ringing kicked in again.

"What is that?" Philip asked.

"*I Touch Myself* by the Divinyls," she answered without thinking.

"What?" Philip asked.

"Shit," Mark said, running for the living room, "that's my phone."

As Mark disappeared through the door, Philip looked at her. "His ring tone is a song called *I Touch Myself?*"

She smiled. "Apparently."

Philip smiled back.

Yawning, she looked over at the clock. Yuck. It was only seven o'clock—they'd been asleep for less than two hours. Then Mark ran back into the room and the complete and utter lack of sleep didn't matter.

"I'm right around the corner," he said into the phone. "Call the police. I'll be there." When he hung up, he turned to them. "That was the alarm company—the alarm is going off again. It's probably nothing, but I have to go check."

Philip was out of bed before Mark finished speaking, and Grace was right behind him.

Mark tried to talk them into staying at the apartment, but they wouldn't hear of it. They were dressed and rushing out the door in record time. Only this time, she thought with a grimace, she'd had the good sense to wear sneakers. The ankle breakers were officially retired.

Well, except in the bedroom. They still had their uses there.

When they swung around the corner to Valentine's everything looked perfectly normal. They had arrived before the police and the street was quiet. Too quiet. So quiet, she got a case of the heebie-jeebies. This was the second time in one night the alarm had been triggered. Something was going on, and whatever it was, it was not good.

When they skidded to a halt in front of Valentine's, all she could do was gape at the massive hole in the plywood. What the fuck? The fine hairs on the back of her neck stood straight on end. Scrap *not good*. This was bad. Very bad. Someone was determined to get into Valentine's. By hook or by crook.

Or, apparently, by axe.

"What the fuck?" Mark shouted, voicing what they were all thinking. "Someone hacked a fucking hole in the fucking plywood!"

She scanned the street. Still empty. A jogger crossed at the light, a few cars followed. It was broad daylight, but few were out and about. Most of the businesses in this neighborhood, like Valentine's, wouldn't open for hours yet.

She turned back in time to see Mark disappear through the hole and into Valentine's. "Mark, no! Wait for the police!"

But he was already gone into the pitch-dark interior of the restaurant. She grabbed Philip's arm. "You have to go get him. Make him wait for the police!"

He put his hand over hers. "I will, baby. But I want you safe."

"I'll stay right here," she promised, pushing him toward the window. He needed to stop worrying about her and hurry. The bad feeling was growing. "Please, go!"

"No." He glanced at the ragged hole then back to her. "I want you to run to the coffee shop around the corner. Don't come out until you see us or the police, okay?"

She wanted to argue that she'd be fine in broad daylight on a public street, but since someone could apparently take an axe to a shop front with no one noticing, she swallowed her arguments.

"Okay, I'll go. Just hurry," she urged as she turned to run for the corner, her heart in her throat as she imagined Philip climbing through the yawning mouth in the plywood.

She had one foot in the door to the coffee shop when she noticed there was someone sitting in the Escalade parked on the corner. She wondered if the driver had seen anything, but before she could turn back, the car was gone.

As soon as Mark climbed into Valentine's, he knew he hadn't been as lucky the second time around.

Why the fuck was someone doing this?

The plywood did a good job of turning his restaurant into a tomb. Within a few paces of the window he could hardly see more than a few feet in front of him, but he knew the layout like the back of his hand and saw the damage, even through the gloom.

The hostess stand lay shattered at his feet, chopped to bits, the drawer and its contents strewn across the floor. The axe responsible for that and, presumably, the hack job on the window, lay to one side. One of his beautiful high-backed corner banquettes had also been destroyed—the table tossed out onto another nearby, both overturned with centerpieces and candles scattered across the carpet. The plush plum velvet seat had been torn to shreds, the back and seat sliced open, the stuffing tossed everywhere.

He moved carefully around the mess and searched the rest of the room. Nothing else had been touched, as far as he could tell.

For the life of him, he couldn't think of a reason why anyone would do this. Had someone been dumped while sitting in that booth? Or fired? It still didn't make sense to him. And this much destruction seemed over the top for a simple robbery. Yet he couldn't come up with any scenario that would inspire so much rage.

But then again, he wasn't a whackadoo who attacked plywood storefronts with an axe on a Friday morning.

Maybe it was all for money and the booth was just some extra fun?

He needed to check the bar register, his office, and the safe. He was already running into the back hall when he saw Philip climbing though the gaping hole in front, his wide shoulders momentarily blocking what little light there was. Mark flipped on the lights in the dining room and the back hall as he ran past the switches. He heard Philip call out and ask him to wait but his momentum took him around the corner.

His heart sank when he saw his office door. It hung from one hinge, cockeyed in the frame, a boot print next to the door knob. The spray of splinters gave testament to how little resistance the lock had offered.

He could only hope the safe was intact.

Shoving the door aside, he rushed into his office. He heard Philip's second shout to wait, but it was too late. A man rummaged through his desk drawers, the contents dumped onto the surface of the desk and the floor. When he looked up, his hands full of the paperwork Mark had spent hours, *weeks* of his life slaving over, the jerk's eyes bulged, panicked.

Some distant and sensible part of Mark's brain told him to run. The kid could have a gun, an accomplice, a black belt. But Mark was too enraged to listen. He lunged as the thief threw his hands up, scattering paperwork in the air, trying to block Mark as he vaulted across the desk and hurtled both of them into the wall.

They hit hard, bones jarring painfully as their bodies slammed together, youth and sheer size working in the kid's favor.

Goddamn, that hurt.

Mark was reeling, trying to recover, when a knee slammed up into his stomach. The air whooshed from his lungs and he doubled over, desperate to catch his breath. The arm he'd wrapped around the kid's neck was the only thing holding him up. A moment later, a huge fist made blinding contact with the side of his face.

Shit. Not a black belt, but a fighter. And a fast bastard. Mark tried to grab the thief again as he bolted for the door, but all he got was air.

Score one for the bad guy, zero for the chef.

Stars swam before Mark's eyes as he collapsed to the floor, barely processing Philip's shout to stop. He fought to drag air into his quavering lungs.

Fear returned. He had to find enough breath to call out to Philip. To tell him not to chase the guy. It was too dangerous.

Philip watched in horror as an enormous man crashed through the office door, slammed against the opposite wall, and then pelted full speed down the hallway and out the emergency exit. He was about to follow when he heard a strangled gasp from inside the office.

Mark.

Barreling through the office door, Philip stopped, disoriented. The room was a mess and for a moment, he couldn't find Mark. The next desperate rasp of breath drew his attention.

Flying around the desk, he kicked a chair out of his way before dropping to his knees beside Mark. He was curled up in the fetal position, his hands clutching his stomach. There was swelling around his eye and blood running down his lower leg.

"Oh, shit." He hauled Mark up from the floor, holding him against his chest. "Mark? *Mark*. Are you okay?"

Grabbing a bar towel off the desk, he pressed it to the wound on Mark's calf, trying to assess the damage, relieved to find that it wasn't bad. The cut was oozing, not deep—thank god. But Mark still wasn't talking and his chest lurched as each breath hitched.

"Come on, Mark. Just hold on. I'm going to call 9-1-1."

He dug in his pocket with one hand, trying to retrieve his phone while Mark shook his head.

Philip really didn't care if the guy didn't want an ambulance. He was getting one.

"Hold on." Mark's voice was hoarse, his breath still heaving but not as erratic. "I'm okay. The cops will be here any minute.

The little shit just knocked the wind out of me."

Philip's thumb hovered over the send button. "Are you sure?"

Mark lifted his head, made eye contact. "Yeah. I'm sure. Just give me a minute, okay?"

Philip hesitated but then slipped his phone back in his pocket. He wasn't convinced it was the right thing to do, but he thought he should trust Mark to decide. For now. Wrapping both arms around the other man, Philip pulled Mark more firmly against his chest and listened while Mark's breathing evened out and his body slowly relaxed.

As it became increasingly clear that Mark was going to be okay, it also became increasingly difficult for Philip not to notice the intimacy of the moment. The hand resting on the warm bulge of Mark's biceps itched to move, to rub and soothe, but he held it still. His other hand grasped Mark's waist, his forearm resting on the tops of Mark's thighs, aware of the tickle of coarse hair against his skin.

He could keep from moving, but he couldn't stop himself from absorbing the feeling of so much muscle, the way broad shoulders and lean hips made holding Mark so different than holding Grace. He also couldn't pretend he didn't like it.

Shit. Time to let go. He pulled one of Mark's arms around his neck. "You ready to try standing?"

Mark tilted his head back and those deep blue eyes locked onto his. *Fuck.* He was sitting on the floor of Mark's trashed office, some nut case had just fled the scene, Mark was bruised and bleeding, and it wasn't enough to shut down his insane urge to kiss this man.

It was crazy. *He* was crazy. He couldn't do it. He shouldn't. He didn't kiss men. Even if he wanted to, which he did, he couldn't toss thirty-odd years of being straight out the window for one man and his hot cobalt eyes. Could he?

Well, hell. Maybe he could.

Bringing his head down, he watched Mark's eyes widen as he got closer. He felt the gentlest brush of Mark's nose against his and let his eyes ease closed...

Then reality crashed down on him like a ton of bricks with one shout from the front of the building.

"Hello? Boston PD. Is anyone in there?"

Chapter Five

The Boston Police Department either had the best or the worst timing in history.

Mark wasn't sure he cared either way. He was desperate to reach up and yank Philip's gorgeous mouth down to his, so close to crossing the last inch separating them. Palms itching, blood rushing to his cock, skin tingling close. There wasn't a doubt in his mind it would be great. Fantastic.

So perhaps the arrival of the cavalry was for the best. Making out with Grace's boyfriend was probably not a good idea, not under these or any circumstances. The fact that Philip had seemed to be in the same place, on the same page, didn't matter.

Much.

Maybe being punched in the head had addled him. God knew, the longer he stared up into Philip's eyes, the more addled he felt.

Staggering under the strain of his own weight as Philip hauled him to his feet, Mark shook his head. He needed to not think about kissing Philip and focus on walking his ass to the door and telling the police what the hell had happened.

Philip kept his arm around Mark's waist, supporting him as they made their way to the front of Valentine's. Mark felt pretty steady by the time they reached the bar, but he let Philip prop him against the wall while he opened the door and identified himself and Mark to the police. Then Philip pulled Mark against his side once more.

Mark thought he should probably suffer some guilt that he let Philip continue to support him, worry over him, just so he could cop a cheap feel, but the way Philip was so gentle with him was nice. Surprising.

And the warmth of Philip's hard body pressed against his wasn't bad either.

He scolded himself, told himself he was a bad man, a letch.

But he still couldn't bring himself to let go completely. Straightening a little, he kept his arm around Philip's neck, his body close, but walked through the door and onto the street of his own volition.

"Mark! Philip!" Grace ran at them, leaving Detective Brown to watch with interest as she threw herself against them, wrapping her arms around their necks as they pulled her close, pulled each other in tighter.

Group hug, Mark thought, bemused. He'd always thought it was corny New Age crap, but no longer. It was heaven to be held close by not one but two people. For the first time since he'd seen the destruction, he felt safe.

Grace pulled back first. "Oh my god! Mark! There's blood on your leg. And what happened to your face?" She reached up to touch the now exceedingly tender spot next to his left eye before searching Philip's face for more damage. "Are you okay? What happened?"

Before he could answer, Detective Brown walked up to them. "I'd like to hear that answer as well, if you don't mind."

Group hug over. Pulling away, Mark turned and held out his hand. "Detective Brown. I wish I could say it was good to see you again."

"I know what you mean," he replied, shaking his hand, "and please, you might as well call me Patrick."

Mark smiled. At least this guy seemed nice. And he was awfully handsome. Black hair, light blue eyes, and the ruddy pink cheeks in a pale face marked him as a member of Boston's Irish community, of which Mark's own mother was a proud member.

"Thanks, Patrick. Come on inside. I'll show you what's happened since we last spoke."

"You sure you don't need a doctor first? Your face looks like it took quite a hit." Patrick cringed in sympathy. "It looks bad."

It felt like shit, too. "I'll live."

"And the leg?" Philip asked.

Philip's concern warmed him, although he didn't want to

63

even look at his leg. It wasn't much more than a deep scratch, but it would hurt more if he saw the blood. He'd clean it up once they'd gone inside.

"I cut it when I climbed through the plywood," he explained. "It looks worse than it is."

Grace rubbed his arm gently. "You sure you're okay?"

He was. Well, except that in the middle of the most significant professional crisis of his career to date, he was falling for these two, hard and fast. What the heck—why not fuck it all up at once? It might have been funny if it weren't so potentially true. And disastrous.

After reassuring Grace once more, he led Patrick through Valentine's, stopping behind the bar for a bag of ice for his face and a damp rag to clean his leg.

It was going to be a long day, longer still because they'd hardly slept the night before. It was all he could do to stay focused as he recounted the morning's events and examined the damage to the restaurant and his office. Grace and Philip followed them, holding hands and quietly murmuring to each other, offering support with their presence.

When they got to his office, he relayed the events leading up to the spectacular shiner blooming under his left eye. Grace gasped, reaching out to take his hand. When they moved to go out into the alley, following the escape route, he didn't let go. Neither did she.

Grace was wiped out. Wrecked. She told herself not to dwell on the fact that she'd had less than two hours of sleep the night before, but—funny—the idea wouldn't quit. She was so tired she could easily curl up on the bar, the sidewalk, Mark's desk, *anywhere*, and promptly go to sleep.

But that was not, needless to say, an option.

It was early afternoon and she figured if she'd made it this far, she could hold out for the next couple of hours until they could go back to Philip's. God, that nice big warm bed, Mark on one side, Philip on the other...

Okay, that wasn't helping.

Fortunately, her stomach took that moment to distract her from her dog-tiredness and focused her instead on her hunger. Philip would be back any minute with their lunch. Thank god. The breakfast they'd picked up at the coffee shop had been an eternity ago.

The morning had been busy. After assessing the damage, there had been a million things to do. Fingerprints, phone calls. Patrick had been kind enough to call the glass man again and have more plywood sheets brought around, then Philip and Mark had installed it, this time with a double screen of chicken wire stapled to the inside of the boards. The glass man swore it would prevent another axing.

Safe to say everyone hoped *that* wouldn't be put to the test. The addition of the patrol car circling the block would no doubt also help.

Once the window had been secured—again—the real work had begun. The upholsterer had arrived promptly and left a quote that made her head hurt. Who knew plush velvet seating cost that much? Apparently Mark had, since he'd approved it, and the upholsterer would be back in a couple of hours to do the work.

While Mark had called all his other employees to let them know Valentine's would be closed until Monday, Philip had been on the phone with his office, arranging for a security guard from the firm they used for their clients. She hadn't realized Philip had clients who required such services, but she was grateful that they were able to deliver a guard by sunset.

All in all, a lot of pretty mundane chores went into resolving a crime scene. The only real excitement had been when Mark had called his insurance company with the latest information. Within a minute of dialing, tension had crept into his voice. Grace had sat down next to him, offering her support, while Philip had stayed at the bar, watching them and jotting down whatever information was being relayed to him over the phone.

Eventually, Mark had lost his cool. "What do you mean you

may not honor my claim? You're my goddamn insurance company! This is what I pay you for!"

She'd heard Philip's quick "I have to call you back" before he'd ended his call, crossed to Mark, and plucked the phone right out of his hand, pressing it to his ear and listening.

Mark was stunned. "Wha..."

Philip had soon heard enough of whatever the insurance agent had to say. "Excuse me, ma'am." His voice was hard. There was no way the woman on the phone hadn't been listening. "My name is Philip Marsten, Mr. Valentine's legal representation. Is there some issue with his coverage?"

Wow. She'd teased Philip about his courtroom voice before, but hearing it in action had been wild. And wicked sexy.

Mark's jaw had absolutely dropped.

Philip had smiled at him as he slid a hand over the mouthpiece. "Don't worry about this. I'll take care of it."

Twenty minutes later, Mark had been back on the phone, listening to a litany of apologies from the insurance supervisor who'd just been reamed out by his *legal representative.* She'd laughed at Philip's smug smile.

It had been interesting—and arousing—to sit by Mark's side and watch Philip work, knowing that Mark was as impressed and, based on how much fidgeting he'd done, as turned on as she was. She'd watched as what she herself had been feeling moved across Mark's face, her heart stuttering when Philip had given Mark a long look before returning to his work at the bar.

She'd contemplated asking Philip right then and there what the heck was going on between him and Mark, but one chore or another had distracted them all.

And now, two hours later, she was trying to psych herself up for the biggest chore of all—putting Mark's office back to rights. It was a disaster. Papers and drawers were strewn everywhere, the lamp shattered on the floor, a nice rust-brown bloodstain on the carpet where Mark's leg had made contact. She couldn't fathom why anyone would have done this, and she was determined to return it to normal as soon as possible.

But the first order of business was definitely food. She was about to raid the kitchen, Philip and his favorite deli be damned, when he came through the office door with Mark close behind. Thank goodness!

She tried to remain ladylike, but was hard-pressed not to scarf down her sandwich as they sat at the bar and ate. When lunch was over, she felt immeasurably better. Still tired, but human.

Mark cleaned up the wrappers, tossing them into the trash. "I better get over to the police station to file the report. I don't want to give my insurance company any reasons to try to take back whatever you've talked them into."

Philip's smile was wolfish. "They wouldn't dare."

Oh yes. Lawyer Philip was definitely Damn Sexy Philip.

Mark wasn't immune either. He appeared nonplussed as he stared at Philip, eventually clearing his throat and reminding them that he was locking the door on his way out and that the police car was out front. He promised to get back as quickly as possible before bolting out the door.

As she returned to the quiet of the small office, her mind wandered back to the one thing she wanted more than anything else.

Sleep.

Climbing up onto the desk, she stretched out on her side, using her arm as her pillow. It wasn't very comfortable, but she'd make do. She wasn't really planning to go to sleep, but she couldn't resist resting for a moment.

She smiled when Philip lay down facing her, his warmth stealing into her, his arms drawing her against his chest.

Now it would be remarkably easy to doze off. Shaking herself, Grace tried to think of something that would wake her up.

Smiling wickedly, she threw a leg over Philip's hip. She wasn't wearing underwear. She told him so.

For a moment, Philip did nothing more than stare down at

the junction of her thighs, his need painfully obvious.

Naughty ideas filled her head, clearing the fog of sleep deprivation. Nothing like a little elevated blood pressure to kick flagging systems back online. Fresh oxygen and blood to her brain inspired her, helping her come up with all kinds of ideas on how to ease their tense muscles and distract their worried minds. Something to remind them both of the recent change to their relationship.

She smiled. Before last night, she never would have considered ravaging her boyfriend on a desk. But now...

She pressed her lips to his, her tongue thrusting into his mouth, his response immediate. Gratifying. She couldn't help remembering the night before. Of being bent over the bed and taken. She loved how he'd controlled their pleasure.

But not this time. Not yet.

Pushing his shoulder, she rolled him onto his back and straddled his hips, her mouth still locked over his, their tongues dancing. When he reached for her, she shook her head and ran her hands up his arms, pulling and folding them above his head with his wrists crossed.

She broke their kiss and stared down at him. His smile was slow, hopeful, completely cooperative.

Smart man. And smart was sexy.

She touched the tip of her finger to his nose. "No touching. I want to play."

"Be my guest." He lifted a hand to indicate that his body was all hers to do with as she pleased.

And oh, how she pleased.

With one hand, she traced the lines of his face, sweeping her fingertips over his smooth cheeks and the faint stubble on his chin. His long, dark lashes fluttered shut when her thumb ran over one lid. She kissed the other. She'd loved his face the minute she'd seen it. Strong. Handsome. Cheekbones so high they should have been feminine, should have made him look delicate, but they didn't.

Her knees slid out over smooth wood and she brought her warm, rapidly swelling folds down on his stomach, wishing she'd thought to discard her shorts before starting this. His abdominal muscles jumped against her thighs and she rode them in a wave. Nice. While his face was pure masculine beauty, his body was pure sin. Underneath the suit and the ultra-conservative lawyer haircut was a body built for hard work. And good, hard loving.

Thank god she'd never have to fight the urge to jump his bones again. To think of all the time they'd wasted by being so damn careful with each other. Never, ever again.

To prove that, if only to herself, she moved down his body, taking her time, exploring him as she never had before. She rubbed her swelling labia along his already hard cock while nibbling a path down from his ear, pausing to bite him at the junction of his corded, muscled neck and those impossibly wide shoulders. It was the same spot where he'd clamped his teeth the night before when he'd dominated her so thoroughly. So perfectly.

He was clearly having a hard time lying still beneath her. *Good.*

She ran her hands up under his shirt, pulling it over his head. She could see her bite mark. She loved it.

Moving lower, she trailed her tongue against the smooth curve of one pec, then dragged her cheek over the small, dark nipple. The nub tightened, darkened to deep plum. She drew her tongue up and over it with a firm lick, fascinated when the muscles beneath flexed. His erection was full and pressed against her stomach.

"Do you like this?" she asked.

"What?" His voice was rough. It rubbed along her skin, heightening her awareness of how tentative her control of him and his body was, and what it could mean if she lost that control.

The thought made her shiver with pleasure.

She licked his other nipple before pulling it into her mouth for a few hard sucks, letting him feel her teeth. His heart beat against her lips, and she reveled in how it sped up with each tug of her mouth.

"You like that, too," she said, pleased.

"God, yes," he gasped.

She was curious at how far she could take the biting before his pleasure diminished.

When his arms moved she lifted her eyes. He'd brought his wrists down to rest on the top of his head, as if he'd begun to reach for her and held himself back. She wasn't surprised. His nature was to dominate, to possess. She'd only had a small taste of what it was to take her pleasure while giving him his. It made her curious and she was delighted that she could now appease that curiosity without worry. She knew in the future she'd more often prefer to submit, to give herself over to his care, but this time, she wanted to try something different.

Crawling back up over him, she put her face close to his. "No cheating," she scolded.

"I want to touch you," he cajoled.

It was tempting, but she refused to relinquish her tentative control. "How about you taste me instead?"

Climbing farther up his body, she whipped off her shirt and lowered her breasts toward his face. When she was within inches, he reared up and captured one peak in his greedy mouth, his neck muscles bunching as he devoured her, taking as much into his mouth as he could and sucking hard.

She groaned. The pressure was delicious, the pull so strong on her aching nipple that it rode just on the good side of pain. Apparently, he wasn't the only one who liked a little bite in his loving. Another thrilling discovery. She felt each tug as if a string ran from her nipple to her clit.

When she drew back he pushed his head up, trying to stay attached. She twisted, yanking herself from his mouth, depriving him with a gasp before promptly offering him the other breast. God, he'd never been this forceful before. It had always been nice when he'd played with her breasts, but this was different. The pressure was ten times firmer, ten times more erotic. She'd always viewed it as gentle foreplay, but this wasn't anything of the sort.

This was better.

The control was rapidly slipping from her fingers. Grabbing for it once more, she sat up, leaving his mouth with a pop that released his groan of disappointment. She could have stayed there for hours, but she was intent on her mission.

Sliding down the desk, she dropped her feet to the floor and rose to stand between Philip's parted thighs, his knees hooked on the edge of the desk. With little fuss, she yanked his shorts down and off, then stood staring in awe at the bounty laid out before her. Gorgeous.

Stretching over him, she lay her hands on his shoulders and drew them down his body. She took her time adoring him, enjoying her careful study of the contours of his hard belly, relishing the six-pack rippling beneath her fingers. The groan of anticipation he couldn't contain as her hands drew ever closer to the prize ratcheted her own need higher.

She ducked her head, her hair tickling along his hips, her mouth parted and ready over his burgeoning cock. When she exhaled, her breath rushed over the swollen head and it jumped, his stomach tightening in response to the need she could imagine rocketing through him.

She'd never minded giving oral sex, but she'd never before looked forward to it this much. She wanted this as much as he did. More. She wanted to give him a taste of what he'd offered her. She understood that groan. The need bound up with relinquishing control. The power of it resonated in her chest and her pussy. That desperate longing. Desire so fierce it actually ached.

She *wanted* him to ache. She'd consider this his punishment for not giving her a properly good, hard fuck in all those months before last night.

When her still-questing hands reached his cock, she diverted around the base to the creases where his thighs met his ass, cupping and pushing his legs apart, forcing him to lift one knee and plant his heel on the desk, the other leg pushed out as far as it would go, giving her as much access as she wanted. She could see and feel how hard he was clenching the muscles in his ass and groin, trying to tamp down his orgasm. His sac was tight to his body. Anticipation had him close.

Just where she wanted him.

Using his spread thighs to brace herself, she lowered her head and licked the pearl of pre-come waiting for her. Salty. The essence of Philip was hot on her tongue. She licked around the velvety head, taking special care to flick her tongue back and forth under the flange. Philip's hips bucked so hard, she almost didn't pull back fast enough to get her teeth out of the way. His hands came down to his sides, his knuckles white where they clenched the sides of the desktop.

She couldn't wait to see what happened when he lost control.

Motivated to find out, she opened her mouth over his cock, taking in as much of him as she could. She wanted to thrill him. To shock him. He was so hard, so thick, that she had to drop her chin to take him without her teeth scraping. Had to remind herself to breathe through her nose as she sealed her lips around the shaft and pulled back with a tremendous upward suck.

"Fuck!"

Philip's shout of pleasure was the only warning she had before his hands tangled in her long hair and his hips thrust up, shoving his cock deeper into her mouth. She'd never let a man control her head before, hadn't intended to hand control back to Philip this way, but by god, she wanted it. She wanted to take all of him.

For those first few thrusts, all she could do was concentrate on her breathing and sucking. Once she had his rhythm, she lowered her head slowly, taking more and more of him farther back in her throat, timing her breaths with his withdrawal. When she had the length of him, her lips touching the base of his shaft with each thrust, his fingers tightened into fists and he began moaning long and loud.

She was enjoying the hell out of herself. Waiting for another deep thrust, she swallowed, her throat muscles trapping his head tightly in her throat for one second before letting go.

"Fuck!" Philip cried, his body thrashing on the desk beneath her. "Baby, I'm not going to last much longer."

If she could have smiled, she would have. Instead, she reached down and pushed a finger along her clit and then into herself, stopping for a moment to simply enjoy before pulling it back out.

Last night, Philip had teased at the door to what had previously been a forbidden playground and she wanted to know if turnabout was fair play. Clenching his raised thigh harder, she closed her eyes and prayed what she was about to do wouldn't bring this whole thing to a screeching halt.

The moment her self-lubed fingertip touched his tight anus, Philip's thrusts faltered.

Uh oh.

She kept up the swallow-thrust and held her finger still, hoping he'd forget it was there. She was surprised when he let out a long low growl and wiggled his ass. She looked up his body and saw his head was thrown back, his eyes closed in utter abandon.

Another wiggle. Not so freaked out after all.

Relief swamped her. Their playground kept getting bigger and bigger. She couldn't wait to try out every piece of equipment. Starting now.

Sucking until her cheeks hollowed out, then clamping the head of his cock in her throat with a swallow, she twisted her finger and pushed past the tight muscles and into his ass, curling her finger to press on that magical spot.

Philip came with an exultant shout, his hips exploding off the desk, his cock down her throat, the ring of muscles clenched around her finger like a vise. Retreating and swallowing fast, she continued her gentle massage with the finger in his ass while her ears rang with Philip's roar of release. He rocked against her, guiding her ministrations until his thighs and butt trembled and fell back to the desk.

She released his deflating cock with a gasp, the urge to laugh bubbling, her grin enormous. Gently easing her finger from his ass, she crawled back up on the desk and along the length of his body, drawn by the gentle tug of his hands, still tangled in her hair. When her face drew even with his, he pulled her down for a long, slow kiss that might have lasted for hours. His tongue explored every corner of her mouth, tasting himself on her tongue, her teeth.

She was consumed. Adored. And she was just getting started.

When he finally released her hair, he slid his arms around her to hold her tight against him.

"Now tell me why, exactly, we didn't do that six months ago?" she asked, her voice hoarse from letting his cock so deep.

His laughter started as a deep rumble in his chest, working its way up and out until it shook both of them.

"Damned if I know. I'll be goddamned if I know at all."

Patrick didn't drop Mark back at Valentine's until the late afternoon. Trying to psych himself up for more work, Mark dragged his sorry ass and throbbing face through the door, only to find Philip and Grace had already cleaned his office, walked the security guard through the ins and outs of his assignment, and supervised the re-upholstery of the booth.

Christ on a *crutch*, what would he have done without them?

Thank god, he didn't have to know the answer to that. Because they were here, with him, helping him, and Valentine's was almost as good as new, minus one very large window which couldn't be fixed until Monday morning.

So, what now? They were both obviously exhausted. Beautiful, sexy, ridiculously tempting, but falling-asleep-on-their-feet tired.

As if reading his mind, Philip turned to Grace. "You ready to go home?"

Grace nodded and went into his arms. Mark felt a pang of jealousy, followed by the now-familiar hum of sadness. He wasn't sure where he stood with these two, but he knew it was on the outside. When Philip raised his head to look at him, Mark tried to smile, knowing he failed.

"You ready?" Philip asked.

Even as his heart leaped, he shook his head. "No, I can—"

"Shut up, Mark," Philip said, cutting him off. "I'm too tired to argue."

Philip's eyes searched Mark's face, no doubt admiring his black eye. At least it hadn't swollen shut—it was just very colorful. Eventually, Philip's gaze drifted over his shoulder and Mark knew Philip was looking at where the hole had been, remembering the axe, the hostess stand. He couldn't blame him. He, too, could think of little else.

When Philip's eyes returned to his, he nodded, apparently having come to some decision. "I'd feel better knowing you were safe."

It was hardly an admission of love, or lust. Hell, it was probably just friendship, but Mark had the wholly inappropriate urge to grin like a simpleton. Instead, he took the safe route and tore his eyes from Philip's to look at Grace.

"Come on, Gracie, let's get you tucked in."

She looked so pathetically grateful, he felt like a heel. Now was his opportunity to take care of the people who'd spent so much time caring for him. Reaching out, he clasped her hand and pulled her toward the door, smiling when she grabbed Philip and towed him along.

He hadn't meant for the three of them to walk home holding hands, but when Grace didn't let go, he didn't either. He was an idiot for letting his imagination, not to mention his emotions, run away with him, but he was too tired to give a fuck.

As they turned the corner onto Tremont Street, Mark saw a black Crown Victoria roll from the corner and into traffic. Strange, he was pretty sure he'd seen the same car outside the police station earlier. Of course, it was a common make and model. Hell, it could be the police keeping an eye on things. Half their fleet were Crown Vics. Just in case, though, he decided to call Patrick and ask him about it once they got home.

Once they got home. It probably wasn't a good sign that he was thinking of Philip's apartment as home. He'd no doubt reassess that thinking after spending the night on the couch. Disappointment formed a lump in his chest. He didn't want to spend the night on the fucking couch.

He was so busy feeling sorry for himself, he almost didn't see the same car passing them again on Tremont in the other direction. Had the guy circled around? Mark tried, but he couldn't catch the plate. Damn. He was officially no longer convinced he was just being paranoid.

Pulling out his phone, he fired off a text message, aware that Patrick had been up the entire night with them and would likely be asleep. Still, he felt better having done something.

He was scanning the street again when Philip caught his eye. "What's up?"

"Probably nothing. I keep seeing the same car."

Grace's head came up. "A dark blue Escalade?"

He stopped walking. "No, a black Crown Victoria. Have you seen an Escalade?"

"No, I mean, not really." She rubbed her hand over her face. "Forget I said that. I'm too tired to think."

Philip looked down at her with concern before making eye contact with Mark. Mark could see the worry. There was little comfort in knowing they were on the same page.

Taking Grace's hands, they started walking again, their pace a little quicker.

When they finally passed through Philip's building's front door, Mark was thankful for the high-tech security system. He scanned the street once more and saw nothing. Maybe he was being paranoid. Who could blame him?

Since no one was up for tackling the stairs, they took the elevator to the top floor, all lost in their thoughts—or just trying to stay awake.

Once they got through the door, they trudged through the

living room, Grace's hand still holding tightly to his. It was getting dark out, so the excuse for his joining them in the bedroom that morning was moot. If he ended up in their bed tonight, it would be because they wanted him there. And, god, it was where he wanted to be.

He watched Philip's eyes stray to the couch, but Philip didn't stop, didn't let go of Grace's hand. Didn't hesitate to pull all three of them into the bedroom.

Mark's heart did a slow roll in his chest. When it resumed beating, it sent all the blood south.

He would have laughed if he hadn't been so goddamn tired. Heck, he would have thrown himself to his knees and begged for one of them to put him out of his misery and fuck him. Okay, maybe he could be convinced to do the latter in spite of his bone-deep exhaustion, but both Grace and Philip were obviously in the same pathetic condition.

So instead he stood there, transfixed, as Philip stripped off his shirt and shorts and climbed into bed wearing only boxer briefs. The sight of his tight, round ass crawling across the mattress sent further inspiration to Mark's cock, but he forced it back, following Philip's lead and stripping down to his boxers.

He checked to see which pair he wore. Plain gray. Thank god. Nothing said "do me now" like SpongeBob SquarePants.

Smiling a little at his wandering thoughts, he walked toward the bed, and almost tripped over nothing when Grace strolled out of the bathroom in one of Philip's T-shirts, its hem skimming her smooth thighs, the peaks of her obviously braless breasts tenting the cotton. When she climbed into the bed, he caught a flash of smooth, bare butt cheek and a wisp of blue satin thong before she turned, smiling, the comforter held aloft in one hand.

"You ready?" she asked.

Was he ever.

With three great lunges, he launched himself onto the bed. Grace whooped and Philip chuckled as Mark bounced once before pulling up the covers and putting his head on the pillow. Within seconds, they were comfortable, but he was still careful not to touch Grace, awkward now in spite of his joking a few moments before. He heard Philip whisper something but couldn't make out the words. Grace sighed in response before snuggling farther under the covers and against Philip.

As with the night before, he was sure he would never be able to sleep. And as with last time, he passed out within minutes.

Chapter Six

Mark woke up in the middle of the night, his body tangled up with Grace and with an erection so fierce, so painful, it was a battle not to groan out loud. Shifting to ease the ache only made it ten times worse, as his cock was jammed against Grace's soft belly.

He wondered when they'd turned toward each other. And when he'd drawn his leg up and nestled it between hers. A slip of cool satin teased his skin, in contrast to the warm, smooth silk of her thighs locked around his.

It was like the best game of Twister *ever*.

He fought to pull himself together. His black eye was sore, but it wasn't enough to deter his raging arousal. He needed to get some control before Grace woke up from all the poking.

Breathe. Breathe. The expansion of his chest made him acutely aware of Grace's arm curled around him, hugging him close.

God, she was beautiful. Even with his eyes closed, he could picture her perfectly. Every detail. Every nuance of her face, the character and humor that shone in her eyes. And Philip. So kind and generous. So gentle with Grace. And so fucking gorgeous.

Okay, thinking about that really wasn't helping. He needed to think about something else, damn it.

Yeah, right. What a way to wake up. He sighed. These two people attracted him in ways he didn't understand. He wasn't normally a romantic kind of guy, but they called to him. And god, he wanted to answer that call so damn badly.

He stopped breathing when Grace muttered in her sleep and snuggled into his chest, her thigh brushing up against his as she shifted. Her hand spread against his back, as if to shield him. To protect him.

And he felt safe. Comforted. Completely at peace. After the

long night and the even longer day that had followed, he should be a little disoriented. Groggy. Hell, someone had smashed his window, vandalized his restaurant—and worse, forced him to close for a weekend. Close for a Saturday night! He should have been the poster boy for pissed-off sleep deprivation.

Instead, he felt rested and cared for in a way he hadn't been since he was little and his mom could make the world right again. In a way, he hadn't even realized what he'd been missing until this very moment. Grace and Philip had stood by him, partnered with him. What had happened to Valentine's sucked. A lot. But after all they'd done, all the ways that they'd helped him, he felt like it was going to be okay. More than that. He felt...loved.

Even putting aside his arousal, the sexual desire that rode him so hard he ached, he wanted to love them back. It was a first for him. And, he thought with a sinking heart, probably the final and most damning piece of evidence that he was the biggest, dumbest idiot on god's green Earth.

He was falling in love. He'd managed to hold off for thirty-six years without ever taking the plunge, and then he went and fell for not one, but *two people.* Two people who were already committed to each other.

Stupid. Stupid. Stupid.

But what if? What. If. Those two words set off a drum in his chest. He'd never even considered the idea of loving *two* people and that they might love him back. Who would? He wasn't caught up in what was and wasn't conventional, but still...this was a little out there.

Anyway, Philip having a thing for him was a long, long, looong way from Philip acting on it. He seriously doubted that Philip would be interested in sharing Grace.

Sweet, beautiful Grace. He drew another deep breath, taking in her essence, her warm, soft scent trapped in the dark spaces where their bodies weren't touching. He held it in his head and lungs to memorize it, like a fine wine, the perfect combination of flavors.

Grace stirred again, dragging her arm over his ribs, bringing her hand between them to rest on his heart. When the hand on his waist tightened, she scooted her butt a little, dragging her pussy across the fine hairs of his leg before settling back to sleep. How the hell she could ignore the lance trying to pierce her hip was a mystery to him. Said lance was sure feeling it.

But wait...if Grace was lying on her side and her arm was trapped between them, then how could she also have a hand around his waist?

Mark's heart raced as realization dawned.

Not her *hand.*

His.

Grace woke up in a tight, warm cocoon of men. It was *heaven*. Sleeping between two men was now her all-time favorite thing.

She couldn't resist snuggling in closer to Mark, hoping Philip would follow. He did, thank god, quickly returning his burgeoning erection to the crease of her ass when he spooned up behind her.

Nice.

Mark shifted and she wondered if he was awake or if he was reacting in his sleep. Whichever it was, he was definitely reacting. It was all she could do to keep her hand on his chest when she so desperately wanted to reach down and test the length and width of the impressive erection nudging her. Was that all him? He wasn't *that* close, for heaven's sake.

Maybe he was asleep. Careful to keep her breathing even and her body still, she dared to peek up at Mark.

He was most certainly awake. Wide awake. And staring at something over her head. Or, rather, *someone*. Philip. And he looked like he wanted to eat him alive.

She felt Philip's quick inhalation before his hips twitched, the head of his cock bumping against the sensitive skin between her cheeks. Mark's hips gave one long, slow pump in response, his cotton-covered cock dragging along her soft belly where her T-shirt had ridden up. She could feel the moisture leaking from the tip, soaking through his boxers.

The boys were working each other up something fierce.

She tried to breathe evenly, to put off revealing she was awake. She was curious to see how this would play out. In her mind, there was no denying the men were attracted to each other. But that didn't mean either would acknowledge it. And regardless, she didn't know where that left her.

In the middle?

God, she really hoped so. Just the thought turned her on, making it almost impossible not to squirm and let the boys know she was awake. As it was, it was only a matter of time before her arousal soaked through her panties and onto Mark's leg.

"I'm straight," Philip said, his voice hardly more than a whisper.

"I'm not," Mark replied.

"You're gay?" Philip sounded surprised.

"Not really that either," Mark admitted, clearly amused.

Philip had no response to that. A slow smile spread across Grace's face. *Perfect.*

"Have you ever been with a man?" Mark asked.

Philip's body tightened behind her. "No." There was so much confusion in that one little word.

Mark must have heard it, too. He swallowed before speaking, measuring his response. "I have. Been with men in the past, that is."

"Oh."

"And I want you. Very much."

Grace's heart pounded in her chest. She wanted to writhe as images flooded her mind. She loved Mark for putting the truth out there. For the possibilities he offered. He'd never been sexier than in that moment of brave honesty.

She didn't think she was alone in thinking so either. Philip wanted him, too. His cock wouldn't be hard as a rock if what

Mark said repulsed him. If it weren't revving him up.

Philip let Mark's admission hang in the air for a moment before speaking. "I can't. I have Grace."

Mark let out a little laugh. "God help me, I want her just as much as I want you."

Yes! It was hard to do a mental happy dance while holding her body perfectly still, but she managed.

Philip's response was so fervent his voice hitched. "Fuck, I'd like to see that."

"You would?" Mark asked, sounding as incredulous as Grace felt.

He would?

In the space of a breath, Grace's world shook. She lost the battle to measure her breathing. So did Philip. Good lord, it had never really occurred to her that Philip would even consider it.

He sucked in a deep breath. "You can't imagine how sexy she is. What she hides under that proper package she presents to the world. To see you...*Christ.* She'd never forgive me for even thinking it."

"You're wrong," she said, her voice gentle but adamant.

Both men froze, the air trapped in their chests, their bodies coiled to spring. She'd obviously startled them both.

Finally, Philip spoke. "What?"

"I said, you're wrong."

Mark propped himself on one elbow to look down at her and then Philip did the same, though more slowly. The glimmer of humor and hope in Mark's eyes gave her courage. Rolling onto her back, her legs still tangled with Mark's, she looked up at Philip, unsure what she'd find.

Mostly he looked confused. And aroused.

Her heart raced. She knew she faced a very small window of opportunity to make a very big change in her relationship with Philip. She desperately wanted to grab that window with both hands and throw it wide. But not at the risk of losing Philip.

They wanted the same thing. *Mark.* Philip had admitted as much, whether he was ready to accept this about himself or not. Still, she needed to choose her words carefully, to help him understand.

"I heard, Philip. I've been awake the whole time." She reached up to touch his cheek. "It was the sexiest conversation I've ever heard."

Philip didn't look any less concerned. "I'm sorry if we upset you."

"What part of *sexy* do you think I found upsetting?" She stared into Philip's eyes, tried to communicate her certainty. Her love. "You don't have to be afraid of what you're thinking. What you're feeling. I'll always love you."

"I...I don't understand."

She wondered if he really didn't understand or if he was just, as she suspected, absolutely disbelieving.

Mark, on the other hand, understood her perfectly. And he believed. His smile was slow, and so damn hot she would have squeezed her legs together if they hadn't already been wrapped around one of his.

"She's trying to tell you it's okay," he said to Philip, his eyes never leaving her face.

"What is?" Philip asked.

She took the last leap, touching her fingers to Philip's cheek, drawing his gaze from Mark back to her. "Whatever you want, Philip. All of it."

Mark didn't think he'd ever been happier or more sexually excited in his entire damn life. His sweet Grace was a fearless wanton, bless her.

She watched Philip closely, holding her breath and waiting for his answer. The poor man was like a long-time prisoner unexpectedly handed his freedom. He stood at the prison gate frozen—unable to step through, at a total loss. Mark couldn't blame him. He was almost at a complete loss himself.

Almost. Enough of his brain was still functioning to know that of the countless possibilities Philip had just created, some tested fewer boundaries than others. Mark chose his path, hoping that he'd get to map them all one day, but knowing he would find immeasurable pleasure setting his foot on just one. For now, it was more than enough.

Reaching out, he touched Grace's cheek, turning her face to his. He saw her worry. And her desire.

"Philip wants to watch us together," he said, loving the fire in her wide eyes and warm cheeks. "He wants to watch me fuck you. Is that okay with you, Gracie?"

Her answer was to nod, once. Slowly.

He looked at Philip. He didn't appear to be appalled, wasn't objecting. His face was flushed, his lips parted and full. Mark couldn't wait to taste them.

One thing at a time...

Taking a deep breath, Mark cleared his rioting mind and gave Philip one last moment to let it sink in, to react. To change the course. When Philip didn't do any of those things, Mark turned back to Grace.

She was so lovely, waiting, her eyes dark with desire. He took his time, savoring his mounting need and her increasingly hectic breathing as he moved closer, hesitating when their lips were just a breath apart.

He'd fought so long against his desires, his need to hold and touch her, that now he found himself hesitating. Drawing out the moment before he stepped off the precipice. He watched her lids grow heavy, her lips full and waiting for his kiss, and knew she felt it, too.

Finally, he brushed his mouth over hers. Gently. Once. Twice. The exquisite silk of her lips rubbing along his.

Philip's hand, still on Mark's hip, tightened, pulling Mark further into their embrace. Encouraging him.

Not that he needed much in the way of encouragement.

Pressing his mouth more firmly to Grace's, he angled his

head to get closer, nibbling, his tongue tracing the seam of her lips, begging entrance. When she opened to him, he hummed, delighted when her tongue flicked against his before retreating, teasing him with her taste, her touch.

He wanted more. So much more.

The precipice was far higher then he'd ever have guessed.

Plunging his hand into her hair, his fingers curled into the long, silky strands as he sank into the kiss, thrusting his tongue into her mouth to slide along hers.

His heart thundered in his chest, his body shaking with the need to get closer to her. To pull her into his very being. He wanted to feast himself on her body, drown in her scent. She tasted exactly as he'd imagined she would, a heady combination of need and desire.

She met him with equal passion, thrust for thrust, their mouths eating at each other. Her fingers locked in his hair as his were fisted in hers, her head coming up off the pillow to maintain the depth and intensity.

He rolled toward her, over her, his thigh sliding down between her legs, slicking along damp silk before trapping her with his weight. His shoulder brushed Philip's chest before Philip eased back. Not far. Still close enough that Mark could feel his warmth down his side, his scent teasing at the edges of Mark's mind. Christ, it wasn't enough.

Grace writhed against him, drawing him down, bucking to press herself against his leg to try to ease her need. He knew just how she felt. His own need to thrust, to sate, rode him hard. He sank back into their kiss.

Her hips rocked again. And again. Her mouth working at his. She was unstoppable as she arched against his leg, desperate for relief from the fire burning both of them. Desperate for release.

He pressed his hips forward to meet hers.

Grace tore her lips from his and moaned, tilting her head back in abandon. Stretched out like that, he couldn't resist tasting more of her, letting his feast continue. His lips traveled the length of her jaw and down to suck at her neck. When he bit at the soft cord of muscle, she gasped and rocked again. So needy. So perfect. He met her hips with his own, shifting his thigh higher, giving her something to ride.

One of her hands released its death grip in his hair and he lifted his head, watching as she reached for Philip, drawing him down to her. Their tongues met before their lips could, twining and dueling. Mark's stomach muscles clenched.

He felt their kiss as if it were his tongue that licked into their mouths. He'd never have believed such a connection was possible, but then, what did he know? Grace was everything he'd dreamed she'd be, and yet hotter and braver than even his wildest imaginings could have conjured. He had so much to learn.

When she pumped her hips again, he couldn't stand the torment any longer. He shifted both his legs between hers and ground his cock against and into her soft folds, silk and lips parting to accept him.

It was a warm, wet heaven.

He had to get rid of their clothes. Now.

Quickly, he shoved himself away and knelt between her legs, running his hands along her body, over her breasts, her whimper lost to Philip's greedy mouth. Fascinated, he drew his hands lower still, skimming work-roughened fingers over her soft belly, marveling at the trail of goose bumps that followed his touch. He wanted to someday spend hours letting his fingertips glide over her calves, her knees, her long, soft thighs, getting to know her every curve. Her every taste.

But he couldn't now. The need was too great. The drive to find release too fierce. He ran his hands over her hips and around her waist, then lodged them beneath her.

"Philip." His voice scratched like he'd run a mile at top speed.

Philip's head came up fast, as if he'd forgotten Mark was there. Mark froze, nervous until Philip smiled slowly. Then all Mark could do was gape at Philip's beauty. His skin practically shone with the warmth of his arousal. His lips were swollen, his dark eyes wide.

Scolding himself to stay on the path he'd chosen, Mark sat back on his heels, spread his fingers under Grace's spine and ribs and lifted her off the bed. With her back arched, she clamped a hand around his neck and rose up to meet him, her legs wrapping around his waist, bearing her down on his aching cock. His hands slid to her ass, keeping her locked against him, guiding the grind and push of her hips, and thrilling at her low moan so close to his ear.

"Philip. Help me get her shirt off," he gasped, his mind spinning. She rocked against him relentlessly, writhing like a flame in his arms.

Philip crawled to them, his chest coming up against Grace's back and pinning her between their kneeling bodies. When he slid one knee between Mark's, Mark closed his eyes to savor the rub of hair-roughened thigh, delighting in how Philip forced his knees apart, widening Grace's legs so that she pressed more firmly down on him.

Jesus. He'd forgotten the texture of a man. The rough hair, thicker thighs. He groaned, his need for Philip expanding even as his desperation for Grace tore him apart. He was losing sight of his goal, the promise of Philip's touch too great a distraction.

Mark's eyes flew open when Philip's hands ran over his wrists, his gaze locking with Philip's immediately. They were mere inches apart. The intimacy unbearable. His chest ached with the desire to reach out and touch the other man. Only the tug of cotton beneath his hands as Philip pulled up on Grace's shirt brought him back.

Shaking his head to clear it, he let go of Grace just long enough for her shirt to be lifted and bunched around her ribs, then wrapped his hands around her delicate waist, driving her against his cock once more.

Grace's eyes were unfocused. Dazed. "Please."

He couldn't resist her mouth and kissed her again. His tongue plunging and retreating, his hands urging her hips forward as they rolled over his, before tearing his mouth away. "Please what, Grace?"

Philip's lips skimmed over her neck as he continued to lift her shirt slowly. Mark watched how he held the fabric taut, dragging the cotton over her body, abrading her tight nipples with every inch.

She arched. Moaned. "*Please.*"

Philip's lips curved against her neck, his deep voice washing over Mark. "Tell us. What do you want?" Philip held the hem of her shirt just below her nipples, the rough edge caught on the hard peaks. "Grace isn't afraid to ask for what she wants. Are you, baby?"

Grace ground against Mark. He gritted his teeth, staring at what Philip held just out of sight, Philip's fingers a startling contrast to Grace's pale ribs. She undulated in his hands, her smooth skin burning with need. Mark could see the gentle curves of her breasts beneath the cotton hem, knew that they'd be perfect.

"Tell us, Grace. What do you want?" he begged, desperate to hear the words, desperate for Philip to release her.

She lifted her hands above her head. He'd never seen a more wanton or beautiful sight in all his life. She was a goddess. "I want you to take this shirt off me," she panted. "I want you to lick and suck and bite. Please. Please, hurry."

With a last smile against Grace's neck, Philip flicked the shirt up and over her head, scraping it hard across her nipples so that her breasts lifted and held before bouncing free.

Mark stared at the cherry peaks knotted above smooth creamy skin, barely hearing Grace's cry of relief over the pounding of his heart.

He'd never guessed. He'd dreamed and wished and foolishly hoped, but as he bent to draw one perfect nub into his mouth, he knew he never could have guessed how shattering it would be to be with Grace. With Philip.

He hadn't known what loving them would mean.

Grace was on fire. Her heart raced, her nipples ached, and her pussy felt so damn empty. She didn't want to be empty any longer. She longed to be filled by one of the beautiful men surrounding her.

Everything with Mark was new, and she delighted in the giddy passion of taking a new lover. She looked forward to learning all his secrets. That it was Mark, her friend, the man she'd flirted with and fantasized over for months, only added to her need. Her desire to learn all she could about him.

As if that weren't enough, to share the moment with Philip was indescribable. The bonds of deep intimacy and trust were strong. Freeing. Being there together with Mark only strengthened them further.

Then Philip finally took her damn shirt off. *At last.*

The look on Mark's face when Philip let her breasts go free was incredible. His eyes darkened, the pupils blown as desire flooded him, his lips full and open as he took in the sight of her straining breasts.

Straining for him. Toward him. Arousal flooded her, slid out into her satin panties and onto her thighs. She should have demanded they take them off when they took her shirt. She didn't want to have anything between her body and theirs.

Mark ducked his head, clamping his mouth over one nipple, and she whimpered, pressing more into his mouth. She didn't care if they made her beg for what she wanted. She was going to get it. And give it.

Mark wasn't gentle, thank god. She rose up to press his mouth to her nipples, sank into Philip's warm, hard chest behind her, supporting her shoulders.

Mark's tongue laved across one peak before he sucked it into his mouth, letting her feel his teeth. She reached over her head and wrapped her arms around Philip's neck, anchoring herself against their passion, loving how Philip murmured encouragingly in her ear. How he slid his hands over her belly and eased closer behind her, his leg under her ass, his lips locked on her neck.

She turned her head to see Philip's eyes, so close to her own, as he stared down at the other man in his bed, the man who held her aching breasts in his hand and mouth. Their trust in each other had never been so clear, her love never so certain.

Mark lifted his head and she whimpered, returning all her attention to him and protesting his abandonment until he cupped her other breast and latched onto that nipple. Strong lips, rough tongue. Each ferocious tug sent an answering pull to her clit. Mark's other hand caressed the breast he'd already lavished with his attention, his thumb brushing over the peak before his fingers pinched and twisted.

Good lord, she wanted to fly apart. One good rub across her clit and she'd come. Hard. Leaning back to allow Mark access to her breasts had tilted her until she was no longer pressed against his cock. She wriggled her hips, searching for contact, growling in frustration when none came. She moved to take matters into her own hands, but then Philip's fingers, which had been rubbing across her belly, dipped lower.

Yes yes yes. Thank god.

The rough pads of his fingertips brushed along the top of the tiny scrap of satin, and her hips bucked. She wanted him to hurry. No more teasing. She needed him to touch her. To fill her.

Instead, he traced his hands over her hips, as if considering, before curling his fingers around the strings of her thong. Grace thought he meant to pull them off, and she lamented the prospect of unwrapping her legs from around Mark.

Then Philip's hands fisted and tugged. Hard.

Her body jerked with the snap that tore the strings of her panties, startling her. Mark's head jerked up, and they both stared down at Philip's fist clenched around the satin scrap as he slowly pulled it from between her legs. As dark blue satin emerged from between her legs, turning to black where the fabric was soaked, Mark's mouth parted, his breath coming in short pants.

Then Philip drew the satin tight to her body, the last of it taut against her clit, running the rough edge of elastic and stitches along thousands of nerve endings that so badly needed more. She fleetingly wondered when Philip had learned the one thousand ways to torture a woman with her own clothing before she clenched her eyes shut and just focused on the exquisite pleasure.

Yes. Just a little more and she'd come. *Please.*

When the tail of the fabric slipped free, she growled in protest. Damn it. Then Philip's long fingers slid between her legs, his palm cupping her while he brushed over her opening once before returning to her clit.

She watched his face as best she could from that angle, his hooded eyes staring down at where his hand disappeared between her legs. When he flicked his fingers across her clit, bolts of pure delight rocketed through her body. She whimpered, unable to find words of encouragement, of love for what he had already given her just by being there with her. With Mark.

His fingers picked up speed. Her moans picked up volume. Mark stared down at where Philip's arms wrapped around her, where his hand worked at her.

And god, how his hand worked at her. Mark's thighs were as slick as her own, now, easing the rub as she squirmed under Philip's attention.

Unwinding one arm from Philip's neck, she clamped a hand at the back of Mark's. He searched her face before pulling her in for a carnal kiss. She wanted to stay like that forever, but Mark pulled back when Philip's second hand joined the first, his eyes riveted to what Philip was doing to her. She could relate. She found it pretty riveting herself.

Anchored by her arms around both men, she rode the ever-growing waves of pleasure washing over her. Beautiful, trusting, sharing Philip eased two fingers into her, stretching her open as the fingers battering her clit kicked into high gear.

Mark watched with open-mouthed wonder as Philip's fingers disappeared into her again and again, his breath stuttering as he reached out with one finger to trace the thin strip of hair barely visible between Philip's clever hands. Her entire body twitched, hard, as she came apart.

Using the legs wrapped around Mark's hips and the hand

clamped on the back of his neck, she thrust herself down on Philip's fingers and cried out. It was too much. It washed through her like fire, spurred on by Philip's agile fingers, hardly fading before she pumped her hips once, her battered clit still aching, and it took her over again.

Philip had never seen anything more exquisite than Grace climaxing in his and Mark's arms. Her joy would ring in his ears for days. She sounded like she was in agony, but he knew it was pleasure so huge it almost hurt. *Le petit mort.*

Mark was staring at Grace, need etched on his beautiful, bruised face. God, Philip could relate. But unlike Mark, who looked desperate to plunge into Grace, to take her, Philip wanted to watch more than he wanted to act.

When Mark's eyes met his, Philip sank into those dark blue pools. Eyes that were always so ready to laugh were serious, narrowed with unspent desire. Philip knew that not all of it was for Grace. He thought that should probably scare him, but the only thing frightening was how much it pleased him.

Taking deep breaths, he looked down at Grace, who had collapsed back against his chest, an arm locked around each of them. She stared up at him in glassy-eyed wonder.

She'd never been more beautiful. And, damn it, he thought, it was his turn to be brave. Maybe he couldn't jump in with both feet, but he could tell them what he wanted at that moment, more than anything.

He looked at Mark. "I want to watch you fuck her."

At Grace's sharply indrawn breath, his entire body locked up with sheer panic. He clutched her tighter to his chest. "Only if it's okay with you, baby. Only if it's what you want."

Her slow smile set his heart to racing with a rush of relief and adrenaline. With a staggering amount of love. She pulled the arm from around his neck and ran her fingers over his cheek before turning to look at Mark. Mark stared back, hanging on the edge.

Reaching out with both hands, Grace ran her hands into

Mark's hair before pulling his face down to hers. When their lips were only a breath away, she stopped. Her voice was hoarse, throaty, barely above a whisper. "I want you in me, Mark. Right now."

Mark captured her mouth and Philip watched in awe when Mark lifted a hand to her face, his fingers shaking. *Fuck.* Philip understood exactly what Mark was feeling. Knew how soft and warm Grace would be, how wild and sultry.

He ran his eyes over Mark's hard body, admiring the planes and angles, so different from Grace's curves. Yet equally appealing. He let his gaze roam, absorbing the perfection and the flaws, the differences from Grace and the similarities to himself. When he reached the place their bodies were twined together, he frowned.

Mark was still wearing his boxers. Those had to go. Philip admitted to himself he wanted to see the truest physical manifestation of Mark's need. He wanted to see Mark's dick.

Wrapping his arms around Grace's body, Philip pulled her back against his chest and drew her up the bed. Grace whimpered. Mark growled, holding onto Grace and following them up the mattress.

Christ, he wasn't about to engage in a game of tug-of-war when they all wanted the same thing. Reaching for the bedside table, he whipped the drawer open and found what he needed.

"Mark, take those fucking boxers off and put this on." His voice was hard command as he slapped a little foil packet into Mark's palm.

Mark immediately let go of Grace and a thrill ran up Philip's spine at how quickly Mark obeyed. He smiled a little, and Mark stared back as he hooked his thumbs in his waistband and pushed his boxers down and off.

Philip absolutely couldn't resist looking down.

Gorgeous. Mark's dick was long and thick. Not as thick as his own cock, Philip thought, but at least an inch longer. Maybe more. So long, in fact, he wasn't sure Grace could take him in all the way.

The velvet head was large and scarlet, straining away from Mark's body, the veins pronounced where the blood engorged the stiff shaft. Never in his life had Philip thought he'd find another man's cock so damn...tempting.

Fighting the urge to reach out, to touch and to taste, he licked his lips and watched in wonder when Mark's cock bobbed in response.

Fuck.

Gathering what little of his wits he had remaining, Philip slid the last foot to the headboard, pulling his own underwear off before leaning back against the pillows and drawing Grace to him, her head resting on his chest, her body lax and trusting in his arms.

Mark finished putting on the condom, then remained on his knees looking down at them, perfectly still as he took in the picture Philip knew they must make. A study in contrasts. Grace's delicate curves on his hard angles. Her smooth, pale skin running along his darker chest and the rough hair on his legs. The appreciation he saw in Mark's eyes as they darted from his shoulders to Grace's breasts and on to where her hips hid his cock warmed Philip. He'd never seen so much hunger in another man's eyes. Not directed at him. He'd never dreamed he would be so excited by another man's admiration.

He glanced down at Grace and saw she was staring at Mark's cock with longing. She reached out and Mark crawled to her, sealing her lips with his. They were so close, touching Philip in a thousand places across his hypersensitive skin. He fought the urge to squirm, to move and rub against them both. As desperate as he was to ease the ache that had been burning in him since he'd woken up to find Mark staring at him, he wanted to watch even more. He wanted to watch Mark fuck Grace.

As if reading his mind, Mark ran his hands down Grace's sides, planting them on either side of her and levering himself up. His hips twitched and Philip knew Mark was seeking entrance, desperate to sheathe himself, not able to wait another minute. By Grace's moan, he could imagine the smooth head was rubbing through her slick folds, teasing her while begging for entry.

He touched Mark's shoulder. When Mark looked up at him, he wanted to sink into that soft mouth and taste it for himself. He held himself in check.

"I want to see you enter her. I want to see you fuck her. See where you're joined."

Grace groaned and arched her back, trying to impale herself on Mark, but Mark held back, understanding his request. He thrust a pillow under Grace's hips, canting them up, then slid his knees forward and lifted his torso up.

Perfect.

Philip could see it all now. See Grace's legs spread wider as Mark slid an arm under one of her knees and pushed it up against her chest. He jolted when Mark wrapped a hand around Philip's hip to anchor himself and Grace's raised leg. The role of voyeur-only was stolen with one touch, but he couldn't bring himself to shake off Mark's grip. Indeed, he admitted to only himself, he found the feel of Mark's strong hand deeply arousing.

Equally arousing was watching Mark draw a finger down Grace's slit before bringing it back to flick across her clit, drawing moans and pleas from her as her hips began to buck. She quickly reached a fever pitch, pleading with Mark to enter her. To fuck her.

Taking mercy on them all, Mark slid the head of his cock past her entrance and plunged.

Philip forgot to breathe, his eyes unblinking and wide, his heart galloping in his chest as countless fantasies were realized. Grace's moan was the purest music as it vibrated through her and into him. Her nails biting into his thigh the sweetest pain. But nothing compared to the sight of Mark's beautiful, long, hard cock disappearing into her pussy.

Mark stopped when he was buried deep, close to the hilt but not quite there. Grace's gasp told Philip that Mark had met the resistance of her womb. He wondered at what she must be feeling. To be so full.

Mark withdrew and Grace whimpered, lifting the leg not

pinned to her chest to hook it around his hips, holding him close. Mark's quick smile was pure masculine satisfaction as he thrust back in, easing his way farther into her channel. Philip could remember every time he'd ever been with Grace, how tight she'd been, how the muscles would ripple and cling, greedy for the invasion. He could see that need reflected in Mark's face and it pleased him. Pleased him that Mark would know this joy.

Mark continued his short, sharp thrusts, each one taking him deeper into Grace. As the rhythm and force of his thrusts increased, Grace's body pressed farther back into Philip. He shivered. His cock was trapped against his abdomen, sliding against Grace's sweat-slickened back with each thrust. It was as if Mark were fucking them both.

Mark and Grace both grunted when, with one last thrust of his hips, Mark was seated fully in Grace's welcoming wet heat.

Mark stared down at Grace. "Are you okay?"

Grace's smile was radiant. "God, yes."

Mark closed his eyes and took a deep breath before he looked up at Philip. "Sweet Jesus, she's so tight."

He could do nothing more than nod in response, his eyes locked on where Mark and Grace were joined. Every muscle in his body was knotted with desire. His fantasies were pale shadows of the reality of this moment. Never could he have imagined *anything* could be this fucking hot.

Mark pulled back, sliding his cock all the way out of Grace until only his head was lodged within her before plunging back in. She moaned, her arching back running up hard against Philip's chest. His cock.

Within a couple of thrusts, all three of them were moaning long and loud. Philip's hips rocked against the bed and along Grace's skin, no longer able to be a passive observer, unable to stop himself from fucking them back.

His climax was coming on like a freight train, and he held his breath in anticipation. He was fascinated by the hard muscles of Mark's flanks bunching and easing as he pounded into Grace. Mark's balls slapped against her ass with each thrust, slowly drawing up tighter to his body. Philip knew the exquisite pleasure was building to a flash point, could feel the looming detonation in his own body.

He gaze went to Grace's face and the ecstasy etched there. Her eyes were closed tight, her face a mask of fierce concentration as her body slid along his, as her pussy clenched around another man's cock. Around Mark's cock.

Philip bucked against her back, his body no longer his to control.

Grace went over the edge first. Her nails raked his spread thighs, her back taut, bowing as she sucked in three quick breaths and let them out in a shout of triumph that should have rattled the windows. He stared at where her body joined with Mark's, knew how her muscles were rippling down along Mark's cock, remembering the intensity of it as Mark tightened his hold on Philip and plunged faster. Harder. Thrusting Grace back against him, pounding into her with enough force to rock her up and back again and again, the shock of their bodies meeting echoing through his, her warm skin creating unbearable friction.

His release slammed through him, roaring up and out of his balls, tightening his arms around Grace as his hoarse cry joined hers. His cock exploded, easing the drag of Grace's body along his as Mark rocked against them for the last time. He heard Mark's shout and opened his eyes to watch joy transform Mark's face as he pumped into her, his hips working in short, sharp circles.

Philip shook, his body quaking with passion spent and the sheer intensity of the moment. The intimacy.

The bliss.

Grace was struggling to collect her completely scrambled brains when Mark collapsed on top of her and Philip. He was kind enough to shift most of his weight to his elbows, but his head came to rest between her breasts, his gasping breaths pushing her into the bed and Philip's chest.

She could feel the warm slide of semen on her back, how the air was heaving in and out of Philip's lungs, just as it was Mark's, just as it was hers, and she smiled.

That had been fucking incredible. Pun intended.

Philip's hand was trapped between her and Mark, rubbing her belly with the pads of his fingers and Mark's with the back of his hand in slow, lazy circles. Had it been just a day and a half ago that she'd been worried about their sex life? It seemed ludicrous now. She laughed, pure joy bubbling up from where it tickled. Delighted.

Mark's lips curved against her skin, his voice muffled. "What are you laughing at?"

"Take it as a compliment," Philip answered, his voice thick. "Grace laughed the last time we had mind-blowing sex, too."

"I did not!" she said indignantly. Then paused. "Oh, wait...okay, I did. I'm sorry. It just feels so good."

Neither man disagreed. Mark still hadn't even managed to lift his head, although his breathing was returning to normal. She wiggled a little and realized she was rapidly becoming stuck to Philip's chest. Kind of sexy, while still kind of gross.

"Okay, boys, up you get. It's shower time. And I'm hungry."

"Bossy little witch, isn't she?" Mark asked, still speaking into her left breast.

Philip ran the back of his hand down her cheek before letting it hover over Mark's head. She held her breath, waiting to see what he would do. He wanted Mark, but he'd held himself in check. His hand was trapped between them, but Mark had collapsed on it—which wasn't the same as Philip reaching out to stroke or caress him.

She nearly burst with hope and happiness when, finally, he let his hand drop into Mark's soft curls, gently running his fingers through them.

"She can be bossy. But perfect, nonetheless," Philip said, his voice gruff.

Mark lifted his head, Philip's hand still threading through his hair, his thumb skimming gently over the bruised skin beneath Mark's eye.

"Yes, she is," Mark agreed.

Her heart rolled over in her chest.

It was a fine thing to feel so cherished. Sated. Her stomach let out a grumble of protest. And, well, darn hungry.

Mark and Philip had the nerve to laugh at her stomach's loud complaint before helping her and each other from the bed, not the least bit concerned about their nudity as they moved around the apartment. She hopped in the shower first, hoping that someone might join her, but managing to get the job done alone. When she came out of the bathroom, she found Philip, naked, sitting at the breakfast bar talking to Mark, who was in the kitchen wearing Philip's only apron. And only the apron.

"What's the point of the apron if you're going to flash that gorgeous ass at us?"

They both turned to her, grinning.

"The point," Mark explained in patient tones, "is to enjoy being naked without exposing myself to possible injury while I cook you two a midnight snack."

She registered the wonderful smells coming from the stove and peeked over Mark's shoulder to see he was making omelets. *Yum*. Having Mark around had already proven to have plenty of advantages, but that he was an amazing cook wasn't going to suck either.

In fact, she couldn't think of anything that would suck about Mark being with them.

They ate at the small dining room table set to one side of the living room. Grace wore only a T-shirt, Mark only the apron, and Philip was stark naked except for the napkin he carefully draped over his lap, which absolutely cracked her and Mark up.

It was easy, being with these two men. Fun. Thrilling. She didn't think she'd ever been happier.

Mark made her laugh. And almost more importantly, he made Philip smile. Laugh. Her serious-minded lawyer with the hidden wild side and the velvet voice was full of love and joy, but he was not always demonstrative. She knew she brought out Philip's nurturing, soft side. His love, his patience, his romanticism. But Mark brought out the flirt. A playful and often neglected part of Philip that delighted her.

She tried not to wonder how long Mark would be around to bring out this side of Philip. It hurt her heart just to think about it. But it wasn't like it could go on without end.

Could it?

Chapter Seven

The next morning, Grace returned to the dining room table, pretending to do her homework while she watched Philip, shirtless and sexier than any man had a right to be in flannel pajama bottoms, move around the apartment. He washed the breakfast dishes and straightened, collecting laundry as he went and putting away the bedding still neatly folded on the couch.

She turned her head to hide her smile. That answered the question about where Mark would sleep tonight. Not that she'd really had any doubt.

Aside from her increasing certainty that Philip was as caught up in whatever was going on with Mark as she was, there was still the matter of whatever the hell was going on at Valentine's.

She'd seen the axe. She'd seen the hostess stand. She didn't have to be a shrink to know a whole lot of rage went into destroying something like that.

Almost as frightening as the results of that rage was the knowledge that not one of them, nor the police, had even the first inkling why someone would do this. How would they find a bad guy if they had no idea where to look?

Philip had told Mark he'd feel better if he knew Mark was safe. She couldn't agree more. Regardless of what was happening between them, Mark was their friend, and he *was* Valentine's, in name and in spirit. If someone had a problem with Valentine's, it was entirely possible they had a problem with him. It was impossible not to worry. Not to need to know he was safe.

The fact that he was particularly safe tucked into bed with her and Philip was all the better. The best.

Excitement zinged through her as she remembered their midnight romp. She was *really* looking forward to a repeat performance.

Well, actually, perhaps not an exact repeat. She wasn't blind or deaf, and a person would have to be both—*and* a fool—not to see that Philip was attracted to Mark. She'd heard it in his voice when they were in bed together, when he had shared her with Mark; seen it in his eyes when they met Mark's and he couldn't look away. Those moments, in spite of them not touching, had been profoundly intimate. Passionate.

Regardless of the depths of his need, though, there was still a big hurdle for Philip to clear. He was close, running headlong toward it, whether he recognized it or not. She fought her impatience, her desire to demand he get over it and do the things with Mark he so clearly wanted to do. That wouldn't be fair.

If she were honest with herself and not thinking about her own needs and wants, she could understand his hesitation. It wasn't a small thing for a man who'd been in straight relationships his entire life to realize that wasn't what he wanted any longer. Well, not the only thing he wanted. Philip had to let that go, to give up the more widely accepted path and be willing to explore the other options. And by god, he had some serious options before him now.

He might not be ready to admit it just yet, but Philip was bisexual. There was no doubt in her mind. What remained to be seen, though, was how much doubt he carried in his heart and if it would hold him back.

She wished she could make it easier for him. Wished she could help him. Reassure him. But she wasn't sure how, and she feared pushing too hard. He had to do this for himself. And when he did...

The delicious image of Philip on his back, his legs pulled up as Mark pounded into his ass, floated through her mind. She held it there, savoring it and the warmth her rushing blood brought to all the fun parts of her body.

When Philip leaned over and kissed her cheek, she just about leapt out of her skin. His look was knowing. Amused. "What were you just thinking about?"

She was determined to help Philip accept what was happening to him, but maybe she'd keep her naughty fantasies to herself. For now. Too bad her brain was too fried from sleep deprivation and arousal to come up with a good answer. "Uhh...nothing."

Philip slapped a hand to his chest, threw his head back and laughed. "You should see yourself—all flushed with your knees locked together. You were *not* thinking about nothing."

Mark had been in Philip's office making calls, but he poked his head around the corner, no doubt following the rare and enticing sound of Philip's laughter. "What's going on?"

"Grace is having dirty daydreams. She won't admit it, though," Philip said, resuming his cleaning, his smile lingering.

She scoffed. "I was not." She managed to hold on to her outrage for all of about three seconds. Who was she kidding? "Okay, I was. And who can blame me? But I'm still not going to tell you what they are. Get your own dirty daydreams."

Philip stopped what he was doing and looked back at her. "Oh baby, I've got plenty of those. And I don't mind sharing." His voice was Barry White deep, a smooth timbre that rubbed along her skin, standing the hairs on the back of her neck to attention.

Mark had been coming toward her but he faltered, stuttering to a stop near Philip. His blue eyes went dark, his hands curling into fists as he gazed at Philip. Nice to know she wasn't the only one Philip could stir up with his voice alone.

She stood and went to them. Her lovers. They shifted, neatly trapping her between their bodies, as if they'd practiced the dance before. Great minds were thinking alike. Oh, goody.

She leaned against Mark, loving his warmth pressed along her back, letting Philip look at them both. Together. His eyes roved over her, over Mark, the heat obvious. If her daydream had been the frying pan, this was the proverbial fire.

She brushed her hand down Philip's bare chest, but his eyes followed Mark's hands as they skimmed under her shirt, lifting it as his palms smoothed up over her belly and cupped her bare breasts. She sucked in a breath when Mark's thumbs traced over her nipples, the peaks tightening to painful points that shot tingling fire through her body. Her heart raced, her need mounting as her mind searched for a way to allow Philip the joy of Mark's skillful hands, his hot touch and warm body.

Mark's hands continued to roam, pulling her shirt up and off her. While her arms were above her head, Philip hooked his fingers in the waistband of her yoga pants and under the hip strings of her panties and drew them down her legs, tossing them aside.

"No fair," she laughed, teasing. "Why am I the only one who is naked?"

Without hesitation, both men stripped before returning to press her between them. Enveloped by their heat, her head swam. She could feel them, soft in places, rough in others, rubbing all over her. She could smell the different scents of their skin as they wrapped around her, their hands weaving a heady spell over her. They worked in tandem, reaching for her, touching her, but not each other.

Sighing, she let her head fall back onto Mark's shoulder. Mark clutched her tighter and rolled his hips, pressing his straining erection to her ass and Philip's to her belly. She groaned, wishing Mark would cooperate and stop distracting her, even while she ground her ass back against him.

When Philip eased back, she reached for him, her protest dying in her throat when he ran the back of one finger down over her belly to the tiny strip of hair. Mark's hands caught hers and brought them to her own breasts. She cupped and lifted them with his fingers pressed over hers, his thumbs continuing their slow torture as she offered herself up.

It was impossible to focus on anything but their touch. With each swipe of Mark's thumbs, the calloused pads brushed across her sensitive areola and tweaked her tight nipples, sending her higher. His cock nestled closer between her cheeks and she pushed back against it, instinctively searching for more, her quest to help Philip temporarily lost to the barrage of sensations.

Mark buried his face in her hair, his lips close to her ear. "My sweet Grace. You're so ready."

She was. She was burning up. Her need for them boundless. They barely had to touch her and she was consumed by desire.

"Please."

"Begging again," Philip said.

She could hear the smile in his voice. She didn't worry if it was right or wrong. If it got her what she wanted, she was begging.

She briefly considered begging Philip to touch Mark, to kiss him, but even with her brain clouded with arousal, she knew that would be wrong.

Then Philip's finger eased between her swollen lips and over her clit, circling and circling with increasing speed and pressure until her knees were weak and all thought was lost. Mark's arms held her up as sensations spiraled out from that wonderful bundle of nerves and Philip's talented fingers.

Mark lifted his head, but she paid no mind until Philip's fingers stopped moving.

NO! She was so close. She opened her eyes to look at Philip, to see what had stopped his glorious torture, and found he was staring at Mark.

She turned her head. Mark was staring right back.

She hung suspended between them, the tension humming. The hurdle was racing toward Philip, or he toward it, and she prayed he saw it coming and wasn't afraid. She prayed that he would clear it. Mark's heart pounded against her back, his arms tightening around her as, united, they watched. Waited.

Only Philip could take the next step, and he had to do it freely.

Reaching up, she placed her palm over Philip's heart. It galloped beneath her fingers, his breath panting short and sharp. Arousal was turning to fear.

She wanted so badly to help him, to quell his fears, but the best she could do was offer her acceptance. Her love.

"Philip, honey, it's okay," she said, hoping he'd hear her desires, but also understand she'd support him no matter what he decided.

He shook his head once, his fingers unconsciously flicking

across her clit.

She wanted to cry with pleasure and frustration, but she kept her voice gentle. "If it's what you want, then it's right. You don't have to be afraid."

Philip looked down at her, unblinking. His thumb was circling. Tormenting. She didn't think he was even aware he was doing it.

She closed her eyes and gritted her teeth against the sensations. When she opened them again, her men were back to staring at each other. Mark's fingers were pinching her nipples endlessly, as motionless as the rest of him. Philip's fingers drew to a halt once more.

Time stopped on the tip of a pin. Grace held her breath.

Philip stared into Mark's beautiful blue eyes and tried to make sense of what was happening to him. He heard Grace's breath hitch, understood he had her blessing—no, her encouragement—and still, he was unable to move.

The fear of the unknown lodged in his chest like a lead weight, holding him back from doing what he so badly wanted to do. It wasn't the sex he was afraid of. Not anymore. Fuck, just thinking about kissing Mark, touching him, tasting him, sent heat spiraling through his body.

No, the fear was because he cared. He cared for Mark a lot. Too much. He was scared of getting hurt. Of Grace getting hurt. It rattled him that he cared so much about what would happen after the sex. This wasn't a one-night stand or a weekend fling. Not to him.

So he stood, frozen, lost in the yearning he saw in Mark's dark eyes and the answering call from deep in his own chest.

"Please," Mark whispered, his voice rough.

Mark's plea broke the dam that had been his last resistance, making him brave, drowning his fear with the need to touch and be touched by someone he wanted and cared about.

Grabbing Mark by the back of the neck, Philip slammed his

mouth down over Mark's waiting lips. Their tongues met, immediate, warring, his thrusting into Mark's mouth without hesitation or apology. He was met with equal aggression and it burned through him, his seduction complete.

Grace's hands clutched at his arms, her moan long and needy. She watched them kiss and he felt her response in the fresh slick against his fingertips.

He'd always believed himself to be more voyeur than exhibitionist, but Grace's response to their kiss spurred him on. He plunged two fingers into her, thrusting as he sank further into Mark's kiss, rolling his tongue across Mark's, licking through every corner of his mouth. He absorbed everything he could, finding joy in the new and different, the rough cheek and chin, harder, fuller lips, the corded neck muscles under his hand.

Grace was desperate, fucking herself down on his hand. It took what little concentration he had left to hook his fingers and find the spot, zeroing in on it as his thumb rubbed over her clit faster and firmer. Mark wrapped an arm around them both, holding them together. Quite possibly holding them up.

He slid a third finger into Grace.

Strong muscles clenched then rippled and she whimpered, shoving herself down on his hand one last time and grinding against it. Mark steadied her, pressing her more tightly between them, their mouths never parting. She groaned, rocking, the ripples spiraling down on his fingers again and again.

When her knees gave out, they broke apart, gasping, grabbing for Grace and easing her down to the floor, following until all three ended in a sweaty heap on the living room rug.

For a moment, Philip lay on the floor in a daze. Disbelieving and triumphant.

He'd done it. He'd kissed a man. No, he'd kissed *Mark*. And now that he'd had a taste, he wanted to feast.

Dazed, he wondered how he'd ended up at this remarkable place, when not three days ago it would have been impossible. Then he looked down at Grace, stretched out beside him. Her chest was heaving, her lips swollen as she stared up at him.

His Grace. Her love and acceptance had set him free.

"Feel better?" she asked softly, proving how well she understood.

He'd never loved her more. "I do."

"I thought you might," she said, her eyes bright, her lips twitching. She looked damn smug. She had a right.

Tapping her nose with the tip of one finger, he reached for Mark's hand where it lay on Grace's hip. Their eyes met. Their fingers laced together over her warm skin. "She's not just a bossy little witch, she's a clever one," Philip said, his heart lurching when Mark's warm hand clasped his.

Mark's eyes sparkled. "Yeah, she's pretty damn clever."

Grace sighed, happy and apparently boneless on the floor. "You two are going to give me a fat head, which is fine." Her voice scratched and she rubbed a hand over her throat. "Too much shouting."

Mark started to stand. "I'll get you a glass of—"

"Wait." Philip grabbed Mark's wrist, tugging him off balance. He was nervous and achingly aroused. It proved a heady combination. "I'm not done."

Mark landed back on his ass with a thud. The look on his face was priceless. He went from shock to lust in the blink of an eye.

Philip's pulse kicked up a notch. There was so much new territory, so many new things to try, places to explore. He knew how a man's body worked, understood all the ways it could be teased, tormented, and pleasured. He wanted to put that knowledge to good use. He wanted to try them all.

He thought back to kissing Mark. His eyes dropped to Mark's swollen lips.

Mark met him halfway, reaching for him as he reached for Mark. They knelt above where Grace lay on the floor, their broad chests and flat bellies pressed together. Their mouths clashed, meshed, and broke apart. Mark's teeth raked over Philip's lower lip before sinking in for a bite that made Philip's entire body shudder.

Everything with Mark was different. He loved it when Grace submitted. Knew he always would. But with Mark, he wasn't sure what he wanted.

As if reading his mind, Mark ran a hand through Philip's hair and tugged. He let his head fall back, giving himself over to Mark's control and liking it far more than he would have guessed. He watched Grace while Mark ran his tongue across his pulse, then bit his jawline with strong teeth. She sat up, her chin resting on her knees, watching them with fascination.

Apparently, he wasn't the only voyeur in this relationship. The possibilities in that one discovery alone seemed endless.

When Mark's tongue traced the shell of his ear, Philip closed his eyes and moaned. Mark's stubble rasped along his cheek, dragged against the sensitive skin under his chin, along his neck, Mark nibbling and licking as he went. It felt incredible. Mark felt incredible. Philip's hands roamed up and over Mark's back and shoulders, appreciating hard muscle and smooth skin. Not soft like Grace, but smooth. Firmer. The rasp of chest hair across his nipples as their bodies shifted was intense. Distracting.

He pressed his hips forward, gliding the leaking head of his cock along Mark's belly, drawing a line through the trail of hair that ran from navel to groin. Mark thrust back, growling in frustration when his cock slid to one side, then reaching between their bodies to wrap his long, lean fingers around both their cocks, bringing them into full contact from tip to stem, his thumb brushing over the swollen heads.

Fuck. The air stuck in Philip's lungs, then exploded out when Mark's warm fist pumped up and down the length of their shafts. The roll of Mark's silky skin against his was mesmerizing.

His moan was hoarse. "Do that again."

Mark's smile was wicked as he did as Philip had asked.

Philip rode another wave of desire, his toes curling as Mark took him higher. He grabbed the back of Mark's neck for support, for control, distracted by the resistance. He loved how strong Mark was. How forceful Philip could be with him.

Their eyes met and Philip felt something inside him shift, his

110

heart stuttering. This was what he'd been afraid of. This was so much more than simple need, and nothing as uncomplicated as *just sex*. The emotions coursing through him proved he'd been right to be scared, but he could find no room for regret as he stared into Mark's dark blue eyes. Instead, he found only hope that he wasn't imagining the look Mark sent back. He found only immense gratitude and love for Grace for helping him find this.

With a slow smile, Philip pulled Mark in for another kiss. Their tongues met and tangled, retreating from one mouth and then the other. Philip moaned into Mark's mouth when Mark's thumb stroked again over the aching head of his cock, smearing the moisture it had gathered from them both. He was going to come and he wasn't ready.

Or, rather, he was more than ready. But he wasn't finished. No, in fact, he was just getting started.

Tearing his mouth free, he planted a hand in the middle of Mark's chest and shoved him back. When Mark's brows quirked in question, he smiled.

"I like how you taste," he explained.

Mark looked at him quizzically. "Okay, I like how you taste, too. So, why'd you stop?"

Philip pushed again, harder, forcing Mark to release their cocks and land on his ass, sprawled out on the carpet.

"I like how your mouth tastes. Now I want to try the rest of you."

Mark winged one brow up before propping himself on his elbows and letting his legs fall open. His cock stood at attention above his body. "Do your worst."

He heard Grace suck in a gulp of air, but he couldn't tear his eyes away from Mark. He felt like a starving man at the all-you-can-eat buffet, determined not to miss a single bite.

Focused, Philip wrapped a hand around each of Mark's ankles, testing their warmth and strength before running his palms up and over calves, shins, and knees, before tickling into the crisp hairs sprinkled across his inner thighs. He stopped within inches of Mark's tight sac, hovering for a moment before stroking out to the points of his hips. Mark's stomach twisted, his breathing picked up speed.

It excited Philip to see the signs he knew so well. The symptoms of desire translated through a man's body. There was a symphony of sexual sensation at his fingertips and this was an instrument he knew how to play.

Careful not to touch Mark's cock, Philip let his thumbs drag along the wedge of muscle that bound abdomen to groin, captivated by how Mark's stomach dipped and knotted, the anticipation tightening his belly. So much hard muscle. He couldn't resist running his hands over every inch of it, eagerly tracing the ridges and bumps of sinew and skin so like his own, but still fascinating, because they were Mark's.

So few curves and soft edges. So different than a woman. But the desire was just as powerful. Just as consuming.

He couldn't resist a taste any longer, curiosity driving him on. Leaning down, he pressed his lips to the divot of Mark's navel, smiling when he hissed in response.

Salty. His tongue slipped out, swirling around the taut outer ring of flesh before licking across the surface of it. A combination of flavors, sweat and soap and *Mark*, danced on his tongue.

He took a bite, then soothed the spot with his lips and a gentle lick. Mark's scent filled his head until his own need clawed at him, but he continued his slow exploration with his mouth and hands, devoted to memorizing every inch of his lover.

Mark's breath hitched when Philip dragged his tongue up and over his belly, sliding sideways to ride the curve under one bulging pectoral before clamping his lips around a nipple. Mark's hips jerked with the first good, hard suck, the head of his cock poking Philip in the ribs, making him smile. He wasn't going to be able to resist paying attention to that for long. Nor did he want to.

Congratulating himself for resisting at all, he moved to the other nipple, biting it once before his lips pressed over the hard little nub and began to suck. Mark's hand ran through Philip's hair, pressing his face to his chest. Philip took this as a cue to suck harder.

"Jesus, Philip." Mark's groan turned into a growl. "I need...I want..."

Philip groaned against Mark's chest. God, he loved it when they begged.

With a last suck and a loud pop, he released Mark's nipple. "What do you want? Tell me what you want."

"Jesus," Mark said again. Still propped up on his elbows, he looked down his chest at Philip, strain evident in every facet of his body, his voice. He writhed restlessly. "I don't care. Anything. Just, please, do something. I want whatever you want."

Philip paused, his pulse pounding, his breath short. One didn't get offered carte blanche often in life, and he took a moment to savor it, to savor Mark sprawled out beneath him. He could do anything he wanted. There were so many things. But he'd determined his prize in this fight the minute he'd pushed Mark onto his back. He'd stick with Plan A.

He kissed Mark briefly, fiercely, tempted to linger, but pulling himself away to lick a trail back down Mark's body, pausing to hover above his erection. Mark's need rumbled from his chest in a long moan that Philip cut short by running his tongue around the soft crown of Mark's cock. The immediate silence might have amused Philip, but he was completely spellbound by what he had discovered. What he had done and wanted to do.

The texture and resistance of Mark's cock were familiar, while shockingly new against his tongue. The flavor unlike any Philip had tasted before. Impatient for more, he licked across the velvet surface, burrowing the tip of his tongue into the slit to steal the dollop of pre-come and roll it around on his tongue.

Mark thrashed beneath him, his body pleading for more, until Philip took mercy, dropping his head and taking a good portion of the shaft into his mouth.

For a moment, Philip remained as he was, Mark's cock stretching his lips, filling his mouth, all thoughts of technique lost to the musky taste, the heat of the shaft pressing so intimately against his tongue. He hadn't been sure how it would be, how it would feel, but he found joy in the act. He whisked and wiggled his tongue beneath Mark's shaft, savoring Mark's low moan, his need palpable in his voice. Fulfilling that need became Philip's only mission.

Wrapping a hand around the base of Mark's considerable length, Philip pushed his lips lower, sealing them tightly about the shaft and sucking hard as he pulled back. Mark's hips shot off the floor, possibly in response to the extraordinary pleasure burning down his cock, or just trying to keep himself buried in Philip's mouth. Maybe both.

Philip knew exactly how good it felt and it drove him to give more. It heightened his own pleasure in the act. He flicked his tongue back and forth under the head, tickling the sensitive divot while he sucked, putting as much pressure as possible on that perfect spot without forcing Mark up against his teeth. Then he plunged once, twice, before doing it all over again. Occasionally he'd detour, his lips wrapped around only the crown and the tip of his tongue tickling into the slit, greedily gathering up the pre-come that continued to leak as he tugged upward.

When Mark's hips bucked, he tightened his grip at the base of the shaft and pumped his hand the length twice before starting all over again, this time pulling all his new tricks into one long course of pleasant torture for Mark. As only seemed fair, Philip was determined to rock his world.

It appeared to be working.

"Fuck!" Mark's shout was hoarse, his head thrown back, his eyes sightless. The tendons in his neck stood out as he fought for the control Philip was doggedly trying to steal from him. His chest bulged with clenched muscle as his stomach contracted and he fought not to lift his hips.

He was amazing. Beautiful. Gloriously masculine. He was laid out in utter abandon, lost to pleasure. Exactly how Philip wanted him.

When Grace crawled up, leaning close to study how his mouth worked over Mark, he cut his eyes over to look at her. She met his gaze and shrugged. "Who better to learn from than someone so familiar with the equipment involved?" Her smile was wicked as she glanced at Mark, panting beneath them. "*He sure seems to think you're a natural.*"

Philip would have smiled back if it had been possible. Instead he closed his eyes and concentrated on giving Mark as much pleasure as he could, knowing that nothing would please him more than Mark's complete surrender. He concentrated on taking more and more of Mark into his mouth. Into his throat. Unfortunately, his gag reflex wasn't cooperating. Drawing back, he caught his breath, using the trail of his saliva and Mark's pre-come to lubricate his fist as he pumped from the base.

Apparently, he wasn't the one to give Grace lessons. How on Earth had she done this yesterday? He could have sworn she'd taken him down her throat and swallowed. Maybe she didn't have a gag reflex?

When he looked at her, she quirked one eyebrow. "Harder than it looks, isn't it?"

He smiled, but before he could respond, Mark cut in. "It couldn't possibly be any harder than it is. Please, one of you, finish me before I die."

Grace burst into laughter and Philip grinned, his heart skipping at the happiness shining in Grace's eyes and the smoldering heat in Mark's. Mark looked like he was almost in pain, and Philip took pity, wrapping his lips around him once more.

He was vaguely aware of Grace moving away, but quickly lost track of her, his sole focus returning to Mark.

Mark's taste was intense. Earthy. Male. His moans and his utter inability to control the twitch of his hips were like a stream of praise for what Philip was doing, urging him on, driving him to increase the suction and speed.

When a soft, warm hand wrapped around his own aching cock, he jolted. Gasping, he released Mark's cock from his mouth. "Jesus. Warn a man! I almost maimed Mark."

Mark's head snapped up. When he saw Grace had wrapped

herself around Philip, her hand pumping between his legs, Mark squeezed his eyes shut. "Please. Please, Gracie, don't distract him. Let him finish it."

Silent laughter shook Grace as Philip took Mark back into his mouth, dipping his head and setting his rhythm to match hers— the only way his scrambled brains could manage to stay on task while being stormed by so much pleasure. Each time her thumb brushed over the head of his cock, his tongue laved over the head of Mark's. Each squeeze of her hand along his shaft was a firm suck along Mark's. It didn't take Grace, the clever witch, long to figure out she was conducting the action and to take full advantage. She kept her rhythm steady, controlled, only taking it up a notch when Mark's groans and Philip's jerking hips told her it was time.

Apparently, there were all kinds of things he could learn from Grace. The pace she set felt right. And god knew Mark was loving it. He was moaning without end, his hips thrashing erratically.

Grace pushed the tempo faster, taking both men with her. Closing his eyes, Philip fought for the focus to give Mark what he needed and not be distracted by what Grace was doing.

So close. So close. His balls drew up, his release at the ready, his gut tightening.

He screwed his eyes closed tight, scolding himself to concentrate. He couldn't go without Mark.

When one of Grace's fingers traced over his ass, he groaned, the vibrations from his lips echoing up Mark's shaft, making the other man cry out beneath him. When she slid her finger past the tight ring of muscles and into his ass, a bolt of dark pleasure rocked through him and he came dangerously close to losing it, his moan louder, longer. He wanted more.

Mark's shout brought him back from the edge. Barely. "Fuck, Philip. *Fuck!* Do it!"

Mark had no idea what he was asking for, but Philip was going to give it to him. Lifting his head for the second it took to moisten one of his own fingers with his mouth, he immediately lunged back down on Mark, taking more of him than he had before. *Fuck the gag reflex*, he thought wildly. Grace was pressing her finger to a spot in his ass that made stars shine behind his closed eyelids, it was so fucking good. Was there anything his witch didn't know, for Christ's sake?

The pace was furious and his head bobbed faster, his tongue swirling over Mark's crown with each retreat before he plunged his mouth down again. As Mark got closer, his knees came up, his heels digging in, giving his hips purchase to thrust. Philip wrapped his fist around the base of Mark's cock to prevent it from being jammed all the way down his throat, even though that was exactly where Philip wanted it, wished it could go.

The thrilling eroticism of letting Mark fuck his mouth took Philip to the jagged edge. Every muscle in his body tensed, desperate to fall on the other side, into the abyss.

Determined to take Mark with him, he pressed his finger into Mark's ass, pushing deep.

Mark exploded. His hips reared up from the floor, forcing himself into Philip's eager mouth as his come burst onto Philip's tongue. Into his throat. Philip swallowed fast, wanting every drop.

Grace was pumping hard now, both on his cock and in his ass. The sound of Mark's roar, the tang of his come, sent Philip flying. Releasing Mark's spent cock from his mouth, he gasped, pumping his shaft into Grace's hand then throwing himself back on her finger. When she pressed that magic spot again, he shouted with triumph and let his orgasm rip through him.

Lightning shot from every corner of his being, his soul burning with it, his body racked with ecstasy. His abandon complete and welcome. He trembled in Grace's arms, bucking against her hands while holding onto Mark for dear life.

And what a sweet and surprising life it was turning out to be.

An hour later, Mark still lay on the living room floor with Philip and Grace, their naked bodies touching his in a thousand places. He wasn't one for superlatives, but this was the best weekend of his entire life. No question.

Sure, his restaurant had been broken into and vandalized. And he knew Philip was concerned for his safety, though they really had no reason to believe he was in any danger, provided he didn't go crashing around any more blind corners. But the restaurant would recover. Mark would recover.

So rather than being upset about it, he thanked the fates or whomever else had conspired to allow him a weekend of scorching sex with not one, but two people he loved.

And love them he did.

Not one more than the other. Not one because of the other. Not the package, or the couple, or the sex. He was in love with Grace. Just as he was in love with Philip.

It was stupid. It was going to hurt so fucking much when they got over him and the thrill of his presence in their bed, but god help him, he couldn't stop it. Wouldn't want to if he could. He just wanted to be with them, as much, as often, and in as many ways as possible.

And he wanted to get started on some of those ways as soon as possible. With a few gentle questions, he'd discovered that neither Grace or Philip had ever had anal sex, or engaged in anal play of any kind before yesterday. Based on that and the gleam in their eyes when the subject had come up, they were both ready. Eager.

He was more than happy to teach them everything they ever needed to know. Hell, he was shaking with his desire to do so, but first he needed to get some supplies.

It took a lot of willpower to peel himself up off the floor. Pulling his shirt and shorts back on, he turned to his lovers. His loves. "I have to run out."

"What?" Grace took hold of his hand, as if to keep him from leaving.

"Just for an hour. I have to check on Valentine's, then I want to run home for some things."

"You'll come back?" Philip asked.

It pleased him that Philip was the one to ask. That he wasn't trying to hide from what had happened. A lot of men would have.

Mark kissed him. A long, hard kiss. "You couldn't keep me away."

Philip's smile squeezed his heart. "And you'll spend tonight with us?"

"Yes," he agreed quickly. Christ, he didn't even want to leave them for an hour.

"I'll call a car for you," Philip said, standing and reaching for his phone.

"That's all right. I can walk, or I'll take the subway," Mark offered.

"No," Philip said in a voice that made clear he was determined, "I want you in a car. I know a good company. I trust them." Philip began dialing. "They'll be here in five minutes."

Mark was generally too cheap to take a taxi, let alone hire a damn car service. He looked at Grace, helpless. Her wink told him not to bother arguing. He'd get no support there.

Sighing, he told himself not to read too much into their protectiveness.

Even if it warmed him from the inside out.

Chapter Eight

With the help of Philip's fancy car service, it took Mark less than five minutes to pop over to Valentine's and confirm with the guard that all was well. He didn't expect any issues now that there was someone on site, but he'd needed to check for himself.

Walking back out onto the sidewalk, he saw a black Crown Victoria parked across the street, just a few cars down from the Lincoln Town Car in which he'd arrived. He was sure it was the same car he'd seen, repeatedly, the day before. Only this time, it was parked and he could see someone behind the wheel—someone who turned away as soon as Mark caught his eye.

A whisper of unease brushed down Mark's neck, his body humming as he stepped off the curb and cut across the street, determined to ask the man who he was, or to at least get a license plate. As soon as he passed the Lincoln, his car-service driver got out and followed him, his hand slipping beneath his sports coat.

Mark jolted, almost forgetting his mission as realization slammed home. Jesus Christ, Philip hadn't just hired him a car, he'd hired him a fucking *bodyguard*.

His hesitation was a mistake. The mysterious sedan gunned its engine, tires squealing as it shot out of the parking space and down the street.

7077—

Mark only caught the first four numbers of the plate before the car roared around the corner onto Tremont Street. He yanked his phone from his pocket, scrambling for Patrick's card and dialing the number.

Voicemail. Crap. He left a quick message sharing what little information he had. Hopefully, he was just being paranoid, but he seriously doubted it at this point.

His bodyguard stood close, listening. How freaking weird was that? When Mark hung up, the driver nodded approvingly

120

before opening the back door of the Lincoln and ushering Mark inside.

All Mark wanted was to get back to Philip and Grace as quickly as possible, but he gave his address, and another for the errand he needed to run en route. If the driver thought anything of their side trip, he kept it to himself, his face impassive.

Sitting back, Mark turned the events of the past two days over in his mind. When they finally pulled up in front of his building, he scanned the street before climbing out of the car and running up the front stairs. His "driver" stood on the sidewalk, surveying the street. It took Mark only seconds to key open the crappy front door lock, damaged by years of tenants tampering with it so they wouldn't have to let their guests into the building. He quickly crossed the small foyer and climbed the three flights of stairs to his apartment. When he rounded the last corner, he stopped cold, clutching the worn wooden bannister.

There was no way in hell he'd left his door open.

Hands shaking, he spun on his heel and ran back down to the street, digging out his phone to dial 9-1-1. Then he called Philip and Grace.

Grace stood in the doorway to Mark's apartment, Philip a reassuring presence at her back. Mark moved carefully around the living room, picking up some of the more precious items from the floor, stepping over others. There didn't seem to be any rhyme or reason to what had been smashed and what had gone unscathed.

She wished she knew what the hell was going on. She wanted to scream and yell and demand the police find answers so Mark wouldn't have to suffer another blow. First Valentine's, now his apartment? And no one, not a one of them, could come up with a reason why.

Philip's hand came to rest on the back of her neck, his thumb rubbing under her hair, offering what little comfort he could. She knew he was desperate to offer the same to Mark, but he held back, watching silently as Mark catalogued his belongings and tried to determine what, if anything, was missing.

Fifteen minutes and two thorough searches later, it was the same story as at Valentine's. The place had been searched, his belongings destroyed and tossed all over the place, but nothing appeared to be missing.

Detective Brown stood in the middle of the mess and shook his head. At this point, Grace had spent enough time with Patrick to add him to her holiday card list.

He was the first to break the silence. "Mark, can you think of *any* reason why someone would target you like this? Can you think of anything you might have that someone would be this desperate to get their hands on?"

Mark ran his fingers through his hair. He'd showered that morning at Philip's, but already the curls were unruly, driven to stand on end by his relentless fingers combing through them.

Her fingers twitched with the need to smooth them back into place.

"No, nothing. I swear," Mark growled. "No one has asked me for anything. Given me anything. *Nothing*. Fuck! What is going on?"

Patrick shook his head. "I have no idea," he admitted. He looked at the door again, and she knew he was trying to make sense of it having been opened without being broken. There was a sturdy lock in the doorknob and a deadbolt above. Both looked new and well-made, but they had both been picked open. According to Patrick, only professionals, really experienced ones, were able to do that.

Not the same thugs who broke through plywood windows with an axe. Which meant that possibly more than one person was after Mark.

Fear and nausea rolled through her.

Patrick pulled his phone from his pocket. "Give me a minute and I'll see if there was any luck with that license plate you gave me."

Mark nodded, turning away and running his hands through

his hair again. Her heart hurt watching him, knowing he felt helpless. Philip growled low then urged her forward, taking Mark's elbow and her hand, pulling them both toward the bedroom. He looked behind them at Patrick. "We'll be back in a minute. I just want to talk to these two."

If not for her nerves, she would have laughed at the look on Patrick's face. Were they that obvious?

She glanced at Mark, saw how he was looking at both her and Philip, and found a smile. Oh, yeah, it was pretty obvious. Perhaps she should be embarrassed, but she wasn't. Everyone should be so lucky.

As soon as the bedroom door closed behind them, Philip reached for Mark, pulling him in as she did the same, sandwiching Mark between them. With their heads pressed together, Mark put an arm around each of them, his sigh uneven.

They held on, barely rocking back and forth. It was a while before Philip spoke. "I want you to come stay with me until this is over." He looked at her. "Both of you."

She nodded, agreeing immediately, but Mark stiffened. Her heart sped up, delighted by the idea of Mark staying with them for a while, terrified that he'd decline.

"That's not necessary. I don't want to impose. And I don't want to drag you both in any further than I already have."

Philip leaned back to study Mark's face. "If you don't want to stay with us..."

Mark looked horrified. He wrapped a hand around Philip's neck. "No. No, that's not it at all. God, I want to stay with you, but I couldn't stand it if I put you two in danger."

Philip's scowl was fierce. *Uh oh*, Grace thought. She could practically see his protectiveness kicking into overdrive. And as ridiculously sexy as that could be, it would be easier if Mark agreed through reason before Philip started making demands.

Sliding around so that she faced both men, she smiled at Mark and put her hand on Philip's arm. "Let's be sensible. Philip's apartment is the safest of our three choices. His building is the most secure, with the cameras and the fancy locks." She spoke as if being separated wasn't even an option. But she supposed it was. Mark still looked unsure. "Don't you understand? If you can't stand the idea of us in danger, how could we possibly stand the idea of you facing this alone?"

Mark searched her face. Eventually he nodded and turned to Philip. "Are you sure?"

"Yes. Damn it, Mark, you need to be safe. *I* need to know that you're safe." Philip's voice was rough with the quiet admission.

Grace's heart fluttered in her chest and, in spite of their situation, she felt giddy. It was crazy and stupid and totally improbable, but she was beginning to believe she was in love with two men.

She hadn't even known it was possible, but it was. She knew that now. And while Philip hadn't just offered a declaration of love to Mark, it was a declaration of possession. She knew how closely linked those two concepts were in Philip's mind. In his heart.

Mark stared at Philip, and she wondered if Mark had any idea. By the look on his face, she thought he might have some. When eventually Mark nodded, Philip brought them both in for another long embrace.

Grace buried her face against her men's chests and hoped to god the police figured out whatever was going on, even while looking forward to every minute Mark was bound to stay with them.

Mark couldn't believe he'd agreed to spend an unforeseeable amount of time living with Philip and Grace. He wanted to dance a fucking jig and pound his head against the wall, all at the same time.

This was insane. When Philip had turned all that possessive he-man stuff on him, he had practically shivered with delight. How fucking stupid was that? If asked forty-eight hours ago what he would have done if a man he was sleeping with pulled that kind of shit, he'd have probably said he'd walk—possibly run— right out the door. Instead, he wanted to rip the man's clothes off.

Good thing Mark was conscious of Patrick's presence in the next room. He resisted the urge to tackle both Grace and Philip to the bed and have his way with them, to celebrate all that was good in spite of all that was wrong in his world right now. Instead, he leaned in and kissed Grace gently before doing the same to Philip. When Philip began to kiss him back in earnest and Grace's hand slid over his ass, his head swam and he almost tossed decency to the wind.

With considerable will, he tore his mouth from Philip's. His breath was already coming in soft pants. "You two are going to kill me. There's a cop in my living room, for Christ's sake. Maybe we should keep our clothes *on*?"

Grace laughed but stepped back, slipping her hand into Philip's as he eased away. "Okay, that's a good point," she said. "I don't want to frighten poor Patrick."

Philip's gaze was ridiculously possessive as it roamed over both of them. Mark's cock filled further, responding to the caress of Philip's eyes as if it were a physical touch.

"Shit, Philip. Knock it off. I need to be able to walk." He reached down to rearrange himself, trying to unbend his growing erection.

Philip's face broke into a slow, sexy smile.

Grace drew Philip's attention with a tug on his hand. "If I'm going to be at your place for a while, I need to get some stuff from my apartment." She looked at Mark. "Will you be okay if I leave you for a couple of minutes to run over to my place?"

"Sure, but Philip should go with you." In his mind's eye, he could see that damn black car passing them repeatedly as they'd all walked home hand in hand yesterday. "I don't want you out alone. Not until we figure out what's going on."

Philip nodded. "Agreed. But what about you?"

"I'll wait for you here and finish up with Patrick. Clean up a little."

Philip looked like he wanted to argue, but, after a long pause, he nodded. That settled, Grace and Philip each kissed him again, promising to return as soon as they could. When Philip turned to leave, Mark held him back with a hand on his arm.

"Did you come using the same car service?"

"We did," Philip answered carefully, measuring his response.

Mark smiled, relieved and amused. Had Philip thought Mark wouldn't notice his driver was a bodyguard? "Good. Okay. Go."

Philip inclined his head with a small smile before following Grace through the living room and out the door.

He watched them go and knew without a doubt he was becoming a complete sap when he missed them within minutes.

He and Patrick spent the next half hour trying to find some event in his recent, or even ancient, history to explain the break-ins, all the while straightening up the mess the intruders had left behind. He knew it wasn't standard operating procedure for BPD detectives to clean house for victims and he appreciated Patrick's help. Their conversation flowed and they worked together well, connecting over shared experiences growing up in the area. It was a fucked-up way for friends to meet, but he thought he might like to hang out with Patrick sometime without there being crime tape involved.

They stopped their cleaning efforts only occasionally for Patrick to jot down something in his notebook. Despite that, Mark knew he wasn't giving Patrick much to go on.

"You don't have any enemies? Anyone at all? Some other restaurant owner who thinks you stole his customers? A chef you fired in a fit one night? Anything?"

Mark laughed. "You've been watching too many of those stupid shows on TV about prima donna chefs. Truth be told, we're just ordinary small-business owners, most of us. And no, I can't think of any rivalry so great that someone would need to search my home. I mean, what the fuck would they be looking for? My newest recipes? Who cares? All they'd have to do is come in to Valentine's one night and try something and they'd probably be able to mimic it readily enough."

Patrick slapped the cover closed on his notebook. "Damn. Well, if you think of anything, you know how to reach me. And I'll let you know if and when I learn anything." Nodding toward the front windows, Patrick smiled. "I noticed you've got a car from McCormick. Stick with them until this is over, if you can afford it."

"Philip's idea. And he can afford it. Speaking of, if you need me, Grace and I are staying at Philip's."

Patrick's snort of laughter brought him up short. "Good for you, man."

"It's not what you think," Mark blurted. Well, actually, it probably *was*, but it felt strange admitting it.

Patrick's brows lifted with surprise. "It's not? Because, not for nothing, but I've seen the way the three of you look at each other, and I just assumed...well, it seemed pretty obvious from the moment I met you."

"It was?" He thought back, remembering when they first met over his shattered window. "But that was before—" he stopped himself mid-sentence. Duh. He'd just admitted that it *was* what Patrick was thinking.

Patrick hooted and slapped Mark on the shoulder. "If that was *before*, then I'm impressed the three of you managed to keep your hands off each other."

"In hindsight, so am I," Mark admitted, relieved. Of all the rooms in his life, the closet had always been the least comfortable. "Shit. Thanks for being cool with it. I wasn't sure how people would react. I mean, Grace and Philip are...um...you know. Together. With each other. I'm just sort of...visiting?" He sat down on the couch. Hard. It felt like his heart had been ripped out of his chest. "*Fuck.*"

Disconcerted, Patrick hesitated a moment before sitting on the coffee table to face him. "Look, for what it's worth, I spend a lot of time watching people, and I think I'm pretty good at it. Philip and Grace don't treat you like an outsider. They treat you just as they treat each other." He leaned back, shrugging a little. "And as far as what other people think, fuck 'em, you know?"

Patrick was what Mark's mother would call a *good egg*. "You're pretty open minded for a cop, aren't you? How'd you get to be so enlightened?"

Patrick shrugged. "What can I say? My best friend is bisexual. And if that weren't enough to teach me acceptance, I went and kissed him last week. Let's just say it's given me new perspective."

"I hope that works out for you," he said, respecting Patrick all the more for his candor.

Patrick just shook his head. "Yeah, well, there's this girl..."

Mark winced in sympathy. "Oh. Yeah. It can be complicated," he agreed.

For a moment, they both sat quietly, lost in their own thoughts. Mark just about jumped a foot when his phone rang. The caller ID identified Philip.

"Hello?"

"Mark! Is Patrick still there with you?"

"Yeah. What's up?"

"We're at Grace's place. It's been tossed. Just like yours." Philip's voice shook. Mark thought of Grace's apartment being wrecked, thought about what it might have meant if she'd been home when whoever had done it had arrived, and his stomach bottomed out.

"Son of a bitch. We're on our way."

Three hours and another police report later, and still they had nothing. Philip was ready to explode, but instead he sat rigid, holding tight to his temper. He had to. Poor Grace was exhausted, sandwiched between him and Mark on her little couch. He didn't want to scare her more than she already was.

Looking around her apartment, he realized that in other circumstances, the situation would have been funny. He and Mark were far too big for her tiny efficiency—one of them alone would have filled the place to capacity—but with both of them there, along with Patrick, who was a giant of a man, it was comical. The studio apartment version of the clown car.

Grace's head rested on Mark's shoulder, one of her hands

warm between Philip's palms. The four of them continued to toss around theories, trying and failing to come up with some plausible explanation. The results ranged from the highly unlikely to the marginally more probable than alien abduction.

The truth was, none of them had any fucking idea what was going on. Still. What they did know was that it was somehow tied to Valentine's or, possibly, Mark. Or both. In other words, they didn't know much.

They'd already called all of Mark's employees, telling them to be careful, asking them if they'd seen or heard anything strange. Twenty-six phone calls later, they'd learned nothing new. While relieved that no one else had been affected, their frustration continued to mount.

When Patrick's phone rang, he stepped into Grace's kitchen to answer it. It was a courteous if totally pointless gesture, as the galley kitchen was less than ten feet from the couch. Hell, Philip thought with a frown, nothing in the apartment was more than twenty feet from any other part of the apartment. It was efficient, even for an efficiency.

When Patrick's voice boomed, "What the fuck is going on here?" followed by, "No way is this guy involved in that shit," they all sat up straighter.

Patrick strode out of the kitchen and took the only seat available to him—the ottoman. Holding the phone away from his ear so whoever was on the other end could hear all sides of the conversation, he looked at Mark. "Do you know or associate with Mario Benedetto?"

Mark looked like he'd been punched in the face—*again*.

Philip had officially hit his fucking limit. He shot to his feet. "What the fuck kind of question is *that*?"

Mark put a hand on his arm. "Philip. Please, sit." When he did as Mark asked, his mind seething, Mark turned back to Patrick. "I'm going to assume you have a reason for asking me if I'm associated with a notorious mob boss, and therefore not take it personally. The answer is no. I've never met him and I hope I never do."

A chill ran all the way down Philip's spine. Hours of confusion congealed into a lump of cold dread in his belly.

Patrick looked at him, then Grace. "Do either of you have any dealings with Mario Benedetto?"

Philip ground out his denial through clenched teeth. Grace, wide-eyed, just shook her head.

Patrick pressed the phone back to his ear, listening to someone, nodding, and scribbling notes in his little book. Sitting there, waiting for answers, trying to be patient, was torture. Philip fisted his hands on his thighs, forcing himself to be still when all he really wanted to do was pack a bag, load Grace and Mark into the car, and get the hell out of Dodge.

Finally, Patrick hung up. "Mark, that license plate you gave me started a shit storm down at the station. It's a fake, but believed to be used by members of the Benedetto organization."

Grace's quietly muttered f-bomb pretty much summed up what everyone was thinking.

"The good news," Patrick continued, "is that you've now got the entire Organized Crime Task Force trying to solve this case. The bad news is that you've somehow attracted the attention of some seriously bad people."

Philip thought Patrick had a strange idea of what constituted good news.

"This is insane," Grace said, anxiety pitching her voice high. "Why would Mario Benedetto want to search my apartment?"

Patrick didn't have any answers. Philip wanted to rail at him for that, but held himself in check. He was worked up enough already. It would take little to sever the paper-thin tether he held on his temper. He knew his anger was a reaction to being scared shitless, but he couldn't seem to rationalize it away.

Patrick stood. "I have to get back. My captain wants a full account of what I know." He sighed and tucked his notebook away. "Which, of course, is jack shit. But it will be a barrel of laughs to tell him that in person."

Mark stood and shook his hand. "Thanks for everything you've done today."

Patrick shrugged. "I wish I had more answers for you. If you think of anything, call me. In the meantime, pack your bags and let McCormick take you home. They're the best. Then I'd suggest you lock yourselves in. We'll keep an eye on the building, park a cruiser out front. We don't have any reason to think they're interested in hurting you, but let's proceed with caution, okay?"

Mark nodded. "We'll lock ourselves in, I promise."

Philip had been staring at his hands, wrestling with his frustration, but he happened to look up in time to watch Patrick wink at Mark and mouth the words *lucky you*. A bolt of surprise and nerves shafted through him.

The detective knew.

Which meant someone knew he was sleeping with Mark. That he was fucking a man. Anxiety fluttered in his chest, a hint of panic ate at the edges of his mind. He'd never given any thought to being *out*. Christ, until two days ago, he'd never given any thought to being bisexual. And now, before he could give it any thought at all, he was both.

Embarrassed, he fought the urge to fidget, unsure where to look. What to do. His roaming gaze eventually landed on Mark, who was watching him with concern. The panic mounted.

Shit. He was fucking this up. He didn't want to fuck this up.

He tried to get his mind around the facts, the lawyer in him collecting his arguments. What did he know? He knew he was, in fact, bisexual, shocking though that was. He also knew he didn't want to lose Mark. Didn't want Grace to lose Mark.

Those last two facts were very important to him. They were absolute certainties.

His priorities fell into place. He knew what he wanted. He knew what he considered unacceptable. And he knew if he tried to shove their relationship back into the proverbial closet, he'd be sending a message to Mark that he was ashamed of him.

That was totally unacceptable.

He wasn't ashamed of anything, least of all Mark. God, it made his chest ache to think of hurting Mark like that.

Instinctively, he reached out to brush his fingers down Mark's arm, just the briefest touch against his warm skin. It wasn't a grand gesture, but it was enough. Mark's shoulders sagged and Philip realized he had something to be ashamed of after all. Himself, for allowing Mark to think for one second that he might deny him.

Grace wrapped her arms around his waist and squeezed. He didn't doubt their clever little witch was aware of what had just happened.

Philip turned back to Patrick. "We'll lock ourselves in."

"Good," Patrick said, his look apologetic. He must have guessed at some point during the lengthy silence that he'd put his foot in it.

"I'm just going to run home for my things and then you'll be able to find us all at Philip's," Mark said.

"No." Philip's denial was quick. Firm. "I don't want you out there alone."

Mark's smile was gentle and his eyes held something that made Philip's heart beat funny. "I meant we'll take the car to get my bag, then we'll go home. Together."

Philip smiled ruefully. For a man who had almost panicked about being outed not even a minute ago, he knew he was now wearing his heart on his sleeve, and he didn't give a good goddamn who his audience was.

The car ride and stop at Mark's apartment were blessedly short and uneventful. As soon as they had settled into the backseat for the drive across town, Mark and Grace slid toward the middle, toward Philip. He put an arm around each of them.

Out of curiosity, Mark watched the driver's face in the rearview mirror as they drove through the city, the three of them quietly talking. He didn't seem to give a damn about the cuddling, but his eyes went wide when the conversation turned to their utter shock over the possible Benedetto connection.

Mark couldn't blame him. It scared the shit out of him, and he wasn't the stranger hired to protect them.

"Sir," the driver interrupted, "am I to understand the Benedettos may be behind your recent misfortunes?"

That was a very polite way to describe the shit storm into which he'd fallen, Mark thought with a smirk.

"The police believe so," Philip answered. "Is that going to be a problem?"

"No, sir. Mr. McCormick just likes to know these things. It helps us to know what we're looking for."

"Good," Philip said, sitting back a little. Mark couldn't resist tucking himself tighter against him and resting his head on his shoulder. "Tell Mr. McCormick we'll be needing his services for the foreseeable future," Philip continued. "I'll give him a call."

"Yes, sir."

At that, they all fell silent for the remainder of the ride. Hell, Mark hardly batted an eye when they rolled up to the entrance to Philip's building and the driver refused to let them out of the car until he'd checked the street, signaled to the cops, and unsnapped his gun holster.

What the fuck was happening to his life?

* * * * *

Two hours later, Mark hung up with his insurance company—again—and stretched his back. He'd been locked in Philip's office since they'd arrived home, trying to plow through claim forms, police reports, and canceled deliveries.

He'd made good headway and the rest could wait. He needed a break. His neck was stiff from being hunched over the desk, and from the tension that had been riding him since he'd seen his open apartment door all those hours ago. He was restless. He needed to relax.

Any other day, he'd work off his energy by running or experimenting in the kitchen.

His first smile in hours whispered across his face as an

alternate idea formed. Maybe he'd just take the experimentation to another room. The bedroom.

What better way to ease tension?

Grinning, he pulled the spoils of his earlier errand from his duffel bag in the corner. When he walked out into the living room, he found the lights out and no sign of Philip or Grace. For one awful moment, he thought they'd gone out without him, and panic took hold, his heart pounding in his chest. Then he saw the little note taped to the bedroom door.

We're napping. Come join us.

The relief was so strong that he staggered under the wave of it. Oh, Jesus, he was in a bad way. How the fuck was he going to survive when they were done with him?

Shaking off the thought, as it was way too freaking scary, he pushed open the door and took in the scene before him. Grace and Philip were curled up in the middle of the bed, his big, strong body spooned around her long, slender back, the covers pulled up to their waists doing little to disguise the fact that they were both naked.

Stripping off clothes as he went, Mark crossed to them, careful to set down his bag of goodies quietly before nudging it under the bed with his toe. Time for that soon. First, though, he wanted to crawl into bed and let their warmth wrap around him.

Sliding beneath the duvet, he scooted over until he pressed against Grace. He smiled at how, even in sleep, their legs shifted to accommodate his. Pulling the covers up to their shoulders, he put his head on the pillow and wrapped an arm around his lovers, his hand resting on the warmth of Philip's back.

He was home.

Chapter Nine

Yep. Waking up between two men, all tangled up in them and they with her, was definitely Grace's new all-time favorite thing.

She hoped she'd never have to live without it again.

She was in love with Mark. She had known it was happening for weeks. Months. But it hadn't mattered before. She'd never once thought that they would find themselves here. Never once thought she might end up in an intimate relationship with anyone *other* than Philip, let alone in *addition* to him.

Heck, she hadn't even considered it a possibility. But it was. It was so unbearably possible, she ached inside. They were so close.

While Mark had been working, she and Philip had sat on their bed and talked. She'd admitted that she'd come to care for Mark a great deal, testing the waters, trying to be sure Philip was feeling some of what she was. She'd been prepared for him to be furious. For his possessive nature to kick in at last, no longer allowing Mark to be the exception. Instead, he'd admitted it wasn't just about the sex for him, either.

He'd sounded confused, possibly even alarmed, by the admission. She loved him all the more for it. Not because it was what she wanted, but because out of all of them, he was the bravest. The strongest, to be able to accept so much change and in such a short time. She'd been so eager for him to throw himself over those hurdles, but she hadn't given much thought to how the landing would go. Philip, of course, had made her proud.

He didn't say it, maybe he didn't even know it, but she was almost certain Philip was in love with Mark, too. Or, at least, well on his way to being so.

She didn't always understand men, but she understood that for someone like Philip to reach out and touch Mark in front of Patrick, to confirm the nature of their relationship, spoke

135

volumes. As open-minded as he was, she couldn't imagine him having done it if it hadn't mattered so damn much. Not to him, but to *Mark*. It also had to mean something that he was so possessive by nature and was still willing to share her, not just for the night or the weekend, but for however long they made it last.

The fact that he couldn't say it meant little. For crying out loud, he'd only just been with a man for the first time. She could cut him some slack if he needed to do some catching up.

But even understanding all that, she still wasn't sure where it left them. The big unknown was Mark. Could he love them back? Could three smart, independent adults actually create a relationship and make it last?

It wasn't a small thing to ask, on a lot of levels. Lifetime commitments scared many people into running away. And this one meant Mark giving up having a woman or a man of his own. One he didn't have to share.

The idea of this other person, who didn't even yet exist, made her furious. That she could be jealous when she was in a ménage seemed ridiculous, but there it was. Mark and Philip were hers, and pity to the poor soul who tried to stop her from keeping them both.

That is, except Mark. If he didn't want this, then she'd let him walk away.

Please, she prayed silently, *please let him want this*.

When Mark stirred in his sleep, she smiled.

Interested in a lifelong commitment with her and Philip? Maybe. Interested in something? Certainly, judging by the considerable erection blooming where their bodies were pressed together.

Now, if she could just wriggle the arm she was lying on out from under her. Trying to maneuver without waking up the men, she pulled her pinned arm free while sliding her other hand back over her hip. She found Philip's flaccid penis where it rested against her ass, cupped her fingers around it, and let them dance. Her other hand wrapped around Mark's already rigid shaft and began a firm, steady pump.

The slow smile that curved Mark's lips was ridiculously sexy. Her heart stuttered and her entire body clenched. She'd be ready before either of them were fully awake.

She was ready *now.*

When Philip moaned softly behind her, Mark opened his eyes. "Are you having fun?"

She nodded, enormously pleased with herself. "I sure am."

Philip stirred, pumping his now hard cock into her fist. "I'm having fun. This is a nice way to wake up." His voice, which always had the power to key her up, was rough with sleep. It was off-the-charts sexy.

She and Mark both turned to look at him.

Philip leaned in and kissed her. His lips slanted across hers, his teeth nipping at her lower lip until she opened to him. His tongue slid into her mouth, sleepy, slow, and hot, before retreating. When he lifted his head, he leaned farther to do the same to Mark.

She lay beneath them, watching how their mouths met and mated, and felt her heart squeeze. This could work. The three of them could work, damn it.

When Philip drew back, she could see how their lips were swollen, their eyes heavy with passion.

Man, was she *ready.* She didn't care what, exactly, came next. As long as it, and she, came soon.

A whimper sounded in the back of her throat and she pumped both hands again. Philip and Mark smiled down at her. Her men. Her wonderful, beautiful men.

Mark leaned down to bite her chin. "I have a surprise for you."

"Yeah?" Her heart pounded in her chest. "I love surprises."

"Then you're really going to love this one," he declared, before pulling himself from her hand and leaning over the side of the bed. With his ass in the air, Philip couldn't resist leaning over and running one finger down the crease to bump over the tight knot below. Mark gasped and sat up, turning to see whose finger tormented him. When he saw Philip, he smiled.

"I have a surprise for you, too." Mark's voice held dark promise. She watched in awe as goose bumps ran across Philip's skin.

Then she heard crinkling and turned to see the plain white shopping bag Mark placed on the bed beside her.

"What's that?" she asked.

"Let's call it *Mark's Bag of Tricks*," he teased, reaching in and rummaging around.

Her eyes just about popped out of her head when he withdrew the single largest tube of sexual lubricant she'd ever seen. Holy cow. Did they sell that at Costco?

Philip's eyes were similarly wide as he stared at the lube, his cock jumping in her fingers. He looked intrigued, a little nervous. Excited.

Mark, meanwhile, had carefully folded the top of the bag over to hide the rest of its contents and shoved it under the far edge of the pillow. "We'll get to the rest of my treats as the need, or needs, arise."

Anticipation shivered through her. She couldn't wait. The need was arising damn quickly, as far as she was concerned.

Mark leaned in and pressed his lips to Philip's while skimming a hand over her breasts, teasing her nipples. She lay back and watched them kiss, aroused beyond measure. She didn't know why, exactly, but watching these strong, virile men make out was such a turn-on. She arched her back to force Mark's hand to stop tormenting her and get down to business. When his fingers twisted around one hard bud, she whimpered.

She let go of Philip—who was too lost in Mark's kiss to notice—and reached over her head for the lube. Squirting a good amount in her palm and spreading it between both hands, she grasped both cocks again. The men broke apart. Philip gasped, closing his eyes. Mark, already panting with need, stared at the hand slicking over his hot flesh.

"There she goes, being clever again," Mark rasped.

"Thank god," Philip muttered in return.

She smiled sweetly. She could watch them kiss all night, but she didn't mind having their undivided attention, either.

Mark took Philip's hand and pulled it to his cock. "Why don't you take over for her while I exact a little revenge?"

The thrill that ran down her spine was pure sexual excitement. She released Mark's cock when Philip's hand skimmed over her fingers. Mark moved to kneel between her legs, his hands firm as they slid up her thighs, pushing her legs wide, then up. When he hooked them over his shoulders, she let her head drop back to the pillow.

Oh yes. She definitely wanted some undivided attention.

For once Mark didn't tease, his tongue traveling the length of her slit, tickling up one swollen lip before slipping down the other.

God, he's good at that.

Burrowing deeper, Mark flicked his nimble tongue across the straining hood of her clit. Every contact sent a bolt up her spine, her thighs tightening until they quivered. He zeroed in on that center of pleasure and took it in his mouth, sucking and rolling it across his tongue before moving lower and licking into her.

She couldn't contain her groans, her body writhing against his lips, until Mark's mouth dipped lower still and she froze, all sound strangling off in her throat. The tip of his tongue circled her tightly clenched anus before wriggling at its center. She gasped at the rush of forbidden pleasure. It felt amazing. And dangerous.

She heard Philip mutter, "Fuck," and knew he was watching. Knew he could see what Mark was doing to her, and that made it even better. Mark's tongue was working at her ass, licking and wriggling against her, and Philip echoed her long moan. God, she'd never even imagined someone doing this, letting someone do this to her. But now…now she wanted to try *everything*.

Philip looked like he was right there with her.

Mark plunged two fingers into her pussy and she snapped.

Her inner muscles bore down like a vise as the first wave of her orgasm crashed over her. She came hard, the climax roaring through her as her spine curled and sensation forced a cry up out of her lungs.

She floated there, enjoying the release from the need that had been gnawing at her since they'd woken up.

Her relief was short-lived.

Still floating on the ripples of her release, she whimpered when Mark's mouth clamped around her clit and resumed its torture. Stunned, she cried out and immediately began climbing back up, only distantly registering the sound of the bag crinkling near her ear.

Philip stretched out beside her, his hand sliding along his own cock, his thumb brushing over the head while he watched Mark closely. She wrapped her hand around his, letting him guide her palm along his warm erection.

Normally, this would have gained Philip's full attention, but he continued to stare in fascination at whatever Mark was doing, presumably with his hands. Her body ached at their absence. Mark's strong lips were still wrapped around her clit, sucking it into his mouth with furious pulses that echoed through her body. She didn't care what else he was up to, as long as he didn't stop doing *that*.

When the cool lube on Mark's finger touched the tight entrance to her ass, awareness of the world around her returned. Acutely. Her legs tightened on Mark's back and her hips bucked—to shy away or to offer better access, she didn't know. As the pressure built, the fog of arousal cleared and she felt a pang of worry, then his finger slid through her tightly clenched muscles and the fog returned in a heavy wave.

She moaned, stunned by the sensations spiraling out from her ass and the incredible things Mark was teaching her about her own body.

When the second finger joined the first, when she felt the sting of pain and pleasure, the kick of her hips was outside her control. Pulling her legs higher, she fisted one hand in Mark's hair, forcing his face harder against her pussy as she writhed against him, desperate for more, searching for the orgasm she could feel building from nerve endings she'd never imagined would have such command over her body.

Her ass felt so full. Every pump of Mark's fingers sent shivers up and down her body, every tug on her clit pulling her taut with anticipation.

Then his fingers were gone and she whimpered with disappointment, instantly deflating. *Was that it?* She'd felt like she'd been on the edge of something...bigger.

Relief swamped her when she heard the rude squirt of the lube tube. She didn't know what was coming next, but she wanted it. Mark's mouth was still working miracles, his tongue flicking in broad strokes across her clit before his lips locked on again.

She looked up at Philip. His face was frozen, eyes narrowed, cheeks flushed with arousal like she'd never seen. He pumped their hands furiously along his cock, his eyes transfixed by Mark and whatever he was doing.

Mark lifted his head.

She tightened her hand in his hair. "*Please.* Don't stop."

"I won't stop, Gracie. I just want to do something a little different, okay?" Mark said, looking into her eyes.

She nodded once before her head fell back to the bed. "Yes. Please. Anything."

Mark's calloused thumb picked up the rhythm his tongue had left behind, battering at her clit with hard, constant strokes that drove her body on. When she felt the push, the cool touch of lube pressing at the already sensitized ring protecting her ass, she tried to relax, letting the muscles ease, her eyes fluttering shut.

At first, she thought Mark was pumping just a tip of one finger into her. Then two. Three? No, two. She groaned. She couldn't stand his teasing. With each press, there was a stretch, a point that rode on the jagged edge of pain, then retreat and loss.

"Jesus," she moaned. "What the fuck are you doing?"

She opened her eyes to see Philip leaning over her, studying her face. "Does it feel good, baby?"

"God, yes. It feels so—" She stopped to catch her breath as she sailed over that point of pain, over the firm stretch before smoothing out again. "So good. I didn't know."

Philip's eyes were feverish as he stared down her body. The pressure kept building, the thrusts coming faster, harder. The pleasure scaling with every push from Mark. She registered it wasn't his fingers. Too smooth. Too even. And she could see by how he was positioned that it wasn't his cock.

"Oh god, Philip. What is it? What is he putting in—" She squeaked, her question cut off as the pain-pleasure balanced for one second on the side of pain. Instinct made her push down on what invaded her, unknowingly opening herself to it. In an instant, the stretch and burn eased.

Only it wasn't the same. She was still so damn full. More than she'd ever been.

She looked at Philip, unsure what had just happened, but trusting in him. In Mark. Loving every new and delicious sensation, she reached up to touch Philip's face, grateful for his love and their common desire to let Mark to take them new and exciting places. She pressed her palm to his cheek and her weight shifted, making her gasp. Every inch of her body was electrified. She couldn't breathe without dizzying shocks rocketing through her body.

Philip's hand shook as it smoothed the hair back from her face. "God, Grace, you're so beautiful. The look on your face when you..." He sucked an unsteady breath into his lungs, swallowing hard. "What does it feel like? Can you tell me? Can you feel it?"

"Amazing," she whispered. "I feel full. God. So full. What the hell is in me?"

Mark's thumb stopped stroking over her clit and he eased her legs down off his shoulders. She groaned, struggling to stay in her head and not just float on the foreign sensations swamping her. Even the most miniscule movements sent waves of pleasure and pressure through her ass.

Mark crawled up over her. "It's a butt plug, sweetheart. I needed—I want...God, I want to fuck your ass. But I don't want to hurt you. This will help. This will get you ready for me."

She felt ready now. She wanted Mark to fuck her. Anywhere. Everywhere. Mark smiled, his eyes knowing, before turning away.

She looked to Philip, desperate for relief, desperate to feel his long thick cock filling her. She was close to begging but paused when she saw his face, a mask of stark need, but with a trace of worry.

She understood why when Mark returned and held up his hand to reveal another plug. "Your turn, my love," he said to Philip.

Her mouth fell open. The plug wasn't any bigger than either of their cocks, far shorter, in fact. Its tapered head flared out to a base no wider than Philip before pulling back in to a relatively narrow waist above the small, round anchor. But still, it looked *huge*.

"Holy fuck. That is *not* what's in me!"

Philip swallowed again before speaking. "Yeah, it is."

Her mind reeled. She could do little more than stare at Mark as he squirted more lube on his fingers, leaving the tube and butt plug on the bed by Philip's hip.

"You don't have to do this," Mark offered, giving Philip an out.

Philip's answer was to grab Mark's hair and pull him into a searing kiss. She would have laughed if she hadn't been having an out-of-body experience. Philip didn't *have* to do anything, but he sure as hell wanted to.

Rolling onto her side toward Philip, another riotous wave of sensation rocked through her. She wanted Philip to know what it was like. For Mark to give him that. She watched them kiss, their tongues dueling, fighting for dominance. Mark was winning, with Philip's full consent. Watching dominant Philip submit to Mark made things low in her body clench tight, muscles clasping around firm plastic, and her eyes slammed shut for a moment while she tried to catch her breath. When she opened them again, she saw that it had taken Mark only those precious seconds to get Philip on his back with his knees drawn up.

She scooted forward, gasping as the movement jarred the plug. She brought her face close to Philip's so she could watch his response and still see Mark. Reaching out, she gently stroked his cock where it lay against his belly, reviving what had begun to recede. Philip turned his head to look at her.

"Tell me," Philip demanded, his voice rough.

"Tell you what?" she asked.

"What's it like?"

She saw his eyes widen, his lips parting as Mark slid two fingers into his ass. She pulled more firmly on his cock, trying not to squirm with delight at the sight before her.

"It feels different," she promised, eager for him to experience it.

"Good?" Philip wondered with a hint of worry.

"Oh, yes. Good. Really good." She reassured him quickly, honestly. Her heart skipped when Philip's face tightened and a third finger disappeared. She cupped his balls, cradling them where they drew up to his body, her fingertips brushing Mark's knuckles. She lost her train of thought while watching those fingers pump and scissor in Philip's ass, marveling at how he opened to Mark. Her own muscles clamped down again on the plug invading her, her head spinning.

Philip growled and her attention snapped back to him. He had his feet planted on the bed, his hips pumping into her hand slowly as he thrust against Mark's fingers.

So brave, fucking himself down on those magic fingers. Prepared to let Mark do whatever he wanted. Leaping into the unknown with abandon. She found herself oddly proud of Philip.

"It feels good, doesn't it? Just wait. You're going to feel so full. Men don't normally get to experience that, do they?" she wondered aloud, only then realizing how significant the invasion might be to Philip. Had he ever been penetrated before? She thought not. Studying his face, his response to Mark, brought a smile. He was going to love it.

Philip's growl abruptly stopped and he closed his eyes. Returning her gaze to Mark, she saw he had pulled his fingers out and picked up the other plug. The lube. She leaned over, kissing the soft bulb of Philip's cock head, trying to distract him from what Mark was doing. What he was about to do.

It also gave her a better view.

She licked around the thick crown, nibbling on the sensitive divot just beneath. She couldn't tear her eyes away as Mark brought the glistening plug up against Philip's tight hole. When he started to press forward, Philip gasped, a shudder passing through his entire body, his legs losing their grip on the duvet and sliding down. She reached out, hooking her elbow under his knee and drawing it back up, turning to look into his eyes.

Mark slid his free hand up the back of Philip's other thigh, pushing it almost to his chest. They had him bent in half. Exposed. His chest rose and fell with his hectic breathing, his eyes wide. She couldn't see Mark's hands anymore, but she could guess what was happening by the changing expressions running across Philip's face.

"Are you okay?" she asked softly, hoping he could see how much she loved him in her eyes and hear it in her voice.

"Fuck. Yes. Grace. What..." His eyes flew open, wild and bewildered, then narrowing to slits.

"Push against it, honey. Open yourself to it. It will feel amazing when it slides home. You won't believe it."

Philip grunted, his hand wrapping around her arm in a painful grip as he did what she suggested. She heard Mark's gasp as Philip sucked a huge breath.

"Fuck!" Philip bellowed, his back arching off the bed.

Grace looked, stunned to see the plug seated firmly and fully in Philip's ass, Mark staring down at it in wonder. She felt an insane urge to laugh. God, she loved him. It was just like Philip to barrel into any challenge head first. Or, perhaps, in this case it would be ass first.

The laughter bubbled to the surface and Philip looked at her, puzzlement barely breaking through the feverish intensity of his gaze.

When she released his leg, Mark did, too. Philip's groan as his feet slid down the bed, as the plug shifted, made her nipples tighten, her pussy and ass clench. Her laughter died and she collapsed on the bed next to Philip, trying to catch her breath.

Mark climbed up over both of them, kissing her thoroughly before turning to plunge his tongue into Philip's mouth.

Mark's breathing was as ragged as theirs. His face was flushed, the strain of arousal pinching the corners of his eyes.

"God, Philip. You took it so fast. You're going to love it when I fill you up. When I fuck you," Mark ground out, pressing his forehead to Philip's. "I can't wait."

Mark's words made her squirm. The images too delicious, too carnal. When he turned to her, she froze. A deer in headlights, her need so great she could scarcely draw a breath.

"Then you. Then I'll fuck your ass, too."

At that precise moment, she couldn't think of anything she wanted more.

Philip had found heaven. Forty-eight hours ago, if someone had asked him what heaven would be for him, he would have said a week on the beach with Grace and no clothes. Imagine his surprise that it was actually right here in his own bed. With Mark and Grace. And a fucking huge plug shoved up his ass, just like the one jammed into Grace.

Jesus. He'd almost come, watching Mark work it in, stretching her open.

But experiencing it firsthand...unbelievable.

He gazed up at Mark, who was smiling down at them like they were his prized pupils. Turning, he looked at Grace, her eyes unfocused, her face flushed. Her nipples were turgid peaks, begging for attention as her breasts rose and fell with her rapid breaths.

Could a person ever breathe normally with a butt plug

lodged in place? It felt as though it went all the way up through him and might blow out the top of his head.

He lifted his legs, groaning as the plug jammed harder against the ring of muscles locking it both in and out of his body. Part of him wanted to wallow in it, but he'd been so fucking turned on for so long, his balls were starting to ache. He needed release.

Mark squinted, studying his face with concern. "Are you okay?"

He gasped as the plug shifted again. "Yes. God, yes. But I have to come. Soon. I can't take this much pressure for so long."

Mark's face immediately cleared. "We can certainly fix that." He turned to Grace, his lips curling. "Gracie, you don't look like you're in any better condition."

Philip vowed to himself that someday he'd get revenge for the smug look on Mark's face.

"I'm not," she gasped. "God help me. I'm not."

That was all Philip needed to know. He rolled toward Grace and Mark scooted out of his way so he could pull himself above her. He was desperately trying to ignore the extraordinary pulsing in his ass, afraid he'd go over the edge from that sensation alone.

She smiled up at him, her back arching as her knees came up to hug his flanks. Her smile faded when she ground her ass against the bed, replaced by a look of astonished need.

"Fuck me, Philip. Please."

He wanted to fall on her, take her quick and hard, but Mark's hand on his hip held him back. "Go slow. She's not going to feel the same. Enjoy it."

He didn't know what Mark was talking about, but Philip trusted him. Implicitly.

Easing forward, the head of his cock pressed against the drenched entrance to her pussy. With a twist of his hips that sent fire racing from his cock to his ass and up his back, the head slipped in. He lowered himself, slowly stretching her open.

Grace gasped and sobbed with every breath as her body worked to accommodate him. Her legs wrapped around his waist, changing the angle.

"Jesus. So tight. Baby, you're so fucking tight," he groaned, trembling with the need to shove himself forward and lose himself in her depths.

Mark's voice was in his ear. "It's the plug. It narrows her down. Is it amazing?"

Grace answered. "Yes!"

Gritting his teeth, he sank down into the tunnel of muscles that clenched his cock with all its might. Grace was always a snug fit. But this…

Tight. Wet. Fist.

When he was fully sheathed, he stopped, desperately trying to grab hold of his control.

He was counting sheep and thinking about baseball, trying to gather the last threads of discipline still remaining to him, when Grace's legs slid to his sides and Mark's chest pressed along his back, his lips to Philip's ear.

"You ready for me?" Mark asked quietly.

Philip froze. The world stopped.

Grace opened her eyes and stared up at him. At Mark. Waiting for his answer.

His heart raced, fear and anticipation mixing in a brew designed to strip him of his hard-won control. He couldn't find the words for what he wanted. How much he wanted it. Instead, he just nodded.

When Mark pulled back, Philip eased a little from Grace before sliding back in again, his teeth clenched tight against the groan working its way out of his chest. Mark trailed a hand down Philip's spine, and he closed his eyes, focusing on Grace. Focusing on how her tight walls grabbed him, trying to hold him in place.

Out. In.

His shoulders relaxed, his rhythm smoothed out. God, how

he loved this woman. How he cherished the tremendous pleasure of being in her. With her. Loving her.

He barely registered the brush of Mark's fingers on the curve of his ass, having successfully lost himself to the joy of making love to Grace. His speed picked up, the force of his thrusts increasing, when on a powerful plunge, the plug was summarily removed from his ass.

Holy fuck.

He slammed into Grace, forcing her plug up against the walls of her ass, up against him. He struggled for control, for breath as she writhed beneath him, her fingernails scratching over his scalp. He hung, suspended above her, unmoving until she pulled him down for a kiss.

And thereby presented his ass to Mark.

Always the clever girl, was Grace.

His tongue traced her mouth, touching every corner, worshipping his beautiful witch. The tip of the lube container pressed against his tender, sensitive hole, and the cool flow filled him as Mark squirted a river of it inside. He didn't know what the plug had done, but he felt open. Ready. He tried to hold onto that. To remain relaxed.

The sound of a little foil packet tearing was almost his undoing.

When the cool lube bottle was replaced by the warm head of Mark's cock, Philip broke from Grace's kiss. She looked up into his eyes, and he down into hers. He couldn't believe what was about to happen. Couldn't believe how much he wanted it. Needed it.

Mark pushed forward. The ring of muscles guarding the entrance to Philip's ass expanded, yielding to Mark's cock. The stretch was incredible, the burn intense. The moment the ridge around the head pressed through the resistance, Philip shuddered, arching his spine, pushing back as Mark slowly sank all the way to the hilt. The intimacy of it was shattering. The plug had been cool, but Mark's cock was hot, pulsing inside Philip. For the first time in his life, he was breached. Penetrated.

149

Well and truly fucked.

Mark's chest curled down along his back, his arms wrapping around Philip's ribs to hold him.

"Fuck. God, Philip. Fuck. Are you okay? Do you feel that? How you took me in?"

Philip turned his head, thrusting his tongue into Mark's mouth for a rough kiss before tearing his lips away and answering. "Can I feel it? Jesus, it feels like you're lodged in my throat."

Mark's face was a perfect combination of male satisfaction and feral need. He looked down at Grace. "Are you okay?"

Her smile was sultry as she arched her back, thus forcing the plug deeper into her ass, his cock deeper into her pussy, and his ass back onto Mark's cock. "I'm great," she purred.

Philip closed his eyes, admiring the star bursts behind his lids. Had he thought he was in heaven with a plug in his ass? *Idiot.* Heaven was being fucked by Mark while he was buried to the hilt in Grace.

And as good as it was, he knew he couldn't take it much longer. It was too good. So good it hurt.

He had to move.

Rocking his hips back, he triggered a chorus of moans as his shaft slid along Grace's tight walls and he forced Mark deeper into his ass. When he thrust forward again, Mark held still, letting his rigid length ease from Philip's burning hole as Philip's cock sank back into Grace.

Jesus. It was mind-boggling. Perfect.

He did it again. And again, setting a rhythm all three could match. So many sensations whipped through him, he could barely hold a thought. He felt full. Embraced. Exposed and completely surrounded. Fucked and thrilled in the act of fucking.

Their groans grew louder, mingled, turning into shouts and calls to god and whomever they could pray to for help in their search for release.

Grace found it first. Her back arched, her neck stretched as she impaled herself on the hard knot in her ass and Philip pounded into her. She cried out, a ragged shout of triumph that bounced off the walls of his brain as he thrust harder. Faster.

Holy god. *Now.*

The ball of lightning that shot up his spine was like nothing he had ever experienced in his life. He wanted to laugh. He wanted to cry. His eyes closed and his mouth opened on a silent scream as his pelvis ground into Grace, wave after wave of come churning from his balls and into her. The ring of muscles guarding his ass clamped down like a vise on Mark's cock, stilling his withdrawal before letting him back in as Mark buried himself to the hilt and shook, his cry hoarse.

And then, at last, Philip finally understood what heaven *really* was.

Chapter Ten

Mark was pretty sure he was dying. Which was okay, actually, since he couldn't think of a better way to go. He lay sprawled across Grace, his body stuck to one side of her while Philip covered the other half.

Philip seemed to think he was dying, too, as he kept muttering into his pillow. Something about heaven? Mark tried to smile, but he couldn't control his muscles yet. He was paralyzed. The only thing working was his heart, which pounded as if it would fly from his chest. All of this was also okay.

Although, the longer he lay there, the more the acceptance of death was passing in favor of a craving for food. When was the last time they had eaten?

He remembered breakfast and groaned. Shit. He was so *hungry*. The morning had been lost to police reports and errands, and when they'd returned home, no one had been thinking about food, all too upset by the revelations of the day. From there, it was work and then, finally, the distractions of napping and sex, which was about the only diet he might someday find acceptable, but which had burned off enough calories to make his body cry out for fuel. He loved food. He didn't diet, he didn't scrimp, and he didn't shy from decadence. He *did* run his ass off for an hour every morning to make up for it, but he'd seen what happened to chefs and restaurateurs who didn't keep up and he wasn't interested. Instead he worked hard, played hard, and ate like a king.

That is, until Grace and Philip had scrambled his brains and his appetites.

He sighed, opening his senses and pulling in a deep breath through his nose. Grace smelled of heather and rain. Philip of lemon and spice. He could smell his own musk mingling with theirs and it was perfect. He'd searched his entire life for the perfect combination of scents and flavors, the perfect meal, and he hadn't known, couldn't have guessed, that this would be it.

He wished he could wallow in post-coital bliss for hours, but it was time to move. Grunting, he pushed himself up and off Grace, smiling down at her and the tangle of chestnut hair framing her beautiful face. When Philip opened the eye that wasn't buried against the bedding, Mark could see he was still dazed.

"I need a shower. And then I need food. And so do you two." He made it clear he wasn't going to brook any arguments. It felt so damn good to take care of the people he loved that he wasn't going to let even them stop him.

Philip closed his eye before responding. "I need a shower, too. Unfortunately, I don't think I have legs anymore. Will you carry me?"

Grace's giggle made Mark's heart stutter in his chest. He returned her grin before lifting his hand and giving Philip a firm smack on the ass.

Philip's head popped up, his eyes wide as he looked around at Mark. "You're going to pay for that."

Mark raised his eyebrows. "How are you going to make me pay if you don't have legs, big man?"

Philip's lunge was so quick and unexpected, Mark nearly toppled off the mattress before catching the bed post with one hand and jumping to his feet. Grace gave a squeak, sounding both amused and alarmed as she rolled to the edge of the bed to get out of the way.

Mark held his ground, letting Philip slam against his chest before dragging him off the bed, kissing his lips once, and dropping him to his feet.

"Look! A miracle! He can walk!"

"Smart ass." Philip's voice was rough with affection.

He couldn't resist dragging one palm down over Philip's sweet, tight ass, reminding them both of what they'd shared. His next breath was shaky, and he berated himself. *Shower, damn it. Food.* Just looking at Philip, holding him in his arms, made him want to forget.

These two beautiful people had turned him into a sex-crazed

slut, which was great. But they seriously needed to refuel.

Taking Philip's hand, Mark turned toward the bathroom before reaching back for Grace. Her fingers curled around his, but when he would have moved away, she didn't budge.

He looked back at her. Her cheeks were stained pink, her eyes bright. If he hadn't known better, he'd have sworn she was embarrassed.

"Aren't you coming to shower with us?"

Grace's cheeks moved from pink to red and his chest squeezed. Oh, god. They'd done too much. Crossed a line. Was she upset with him? With Philip? Jesus, he'd just fucked her perfect boyfriend's ass. That might be upsetting to some people.

He tried to get a handle on his rampant emotions and imagination. "Sweet Grace, what's wrong?" He let his love show in his eyes, his voice, in the squeeze of her fingers in his.

"Uh…" Grace's free hand waved around vaguely. "Well, in the course of…uh…sitting here, I was…uh…forcibly reminded that I still have…um…well, I still have…you know…a plug in my ass?"

He let out the breath he hadn't known he was holding. Was that all? He smiled. "Just leave it."

Philip's fingers tightened where they were laced with his.

Her eyes widened. "What? I can't!"

His brows drew together with concern. "Is it hurting you?"

"Um…no." The way she said it made it clear it was doing something to her, but it wasn't hurting.

He tapped her nose with his finger. "Then leave it. I'm sure we'll find the right time to take it out soon enough. Now, come on," he said, as he hauled her to her feet, "let's get cleaned up."

He carefully herded his charges into the bathroom and turned on the shower. It took a while to get all three of them cleaned up, but he poked and prodded them along, forcing himself not to get distracted as he went.

Philip, while having regained use of his legs, wasn't entirely steady on them. Mark soaped and rinsed him quickly before propping him up in one corner under a warm spray of water and soaping up Grace. She basked in the steam and water under his ministrations. As he worked the shower gel across her back and buttocks, he couldn't contain his grin. She wore the most bewildered look on her face, her eyes far away, as if half her brain were in the present, and the other half devoted to the sensations caused by the plug Mark was shamelessly manipulating under the guise of helping her wash up.

He took care of himself last, then shut off the water and gently dried his docile lovers, ushering them back into the bedroom and instructing them to get dressed. When all Grace did was pull a T-shirt over her head, he laughed.

"Grace, you have to put on more than that if we're going to go out."

"We're going out?" She looked nervous and aroused as she stepped into the shorts he handed her. He watched, fascinated, as sensation and response moved across her face.

"Yes. Just to Valentine's. With an escort, of course. I want to check in and cook you two dinner. And the guard needs a break to eat as well."

Philip came up behind him, wrapping one arm around his waist as he dropped his chin to his shoulder. "That sounds great. I'm starving."

He wasn't surprised. He watched Grace's brows drop before she added, "Me, too." As if she'd only just figured it out when she'd forced herself to think about it.

He clamped down on his need to address Grace's obvious and constant state of arousal and returned to the task at hand, pulling on the sweatshirt Philip gave him before helping Grace into hers. He called Patrick to let him know they were on the move. Soon after, he led the two of them from the apartment. When they stepped out onto the sidewalk, he scanned the street. He didn't see the Crown Victoria, but spotted the Boston PD cruiser and their McCormick car and driver.

It was another gorgeous late-summer night, cool enough to warrant their sweatshirts, but warm enough that the breeze felt great on bare legs and upturned faces. He hated to have to climb into the Town Car rather than enjoy the walk, but he wouldn't even consider putting Grace and Philip in danger.

Valentine's plywood window was firmly in place when they arrived. Mark unlocked the door and ushered Philip and Grace inside. Grace popped behind the bar to turn on the music while Philip spoke quietly with the guard before letting him out the front door, waving to another Boston PD cruiser and the McCormick driver before locking them in.

"The guard is going to run home for something to read tonight and some dinner. I said he should come back in an hour and a half."

Mark nodded, taking Philip's hand and then Grace's as they made their way to the kitchen, towing them to the pastry chef's work bench where he pulled out two stools and dragged them to the center aisle. "You two sit," he said, pointing.

Philip climbed onto his seat and crossed an ankle over the opposite knee while Grace carefully eased herself up onto hers, her thighs spread, her weight pitched forward. Mark kind of zoned out while watching her, and had to shake himself to get back to business.

Food then sex. Food then sex.

He chanted it in his mind, trying to hold onto what little discipline he had left.

He explained, shouting from the back of the walk-in refrigerator at the end of the aisle, that he had to see what was still good. As he spoke, he tossed what had gone bad into a large trash can outside the cooling unit's door, turning to see Philip holding Grace's hand in his lap while they watched in fascination.

Mark couldn't play basketball for shit, but he knew the exact distance from the back of the fridge to that trash can and could toss things over his shoulder and into the bin without a glance. When a particularly large head of lettuce made a perfect landing, Grace and Philip applauded.

He was damn strict about what he would serve at Valentine's, so the trash can filled quickly. He'd get another delivery Monday morning, along with his new window, and with a few tweaks to the menu to compensate for the delivery he'd canceled that morning, he'd be back in business. Provided the fucking Benedettos didn't screw it up.

Sighing, he told himself to put it away for now. He was here to cook his lovers dinner. He would focus on that.

When he emerged from the fridge, slamming and locking the door behind him, Grace and Philip were still watching. Waiting.

"Hungry?" he asked, indicating the fresh vegetables and steaks he spread across the countertop.

"Yes," they answered in unison.

He set to work, picking an interesting mix of veggies for a salad, cooking the steaks in a sinful amount of butter. He whipped up a light dressing from scratch and a balsamic reduction for the steaks. He'd cooked for thousands of people over the years, but never in his life enjoyed preparing a meal more. He picked out a wine from behind the bar and carried it and three glasses to their table.

They ate in the round booth in the corner, sitting far closer than necessary at a table that could easily seat six. He sat in the middle with his thigh pressing against Philip's, one of Grace's legs hooked over his knee. They barely spoke, focusing on the joy that could be found in good food and wine.

Once finished, they carried their plates back to the kitchen. When he went to the sink to start washing the dishes, Philip hip checked him out of the way.

"No dishes for you. In this family, if you cook, you don't have to clean."

In this family. Mark felt like he'd been punched in the chest. He admonished himself not to read too much into it as he stepped back to let Philip take over. He turned to look at Grace. She was smiling at Philip as she picked up a towel and held her hand out for a clean plate to dry.

Jesus, he thought, his heart aching. What a family they would be.

It hurt too much to think about. Instead, he turned back to

the food he'd left on the counter. It wouldn't be good enough on Monday, so it would have to go.

"Are you going to throw all that away?" Grace asked, a hip leaning against the edge of the sink counter.

"Yeah, I have to." Playfully, he picked up a cucumber, waggling it back and forth between his fingers. "Unless you have any other ideas of what I can do with it?"

Her eyes grew big as the dinner plates and Philip chuckled, shaking his head as he turned back to rinse a wineglass. Mark couldn't tell if she was frightened or intrigued. Putting down the cuke, he picked up another vegetable and held it out, his eyebrows raised, as if to say, what about this?

Grace gasped. "Mark Valentine, you put that eggplant down, you pervert!"

Philip's bark of laughter echoing through the kitchen was music to Mark's ears, feeding his soul. Philip didn't laugh as much as he should. Mark wanted to work on that. He wanted to spend weeks, months, *years* working on that.

Chucking the eggplant and the remaining veggies into a crate, he dragged it and the trashcan to the back door, making a note to ask the guard to put it out later. When he returned, he set to work on wiping down counters and mopping the floor. The everyday chores of the business that normally he found annoying seemed far more pleasant with Philip and Grace to help.

He put the cleaning supplies away, then turned to see Grace bending down to grip one of the stools. Before she could lift it to put it away, he came up behind her and gave her ass a light spank, taking care to tap the anchor of the butt plug.

Grace gasped, her hands tightening around the stool seat until they were white. From experience, he knew her head was swimming. Her eyes closed and her mouth thinned to a pale line as she tried to catch her breath.

The poor woman had probably been floating above the surface in a constant state of arousal for almost two hours now, feeling bursts of pleasure with every movement. One small pat on her ass and she looked like she was hanging on to sanity by a thread.

Philip stopped in front of her, stroking the back of his hand down her cheek. "Baby, are you okay?"

She didn't open her eyes when she answered. "Yes. God yes."

Mark watched Philip's erection grow, his loose clothing allowing it to reach out toward Grace. Toward Mark.

His own blood raced to his cock. He'd thought they might make it home before their next bout of loving, but the car ride alone might kill Grace. He checked his watch. They still had time.

Reaching out, he smoothed a palm over one cotton-covered cheek, then the other, before giving her ass another gentle spank.

Grace threw her head back and let out a keening cry. "Please. Please, Mark, don't tease."

He wrapped his arms around her waist, pulling himself tight to her back, pushing his cock against her ass, knowing how the pressure sent electric shocks of pleasure zooming through her body. "You don't have to hold on, Grace. You can let go." He reached down, skimming his hand over her belly before delving his fingers past her waistband and beyond. She was wet. Soaking with it, unable to do more than widen her legs and cant her hips, begging for more with her entire body. He used the tips of two fingers to pinch and tug on her lush and swollen clit, listening to her cries as they grew louder and more desperate. He pushed his fingers farther, easing them up into her tight pussy.

With a gasp and another keening wail, she came, shattering in his arms, her hips bucking as the muscles in her sheath bore down on his fingers.

"Jesus." Philip's voice was reverent as he stared down at them. "Jesus."

Grace was panting, grinding her hips back against him as the pulses of her orgasm still shimmered through her. "It's not enough. Help me, Mark. It's not enough."

He tried to soothe her, easing his fingers from her before nuzzling her neck. "Shhh. It's okay, sweetheart. We'll go home. We'll take care of you."

"No. Now. Please," she wheedled.

He groaned. He was such an idiot. He'd made her wait too long. "I left what I'll need back at the house."

He looked up when Philip cleared his throat. Philip shrugged before reaching into the front pocket of his hoodie and pulling out a small tube of lubricant and a strip of condoms.

Burying his face in Grace's hair again, Mark shook with laughter.

Grace moaned. "It's not funny. Please. You have to do something."

He smoothed his hands over her again, lifting one to hook her hair behind one ear. "I'm not laughing at you, Gracie. I'm laughing at Philip. We've made a wild man out of him."

Grace looked up, saw what Philip was holding, and whimpered.

Mark also looked at Philip. "Do you want to be the one?"

Philip's voice was hoarse. "No. I want..." He pulled in a deep breath. Swallowed. "I want to watch you do it."

Mark smiled into Grace's hair. He would have happily coached Philip through it, but holy fuck, he was even happier being the one to experience this with Grace for the first time.

He ran his hands down her body, over her breasts and along her ribs before traveling back up, pulling her upright as he lifted her shirt up and over her head. As soon as she was free of it, she bent to brace herself on the stool, forcing her ass back against him. He grunted, his own need rising feverishly as he hooked his thumbs in her shorts, pulling them down. She stepped out of them quickly, kicking off her sneakers.

Rising, he turned to look at Philip, who stood stock still, one hand clamped around the base of his cock through his shorts, the other clenching the lubricant in a death grip. When Mark reached for it, Philip's movements were jerky as he pressed it into his palm.

Looking down at Grace's smooth, sweet ass, he tried to focus on what he was about to do. Philip's ability to take him so deep, so quickly, was not the norm. Far from it. He needed to keep his head screwed on straight long enough to take care of her. Nothing was more important than that.

Stripping, he sheathed himself, then drenched his cock in lubricant, enjoying the stroke of his own hand, enjoying the look in Philip's eyes as they tracked his every move. He tried to be quick, as Grace was struggling just to keep her hips still, even with no one touching her, rocking back against nothing more than air. Her head hung down, her hair hiding her beautiful face in a fall of chestnut silk.

He ran a hand over the firm globes of her ass, listening to her whimpered pleas before skimming the line where cheek met thigh, and under, to the core of her need. With quick fingers, he flicked at her clit, dancing over it, plucking and circling and then dancing some more. He loved her response, her breathy moans and how her hips shook against him, begging for more until he sank two fingers into her wet depths. Before he could withdraw, Grace was rocking her hips like a piston.

Her absolute lack of inhibition sent more blood coursing into his cock, spiking his already aching shaft even harder. He felt the telling ripple of muscle and grasped the anchor of the plug with his other hand, telling himself to wait, to be careful. When she cried out and threw herself down on his fingers, clamping them tight as another climax rolled over her, he gave the plug a firm tug and pulled it from her body. Her cries turned to gasps, her eyes sightless as another orgasm roared through her.

There was no better time. She was ready and his need had reached desperate levels.

Moving behind her, he positioned the fiercely swollen head of his cock at her entrance and eased it through. Grace's groan of release ended on a sharp gasp as the flared head popped inside. The plug had opened her to him, but she was still small, and so damn tight. He held himself still, only his head lodged within her, and tried to let her adjust.

Before long, a slow moan rumbled up from deep inside her. "God, please, Mark. Do it."

He eased forward, making steady progress for a few inches until she whimpered and clenched down on him, the muscles in her ass rejecting his invasion even as the rest of her shook and begged for it in words and motions. He ran his hands over her back, soothing her as his hips started to make little thrusts, each one taking him just a little farther.

When Philip stepped closer, he had his shorts down, his hand still fastened around his cock, his eyes transfixed to the spot where Mark was locked in Grace's ass.

Grace let out a shuddering sigh, and, like magic, her muscles yielded, opening to him. His thrusts got more powerful, more demanding. Her body responded, taking him in. When he was within an inch of his goal, she groaned, internal walls pushing back against him, grabbing hold of his cock and pulling him the rest of the way in.

"Jesus." Philip's raspy timbre washed over them, giving him chills.

Grace's head came up, her eyes bright with pleasure as she looked at Philip. "Come here."

Philip moved in front of her, tucking her hair back to look down into her face. "You're so beautiful."

She closed her eyes for a moment, as if to bask in Philip's adoring gaze. "Come closer."

Philip did as she asked, his breath leaving his lungs in a long hiss when she bent lower and brought his cock to her lips. When the head, swollen and dark purple with need, disappeared between her soft lips, he reached back to grab the counter with one hand and let his eyes roll back in his head.

Mark was distantly aware that he was shaking. Shaking with need. Lust. Love. When Philip's eyes came back to forward, he looked at Mark, his grim smile wobbling when Grace's cheeks hollowed and more of him slipped deeper into her mouth. Then Philip's eyes dropped to her ass and stared.

Mark couldn't stay still any longer. Grasping Grace's hips, he pulled out slowly, then eased back in, the clamp of her muscles sending thrills through his body. Her groan vibrated through him and did things he could only imagine to Philip's cock, deep in her throat. Mark withdrew and plunged again. Picking up speed. Finding each stroke easier and meeting that ease with more powerful thrusts. Each time he thrust forward, she took Philip all the way in her mouth and down her throat, until Mark eased back and she sucked the length of Philip's cock until only her lips clung to the crown.

The sight snapped the last of his tenuous control.

His legs braced, he pounded into her, unable to look away from where her mouth surrounded Philip, knowing that Philip was unable to look away from where Mark's cock slammed over and over again into her ass.

The connection with Philip only added to the turmoil raging in his body. He could only imagine what Grace felt, filled up and adored. So thoroughly loved and fucked by both of them at once.

The boil of release churned in his balls, tightening them to his body before the tidal wave of his climax crashed over him. It felt like his hair stood on end as his release shook him. When she met his release with her own, she moaned around Philip's cock, her ass clenching as she milked more than Mark had ever thought he had to give, each pulse like electricity roaring up his cock.

Philip rocked onto the balls of his feet, his knuckles white where they gripped the counter. His hips bucked and he shouted his release, cutting off Grace's moan as she desperately swallowed around him. With a last gasp, she turned her head, releasing Philip's still-hard cock and dropping her head to the stool seat, panting for breath.

Easing from her, Mark left her to collect her wits as he quickly disposed of the condom and threw on his clothes. He slipped out to the bathroom to clean up before grabbing a take-out bag for the lube and the plug. When he returned, he helped Grace stand, holding her as Philip gently dressed her.

She still hadn't said anything by the time the guard returned and knocked on the door. Based on her relaxed expression and half-lidded eyes, he wasn't particularly worried, but he needed to be certain.

"Are you okay, Gracie?"

A smile lit her face. "Never better, actually."

Philip grinned as he scooped her up into his arms. "Come on, Mark and I will take you home now."

She sighed and let her head rest on Philip's shoulder. Mark couldn't resist reaching out to stroke her soft cheek.

Philip looked at him then back down at Grace. "Baby, you were right."

She turned her face up to Philip, confused. "I was?"

Philip, though, looked right into Mark's eyes. "Yeah, Grace. Three *is* better than two."

Mark knew his heart was in his eyes and on his sleeve and lodged in this throat. He didn't give a flying fuck.

He wanted Philip to see it. He wanted him to know.

When they got home, Mark sat Grace on the edge of the bed and left Philip to strip her clothes off. She claimed she could do it herself, but Philip enjoyed helping her. It wasn't sexual, it was comforting. He wanted to take care of her.

Mark brought a warm wet towel from the bathroom. Philip stood back and watched while Mark gently washed Grace, wiping away the remains of their loving before pressing the soothing heat to the undoubtedly sore muscles of her anus.

Philip found he also enjoyed watching Mark take such thoughtful care of Grace. Enjoyed how Mark had taken such good care of him in the shower earlier, and by cooking them dinner. He just flat-out enjoyed Mark.

Could something like this work? he wondered as he stripped off his clothes and crawled into bed. Making sure Mark was in the middle, Philip lay down and pressed himself along the length of Mark's back, wanting him to feel surrounded by love and comfort. Cared for, as he had cared for them.

Mark pulled Grace back against his chest, curling into Philip until his butt rested on his thighs. Mark sighed then, a deeply contented sound that made Philip smile as he pulled the covers over all of them, letting his arm rest over Mark's waist and his hand on Grace's belly.

A threesome. No, not a threesome. That made him think of two people sharing one other person. This was different. Better. Three people, all sharing each other. A triad.

And yes, he knew it could work. Emotionally, sexually, it was already working. He'd seen the look in Mark's eyes and heard the love in Grace's voice. They were already there. Admitting it, accepting it, wouldn't be difficult.

It was the world at large that might have a hard time. Could he take two people to the company Christmas party? Sure, people would be shocked, but if they were smart, they'd also be jealous.

And, okay, it might make Thanksgiving dinner with his family a little awkward. He imagined the look on Aunt Mavis' face when he introduced his two mates.

Yeah, that was going to be interesting. And also, kind of hilarious.

But ultimately, what really mattered was that he didn't care what his coworkers or his family thought. With the shock of the unexpected come and gone, he found he didn't really care about being "outed". Not to the world. Not to his coworkers. Not even to his family. They'd have to accept Mark as they would Grace, or the three of them would skip the party, or spend their holidays elsewhere. Perhaps with Grace's family. Or Mark's.

That is, if Mark would accept him and Grace. Permanently.

His arm tightened around his lovers and he buried his face in Mark's soft curls. Mark murmured something, obviously well on his way to sleep.

Philip's last thought before falling asleep was that he'd find a way. He was determined to find a way to make it work.

Chapter Eleven

Nine blissful hours later, Mark woke up. Holy crap, he'd needed a decent night's sleep. Apparently, Grace and Philip had as well, as they were still curled up with him.

Falling asleep as the middle spoon in a row of three was amazing. Waking up flat on his back with Grace's hand on his chest and Philip's wrapped around his morning wood was even better.

They lay sprawled across the bed, the covers kicked to the floor at some point in the night. Philip snored softly. Clearly, he had no idea where his hand was, let alone what it was doing to Mark. Because of that, Mark was happy to just lie there and enjoy the experience of waking up with two people he loved. Two lovers, one whose warm, soft body was draped over his, her head resting on his shoulder, her hand over his heart. The other, whose hotter, harder body stretched out on his back beside him, their hips touching, Philip's other hand on his own dormant cock.

Mark smiled. Apparently, Philip liked to have a handle on things, even in sleep.

Moving slowly, he eased Grace onto her side and slid Philip's hand over to his own hip before crawling out of bed. Sneaking out to the kitchen, he started rummaging through cabinets and the refrigerator, looking for breakfast ideas. He was going to have to use up the last of their stores, but he could pull together something decent.

Twenty minutes later, he returned to the bedroom carrying a tray loaded with three glasses of orange juice, three mugs of coffee, cream, sugar, three forks, a bottle of syrup, a small plate loaded with crispy bacon strips and a foot-tall stack of seriously well-buttered pancakes. He had the *Boston Sunday Globe* he'd found on the stoop folded under his arm.

The fact that he'd also found a uniformed police officer

sitting outside their door was something of a concern. Patrick had apparently stepped up security overnight, and Mark wanted to know why. He'd asked, and had been assured he'd find out later that morning when Patrick came by to see them. Until then, Mark told himself not to borrow trouble and to focus on Philip and Grace instead.

"Wake up, my lazy loves. Breakfast is ready."

Philip's eyes snapped open and zeroed in on him immediately.

Yikes. *Somebody* was a morning person.

Grace, however, groaned before burying her face in the pillow.

Mark laughed. Definitely *not* a morning person.

When he set the tray on the bed, she lifted her head. "Do I smell coffee?"

"You do. And pancakes."

That did the trick. Rolling over, she pushed herself up and against the headboard. Philip did the same. Mark put the tray down between their outstretched legs, then sat cross-legged, facing them.

The food was devoured, the tray removed. He moved to sit between Philip and Grace, all three propped up against the pillows with the covers pooled in their laps as they finished their coffee and shared the paper.

Philip, their serious-minded lawyer, went right for the comics. Go figure. Grace actually read the front-page news, and Mark, as usual, started with the sports section. At various intervals, the sections were sorted, passed, shared, and discarded. The easy intimacy made his heart sing.

God help him, but the hope was growing. What had started as an ember hidden in his heart now glowed like the sun trapped in his chest. As he stared down at the stock reports blindly, he prayed that they felt it too.

He had been staring at the same graph for five minutes when Philip stuck his tongue in Mark's ear. Mark jerked back and stared at Philip's impish smile, astonished.

"I was afraid you'd fallen asleep with your eyes open," Philip said.

He quirked one brow. "And your test for that is to stick your tongue in my ear?"

Grace laughed, pulling the last pieces of the paper out of his hands and chucking them over the side of the bed. "I doubt Philip was attempting resuscitation." She glanced down at the sheets rising from his lap. "Although it seems to have worked."

Mark's grin was shameless. "What can I say? Breakfast revived me."

"I can see that," she said as she leaned in to kiss him.

The moment their lips met, the little blood remaining in his head drained. She tasted sweet. Like maple syrup, coffee, sugar, and love. Like Grace.

He speared his fingers through her hair, tilting his head to deepen the kiss, to lose himself in her mouth. Her taste. He rolled, taking her with him, kicking off covers as he trapped her beneath his warm body instead. When his erection pressed into the folds hidden between her legs, he exalted in the warm, wet heat waiting for him.

He broke their kiss to look up at Philip. He was staring at them, his hand running up and down his erect cock, his eyes glazed with growing passion. Mark reached out, his hand joining Philip's around his shaft. "Are you going to join us or would you rather watch?"

"I think I'll join," Philip said slowly, his eyes lingering for a moment on Mark's ass.

His heart jumped in his chest. If Philip was asking permission, he *so* had it. Mark's smile felt tight, his ass clenching in anticipation. "Please do."

Philip reached behind him and opened the little bedside table drawer, pulling out the lubricant and two condoms. Mark made quick work of one of the condoms before returning to lie between Grace's silky thighs. He closed his eyes, determined not to follow Philip's every move. Drawing a deep breath in through his nose, he pressed his mouth back to Grace's.

Philip's palm skimmed over his back and down to smooth the curve of one cheek, chasing his hips up against Grace so that his shaft ground into her clit. She groaned into his mouth, pulling her legs higher, lifting her hips to cradle him fully.

He eased back, his ass bumping against cold lube and Philip's hand. He hesitated for a heartbeat, hovering there, desperate to feel Philip enter his body, before he moved forward again, this time sinking into Grace, her body accepting him with one long, slow slide. She was ready, wet and yielding, but with so little foreplay, she was also tight, squeezing around his shaft with unbearable pressure.

Shit. He clenched his teeth as a generous squirt of cold lube filled his ass. As much as he wanted it, they were going too fast. He wanted it to last. And Philip was not a small man. Wide. So damn wide. It was going to feel so fucking good and Grace already had him on the verge.

Breathing in little pants, he gathered his wits. When he was marginally more in control, he pulled his knees up, changing the angle so that his cock head ran along her walls with short, sharp thrusts. He lowered himself to his elbows, staring down into Grace's shining eyes as he presented his ass to Philip.

He ran one hand over her brow, smoothing back the hair. The bed shifted as Philip came up behind him and the thrill of anticipation alone sent him soaring again.

"I'm so sorry, sweet Grace. I have to stop moving for a second." His voice was hoarse, and he despaired as his hips settled against hers. "I don't know if I can last if I don't stop moving." He whimpered, hips jerking, as Philip slid two well-lubed fingers into his ass.

She groaned. "I thought you said you weren't going to move?"

Mark's breaths were already little more than gasps. Good god, Philip didn't waste any time, his fingers scissoring and thrusting. Mark shuddered bucking against Grace without control.

He dropped his forehead to Grace's when Philip inserted a third finger, upping the tempo and pressure of his thrusts. God, he was just jumping right in, wasn't he? And he could, because Mark wanted this so much.

Desperate, he squeezed his eyes shut. It felt *too good*. The stretch. Opening for Philip's fingers. Knowing what would come next. Just thinking about it was enough to send him over the edge, but he forced himself back.

Holding on to his control was tearing him apart. Tears leaked from the corners of his eyes, sliding down his cheeks to drop onto Grace's soft skin.

Her hands came up, cupping his cheeks and running her thumbs through the salty trails. Her voice was soft but firm. "Philip, stop."

He did. Immediately.

Mark groaned, the agony exquisite, relishing Philip's fingers stretching his ass, but wanting more. "For god's sake, Philip, please do *not* stop."

He opened his eyes to see Grace's worried frown as Philip's fingers thrust deep once more, stopping there to stretch him wide. Mark glided on the ragged edge of pain and pleasure, not sure on which side he would fall. Not sure if he cared either way. He couldn't seem to stop the tears, even though they were freaking Grace out.

"It's okay, Gracie. I'm okay. It's just so good, you know?"

Her brows pinched together. "Are you sure?"

He closed his eyes again. He wanted her to understand, he wanted to tell her the truth, but it was hard to hold on to a thought when Philip was slowly pulling his fingers free of Mark's ass. Christ, he tried to force back the anticipation. He had to find a way to relax and stay in control or he'd come the minute Philip's cock brushed his ass.

"I'm okay. *Fuck*," he gasped as Philip's hands gripped his hips, spreading him wide, "better than okay. I don't know why I'm crying, but it's not because it's bad. It's because it's so damn good. It's just so—"

Whatever he had been about to say flew out of his head when the cool, smooth head of Philip's cock pressed against his anus. Mark stared down at Grace as the head slipped past the outer ring of muscles. He was unable to prevent the grunt that tore from his chest as he tried to adjust to Philip's girth.

"You're not crying because it hurts?" she asked.

Philip stopped moving. Waiting for his answer.

Mark fought to hold still and not shove himself back on Philip's cock. "No, my love. That's not it. It's just never felt this way before. It's a little overwhelming."

"Bad overwhelming?" Grace asked.

"*Good* overwhelming," he promised.

Philip must have been reassured, as he resumed impaling Mark with his thick shaft. Mark wasn't sure, but he thought his eyes might have rolled right around backward in his head. He burned where Philip stretched him, but the pressure triggered shocks of pleasure that ran over his body, his skin twitching, electrified.

It must have shown on his face, because the frown marring Grace's forehead smoothed, the corners of her eyes crinkling. "It's incredible, isn't it?"

"Which part?" His voice was raw. He was impressed he could speak at all. Philip had stopped his slow plunge and begun gentle strokes, quick, short thrusts that took him deeper and deeper. Mark's cock mirrored each thrust into Grace.

She moaned before answering. "All of it. Us."

"Yes!" The shout erupted from his lips as Philip's hips bumped against his ass, his chest coming to lie along the length of his back. God, at the base, Philip was *thick*.

Philip's hand ran through his hair, his lips brushed his ear. "It's so hot. Your ass is so hot."

He nodded, as if maybe he agreed. Maybe he did. Who cared? All he wanted was for Philip to fuck him. Hard.

Fisting his hands in the sheets next to Grace's head, Mark anchored himself and arched his back. His hips lifted, pressing that thick cock more firmly into his ass, his own cock sliding from Grace until only the head remained inside her channel.

A riot of emotion and sensation stormed his mind and body. The muscles in his neck ached as he strained back against Philip, then pumped his hips forward and slammed back into Grace. Mark shouted with pleasure when Philip held himself still, his heavy shaft running along Mark's sensitive, stretched rim.

Desire and need crashed over him and he dove into it, setting a steady pace, his thrusts into Grace as powerful as his retreat onto Philip's cock.

It was perfect. He had never been so completely engulfed in desire. In the anticipation of climax. Grace's moans mingled with his, Philip's grunts punctuated by a tightening of his fingers where they gripped Mark's hips, the slap of his skin against Mark's ass.

He wanted it to last forever even while each breath he took without release felt like a breath closer to death. He thrust harder, pounding into Grace as he forced Philip into his ass over and over. They let him set the pace and he set it hard, rough. His lovers shouted their approval, the sounds surrounding him like they did. Filling him, as they did.

When he reached the breaking point, it was as if he'd been thrown from a cliff, and for one indescribable moment he hung in midair, suspended in perfect peace and without gravity, before the shattering wave of his orgasm tore through his body and he plummeted back to Earth. He thrust into Grace, slamming his hips to hers, jerking and pumping with his climax, and she cried out her pleasure. Her muscles rippled and clenched over him, sending more sensation through his shaft and into his body. Philip followed, sinking into his ass, stretching Mark wide and roaring his release.

Mark stayed pinned between his lovers, their climaxes rolling through them for long, timeless moments before Philip eased back, pulling himself free. Mark grunted when Philip's head popped free, just as Grace whimpered when he withdrew from her.

Fuck. Collapsing onto his back, he held one of Grace's and Philip's hands in each of his, his heart pounding. His head spinning. His lovers didn't look to be in any better condition.

Philip broke the silence first. "Okay, seriously, I don't know how many more times I can live through that. I need a break. My junk is killing me."

Mark and Grace grinned at each other.

Once they finally recovered—and it took a good fifteen minutes—they showered. Mark might have been convinced to make the shower into play time, but Philip apparently hadn't been kidding. He'd been so turned on, so often, had climaxed enough times over the weekend, that he actually hunched over and groaned when they started soaping him up in all the best ways.

Grace hadn't known such a thing could happen to a man, but Mark assured her it could. He had to admit he was feeling it, too.

By the time Patrick arrived, they were dry, dressed, and Mark, at least, was enjoying the loose-limbed lethargy that can only be brought on through mind-blowing sex.

That calm left him the moment Patrick sat down and announced that someone had tried to break into the building the night before. While they'd been home, asleep in bed.

While Patrick explained their new security detail's workings, Mark couldn't sit still. He went to the kitchen, listening to Patrick while he cleaned up the dishes from breakfast and took stock of what was left for food. As he fed the last bagel and the remainder of the cream cheese to the patrolman stationed outside their door, a plan began to form in his mind.

The idea that he'd brought, unknowingly or not, danger to Grace and Philip's doorstep was untenable. His only thought was how to make it stop. As quickly as possible.

Popping around the corner to the living room once more, he plastered on an innocent smile. Philip and Grace sat silently, holding hands, while Patrick checked something on his phone.

"If we want lunch, I need to go to the market."

Philip immediately wondered what the hell Mark was up to. Call him suspicious, but he didn't like Mark's smile. In fact, he'd been watching Mark since Patrick's frightening announcement that someone had tried to break into his building last night. Mark was fidgety, anxiety practically radiating from him. And now this smile?

Years of questioning witnesses had taught him when to go on high alert. When to poke and prod for answers, and when to walk away before a witness said something you'd rather they kept to themselves.

Mark exhibited all the signs of a person who was hiding something.

Patrick chucked his phone onto the coffee table, making it clear that whatever he'd heard was of little use. "I have an hour or two. Pull together a list. I'll get whatever you need." Rising to his feet, he rubbed his hands together, as if shopping for three virtual strangers was what he lived for. Philip had to admire his attempt to defuse whatever Mark was planning.

Mark scoffed. "You're going to shop for us?"

"Yeah. Why not?"

"How do you know if a melon is ripe?"

For a moment, Patrick stood staring at Mark, nonplussed. "I don't know. It sounds hollow when you thunk your fingers on it?"

Mark scoffed. "Okay, you're officially not qualified to shop for us."

Patrick jammed his hands on his hips and raised his eyebrows. "Bitch."

Patrick's retort hung in the air. Mark looked at Philip as if he expected him to be leaping up in defense of Mark's grocery shopping honor. It didn't take Mark long to realize Philip was desperately trying not to laugh.

When Mark shot him a dark look, Philip shrugged. "What? It's funny. He called you a bitch."

"Oh for heaven's sake. *Boys*," Grace admonished. When

everyone stood their ground, she rolled her eyes. "I'm going to go call my study group and tell them I can't make it today. Try not to come to blows over produce selection, gentlemen."

The moment Grace closed the door to his office, Philip stood and locked eyes with Mark. "What are you doing?"

Mark tried to look innocent. He failed. Miserably. "Nothing. We need food. I was just going to go to the market on the corner. Not far."

In a flash, Philip understood. What Mark meant was that he was going to put himself out on Tremont Street as bait for the fucking mob. Before Philip could tell Mark where he could stick that brilliant plan, Patrick stepped forward.

"It's not a bad idea."

They both turned to stare at the detective. It was hard to say who looked more surprised. Mark regrouped first.

"Great. I'll just get going then," Mark said.

As soon as he turned to the door, Patrick grabbed one arm and Philip the other.

"You don't honestly think I'm going to let you walk out that door alone, do you?" Philip asked, his anger mounting.

Patrick nodded. "Yeah, not for nothing, but if you go out and get killed, I could get fired."

"I have to do *something*," Mark said, quietly determined. He faced Patrick. "The danger to Grace and Philip...it has to stop."

Philip almost felt sorry for Mark. He couldn't fault Mark's fear when Philip was forcing his own back by sheer willpower alone. But Mark was letting it cloud his judgment. Philip was desperately fighting to keep a clear head so that he could protect them all. Starting with Mark, who seemed determined to put himself in harm's way.

When Philip began to consider what he would do if something happened to Mark, he quickly shut those thoughts down. Too big and scary.

Patrick put his hand on Mark's shoulder. "I understand, but you don't have to make yourself into some sacrificial lamb. We'll do this, and we'll do it smart. I'll be there."

"So will I," Philip said firmly.

Mark shook his head. Before he could start, Philip leaned in close. "I'm going. No arguments."

Mark didn't relent. Instead he went straight for his most powerful argument. "What about Grace?"

Neither of them were dumb enough to believe she'd go for this plan if she had any idea of the outcome Mark was hoping for. Truth be told, Philip didn't think she'd go for it at all.

"No fucking way," Grace snapped, standing toe to toe with Philip.

Mark sat back on the couch and waited for Philip's response. Watching them argue was both educational and entertaining, though his neck was starting to hurt. It was like sitting courtside at Wimbledon.

He already knew Philip had a possessive streak a mile wide and he wasn't afraid to show it. But he was also the consummate lawyer, presenting a different line of reason for every argument Grace offered.

Wickedly clever, Grace continued to come up with counterarguments, relentlessly. They were putting themselves in danger. They were leaving her alone. Patrick could do the shopping. She should go, too. They could order in, for crying out loud! She tried every argument, but Philip, with Mark and Patrick backing him up, ultimately prevailed. Barely.

Standing in the hallway outside Philip's door, Mark waited with Philip and Patrick to hear the deadbolt and chain slide into place before leaving the patrolman on duty and jogging down the stairs and out to the street. Mark wondered if he would ever leave the house again without scanning traffic for a black Crown Victoria.

This time, though, he didn't see any evidence of the Benedetto family. For one deluded moment, he wondered if it all could have been a misunderstanding. Fat chance. While he was an optimist in many ways, he didn't really think he was that lucky.

Someone had tried to get to them last night. The threat was still very real.

Walking along Tremont Street, he and Philip stayed close, their shoulders brushing as they made room for other pedestrians. He wondered how everyone on the street didn't notice that their eyes were constantly moving, scanning the people, the passing cars, every doorway they crossed.

Patrick walked ten feet behind them, sometimes drifting farther back. He clutched his phone in his hand, and, for all appearances, had not a care in the world. Mark kept an eye on him by looking into the windows of the passing shops. At one point, he thought Patrick might actually be texting someone. He had to force himself not to look back and check. Instead, he reminded himself to focus on everything else around him.

It was a nice afternoon and many of the restaurants had tables outside to capture the last days of the outdoor eating season in New England. Farther down the block, he could see a throng of people in front of one of his favorite competitors and he shook his head. They'd started a "pajama brunch" years before and he had to admit it was pure genius. The patio was crowded with people in their fall sleepwear, a particularly boisterous group of women holding court along the front rail.

When they got a little closer, one of the women caught Mark's eye and he smiled back at her broadly, for just a moment enjoying the day, and the spectacle she and her girlfriends made in their sleepwear on a busy street.

Within a nanosecond, he had the undivided attention of the dozen women at the table. *Oops.* Not exactly what he'd been trying to do. And while it was flattering, it was also a bit unnerving. The women looked...hungry. And maybe not just for brunch.

Philip turned to look at him. "What have you done?"

Philip agreed with Patrick that the Benedettos were unlikely to do anything on a crowded street in broad daylight. If he didn't believe that, he would have duct taped Mark to the bed before he allowed him out the door. But then again, Philip *wasn't* confident enough in their safety to stop constantly searching the street for any signs of trouble.

So far, nothing. Thank god. Of course, he didn't know what he was looking for, exactly. And he wasn't sure what he would do if he saw it.

Part of him wanted to tear off after whoever or whatever and force, by any means necessary, the truth about what the fuck was going on. The notion of getting answers was deeply satisfying, even if he knew he wouldn't do anything of the sort. He'd let Patrick do the chasing and catching. His only concern would be making sure Mark was safe.

He felt fiercely protective, and while he was still a little uncertain about this thing with Mark, what he did know was that Mark was his. *His.*

Glancing over at Mark, he watched him send someone a long sexy smile. What the hell was he doing? When Mark's eyes went wide with horror a moment later, Philip turned to see what had captured Mark's attention.

A large and rather aggressive-looking group of women lined the patio railing of one of Grace's favorite cafés. It was pajama brunch day, and these women were clearly determined to enjoy the last of the summer's sun and warmth. He couldn't believe some of them had left the house dressed as they were. Not that he was complaining, since there were a lot of bare shoulders, legs, and cleavage. And every single pair of eyes was glued to Mark.

He also turned to stare at Mark. To his chagrin, his cock twitched as his possessiveness roared to life. "What have you done?"

"What?" Mark glanced at him nervously. "Nothing. I just smiled."

Philip couldn't contain his laughter, holding his stomach as the sound echoed down the street. Mark appeared genuinely confused.

Reining in his mirth, Philip smiled at Mark. "You have no notion of your appeal, do you?" he asked softly, moving closer, their arms brushing.

Mark answered his question with his grimace.

Philip watched, amused, as blood rushed into Mark's cheeks and his eyes scanned the street, no doubt searching for a distraction. Christ, he was blushing like a teenage boy, his fair complexion ruddy with it. It was remarkably endearing. Sweet, even.

Philip sighed heavily. Mark might as well have waved a giant red flag at him. Big, strong, funny Mark made him want to play. To fuck. But, god help him, sweet, blushing, self-conscious Mark made him want to emblazon the word MINE on Mark's chest for everyone to see.

Grace often teased him about his possessive nature, but goddamn, he couldn't turn it off. The women were staring at Mark like he was a side of bacon for their brunch. It made Philip want to drag Mark somewhere dark and warm where only he and Grace could find him. Have him.

Which realistically wasn't going to happen. Unfortunately. Instead, Philip slid his arm behind Mark, running his fingers along the bare skin beneath Mark's T-shirt, laughing when Mark stumbled, tripping over his own feet before catching himself, his mouth open in surprise.

Philip couldn't blame him. Only yesterday, Philip had nearly panicked in front of Patrick. Now, he couldn't remember for the life of him why he'd cared. He wanted not just Patrick, but every single person on Tremont Street to know Mark belonged to *him*.

He smiled and wrapped his hand around Mark's waist, pulling him tight against his side. As they passed the front rail lined with smiling, laughing women, he flashed his brightest smile. "Sorry, ladies, this one is spoken for," he said in the deepest voice he could muster. He delighted in seeing the hairs on the back of Mark's neck stand on end as goose bumps raced across his skin.

Mark's face flamed to scarlet. Patrick's choked laughter was barely audible once the patio erupted in hoots and shouted congratulations. Shameless, Philip grinned over his shoulder at the women, winking at their suggestions and compliments, laughing at himself. Now he was being just as big a flirt as Mark had been.

He hauled Mark in even closer and turned until his lips were a mere breath away from Mark's ear. The women's calls increased in volume and suggestiveness, drawing even more attention. He didn't care. He'd consider it free advertising—more people who would know Mark belonged to him.

Mark shook his head. "Are you having fun?"

Philip knew his smile was wolfish. "Yes, I am."

"You're very possessive, you know that?"

"Yes, I am," he said, taking in Mark's flushed cheeks and how his tongue poked out to wet his full lower lip. "You like that about me, don't you?"

Mark turned his face away to look down the street, drawing in a long shaky breath. "Shit yes."

Mark wished he could will away the bright red in his cheeks. He wished those damn women would stop cheering. He wished it weren't so hard to walk with an erection.

The entire street had to be staring at him and Philip. Which he didn't really mind, but his jeans were only going to cover so much and, while he didn't mind sharing between Grace and Philip, sporting a hard-on for half the city to see seemed like over-sharing.

At least the Benedettos were unlikely to jump them with a hundred people watching closely.

He looked up at Philip's wicked grin and more blood flooded south, forcing his cock up against his unforgiving zipper.

When had possessiveness become so damn attractive? Shit. Probably right around the same time he'd figured out he wanted to be possessed. He'd never wanted to be with anyone as much as he wanted to be with Grace and Philip. Had never felt the same level of connection. Truth be told, he'd wanted to tell those women—and everyone else who would listen—that he belonged to Philip and Grace. It didn't bother him in the slightest that Philip had done so first.

No, all that did was fill him with another surge of hope.

When Philip released him, he tried not to be disappointed. Damn. The show was over, the women having resumed their seats. He missed Philip's warmth immediately.

Then Philip's hand brushed his, their fingers lacing and holding on as they walked the last blocks to the market. Mark's heart resumed pounding in his chest. Hard. He heard Patrick clear his throat and looked back, knowing he shouldn't but unable to resist flashing a smile. Patrick pointed his chin at their linked hands with a small nod, as if to say *I told you so.*

Facing forward, Mark wondered if, by some miracle, Philip could be falling in love with him. As happy as the very idea made him, he didn't have the guts to ask. Even on his most masochistic day, he wouldn't run headlong into a rejection so painful he couldn't fathom how he'd ever recover.

Just the thought scared him stupid.

He remained lost in those thoughts, battling hope and fear, as he and Philip walked into the grocery store on the corner. Fifteen minutes later they emerged, each with a grocery sack in one arm. They'd bought enough to get through a couple of days locked away. He prayed the nightmare would be over before they needed more provisions, even while the thought of what would happen when it ended made him a little sick.

Scanning the street, he found Patrick sitting on a bench halfway down the block, pretending to be enthralled by his phone. It was a good show, since his eyes met Mark's immediately. At his nod, Mark moved to the corner, confident that Patrick would be able to catch up before the light changed.

Philip laughed at him for insisting on crossing Tremont Street now and walking up the opposite sidewalk from their group of lady admirers. No way he was going to walk that gauntlet again.

Waiting for the light, he didn't see the dark blue Escalade coming up the side street until it was practically on top of them.

Instinct alone had him grasping Philip's arm and yanking him back.

The SUV was still rocking to a stop when both passenger side doors flew open and two enormous men leaped out.

"Philip, run!" Mark shouted, dropping his groceries and pushing Philip away. He was about to yell for Patrick when his air was cut off by a tree trunk of an arm wrapped around his waist, pinning his arms as the life was squeezed out of him.

Holy Christ, this guy was strong.

When Mark's feet left the ground, he realized he was about to be chucked into the back of the SUV. He began to struggle in earnest, slowing the bastard's progress, but still being dragged farther away from Philip.

Looking back, he saw Philip throw his bag to the ground and begin to charge. Bracing for impact, Mark's entire body clenched, then shuddered when Philip skidded to a halt, his attention riveted to the second man somewhere beyond Mark's field of vision.

Mark watched with dismay as pedestrians scattered and dove into stores, crossing the street mid-block or simply running away. His heart sank when Patrick abruptly ducked into an alley, his hand leaving the grip of his holstered gun and bringing his phone to his ear as he stepped out of the line of sight.

The sound of a gun being cocked next to his ear halted Mark's struggles. He hung frozen, suspended above the ground.

He didn't dare turn his head, afraid to see the gun pointed at him. More afraid to see it aimed at Philip. He prayed that Philip wouldn't get hurt. And that the bad guys hadn't seen Patrick. And, please, god, that the cavalry would arrive really damn soon.

When the giant ape holding him began to drag him toward the car once more, Philip held up his hands.

"What do you want?" Philip demanded, his eyes searching, never looking directly at Mark. In the reverse situation, Mark knew he wouldn't have looked at Philip for fear of losing his shit.

"You'll find out when we contact you," the second man promised.

"No, please. Tell me now. So I can get it for you quicker." Philip's voice was persuasive, a courtroom voice meant to elicit answers. These guys were probably immune at this point in their careers, given they didn't mind a good broad-daylight kidnapping, but if nothing else, Philip was stalling them, and that had to be good.

Movement drew Mark's eye and he watched in horror as the gun swung from him to point at Philip. Mark immediately resumed struggling, his heels smashing back into his captor's shins. He tried for the knee and threw his head back into the man's face with all his might. When the arm around him loosened momentarily, he braced to do it again.

The piercing wail of a siren shattered the quiet hum of the busy city, and Mark's feet hit the sidewalk hard. He turned in time to see the gunman leap into the backseat of the SUV as the engine roared. It hesitated only a moment, but when Mark's captor didn't move, the tires squealed and the SUV took off, nearly clipping the ambulance responsible for scaring them off.

Holy shit, they left the ape man behind. Mark felt a surge of satisfaction to see the big thug shaking his head, his nose bleeding. He seemed befuddled, which was all the opportunity Philip needed. With a lunge, he sent the thug sprawling to the pavement with Philip landing on top of him.

Mark immediately fell to his knees and helped Philip pin the tree-trunk arms.

Patrick arrived just as they'd managed to flip him over onto his back. Philip grabbed fists full of shirt and hauled the guy's face close to his own.

"What the fuck do you want with us?" Philip barked, all courtroom finesse lost to his rage.

The dumb thug smiled, shockingly unconcerned. "It doesn't matter. You'll give us whatever the fuck we want to get your woman back." Only then did the bastard notice Patrick pulling his handcuffs from behind his back. His eyes widened before he clamped his mouth firmly shut.

But Mark already knew enough.

They hadn't taken the bait. This was just a stall tactic. Christ. Even the fucking mob didn't think they would successfully kidnap someone in broad daylight.

Impossibly, another surge of adrenaline burst through Mark. He was, for the very first time since the nightmare had begun, absolutely terrified.

"Jesus, Philip. We have to get to Grace."

Chapter Twelve

Grace.

Philip grabbed Mark's hand and hauled ass across the street and down the busy sidewalk, barely dodging cars and the people shouting at them to slow down as they sprinted full out for home.

They'd left Patrick kneeling next to Mark's attempted kidnapper, surrounded by groceries and onlookers coming out of every door on the street. Philip had heard him shouting for them to stop, to wait, but he and Mark never hesitated in their race for home.

As they neared his building, Philip dug out his keys, his hands fumbling with the lock, his mind screaming at him to hurry. When it released, he thrust Mark through the door and made sure it was locked behind them before thundering up the five flights of stairs.

Mark was ahead of him, swearing as he leaped over the unconscious—please, god, not dead—cop on the hallway floor before banging on the door, shouting for Grace to let them in.

There was no answer.

Philip saw the circle of scorched metal around the lock on his heavy steel door and his heart stopped. As he thrust his key into the lock, it held firm in its place, issuing a loud snick when it released. He could see the burn didn't make it all the way through the door.

They burst into the apartment, hollering for Grace. She flew out of the bedroom, tossing a chef's knife and her phone to the floor as she launched herself against his chest.

Philip held on for dear life.

Mark staggered against the breakfast bar, sucking wind as hard as Philip was from their sprint. Then Mark spun and ran for the door.

Where the fuck was he going?

Letting go of Grace, Philip was fully prepared to tackle Mark to the ground. Then he heard it. The echoing creak of the door to the fire stairs.

He made it to the front door at the same time as Mark, prepared to wrestle his ass back into the apartment, but Mark bent and grabbed one of the unconscious officer's arms, tugging it hard enough to tear it right from the shoulder.

Scanning the still-empty hallway, Philip clutched the officer's other arm, hauling as fast as they could to get him through the door. Grace came to support his head with one hand, even as the other dialed 9-1-1 and said the phrase that would get more cops there in less time than any other.

"Officer down."

As soon as the officer's feet cleared the door, Philip slammed it shut and threw the bolt.

He watched anxiously while Mark took the officer's pulse and Grace examined the nasty blue-black welt blooming over his temple. When Mark quietly murmured, "Thank god," Philip dropped to his knees.

Thank god was right. Crawling to Grace, he pulled her into his arms, then hauled Mark over so they both very nearly sat in his lap.

They stayed liked that until the police arrived.

Grace sat at the breakfast bar, quietly sipping tea and listening to Mark and Philip give their statements to Patrick and the other detective he'd brought with him.

She'd already given her account of the Benedettos' attempt, she now knew, to kidnap her. She shuddered again, remembering the banging at the door and looking through the peephole to see strangers claiming to be cops. And no one in uniform.

As she'd stood there frozen, terrified that they knew she was on the other side, the door had begun to heat up under her hand.

The flashes of light in the hallway had suddenly made terrible sense, the first sparks sending her to her phone to call 9-1-1 and to the knife block for what little protection she could find. Even in her panic, she knew it was more likely they'd take it and use it against her before she'd do much damage, but there was no way in hell she wasn't going to at least try.

Thank god they hadn't made it into the apartment. Thank god Mark and Philip were safe. She thought about what she would have done if something had happened to either one of them. If she'd lost one or both. The mere consideration was agony, her hand coming up to rest on her chest where her heart felt as if it might crack in two.

She shoved the what-ifs aside. Pushed the fear back. It hadn't happened. It wouldn't happen.

She looked up when Patrick got a call, her hope dimming when he frowned into the phone. When he hung up, he looked at Mark.

"Our favorite thug in custody is cracking. Seems he thinks all this is about a flash drive? One of those USB memory stick do-hickeys?"

Mark and Philip stared at Patrick blankly, shaking their heads. When Patrick looked over to her, she just shrugged.

They still had nothing. Her frustration could hardly be contained. She willed herself to relax.

The police had patrol cars circling the neighborhood, searching for the black Crown Victoria, the dark blue Escalade, looking for anything suspicious. Officer Sullivan was at Mass General Hospital and awake. He was going to be okay and could describe his attackers better than she could. They would figure this out.

Maybe it was that she felt safe for the first time in hours, or maybe it was because the adrenaline had finally started to work its way out of her system, but suddenly, her brain kicked back in.

"It's in my pants!"

Everyone turned to look at her.

"Excuse me?" Philip asked.

"The drive! The flash drive! Someone dropped one at Valentine's Wednesday night...shit...we found it at cleanup. At table thirty-seven!"

Mark leapt to his feet and turned to the others. "That's right next to the booth that got cut up."

"That's it! I have it." Launching from her stool, she ran for the bedroom, her men and both cops hot on her heels.

She fell to her knees in front of the bedroom closet and dug furiously through her bags. Where was it? She found the merry widow and the fuck-me pumps, tossing them over her shoulder with total disregard for her audience, but no dress slacks.

Shit. Philip had done laundry. "Where are the pants I was wearing on Thursday? I had it in my pocket because someone called to say they were going to come get it. Shit. And I never called him back." Things were beginning to make more and more sense. She looked at Philip. "You know, the black pants. The ones I had on with the corset."

The detectives' eyebrows went up, but they wisely refrained from comment. Philip thought for a moment before snapping his fingers. "I think I put them in the dry cleaning." Turning, he hauled a laundry bag from under the big bed and unceremoniously dumped it out on the floor in front of her.

There they were. Yanking the pants from the pile, she thrust her hands in the pockets and found the little plastic stick, pulling it out and presenting it to the rest of the room.

For a moment, they all just stared. What in hell was on it?

She wasn't waiting for some police geek to tell her. She wanted to know why and what. Now.

Jumping to her feet, she brushed past Patrick's outstretched hand and ran out of the bedroom and into Philip's office. His computer was on and she inserted the drive. Mark, Philip, Patrick, and the guy whose name she couldn't remember, all piled in behind her, hovering as she sat and waited the longest fifteen seconds of her life for the damn machine to recognize the new hardware and pop up a window of its contents.

One file. A spreadsheet.

She opened it and everyone leaned forward, prepared to see god-only-knew-what. Instead, all they got was a list of numbers.

At the quiet "oh shit" behind her, she turned to look at the nameless detective. *Now* she remembered. He was from the Organized Crime Task Force. Brandon something.

"What? What's *oh shit*?" she asked.

"Those long strings of numbers are bank accounts. I recognize the routing numbers for the Royal Bank of the Cayman Islands."

"Is that good? That sounds good," Mark offered.

"Very good. We've searched a long time for a money trail on the Benedettos. Our best bet for prosecution is always the RICO statute, and you need to find the money to make that work."

Grace smiled. They were finally getting somewhere. Turning back to the computer, she saw the workbook had multiple sheets and clicked on the next one, bringing up another long list of names, phone numbers and dollar amounts.

"What is it?" Philip asked.

"No idea," Patrick admitted. "Although there are some familiar names on that list."

She also recognized a couple of the names. Like her state representative. And the dean of her college. Oh, and the mayor of Boston.

"Blackmail? Extortion?" she asked.

Brandon shook his head. "Maybe. Most of the amounts are too low. No one extorts for hundreds of dollars or even thousands of dollars. That's a tens-of-thousands-dollar kind of business."

"Interesting...although," Grace said thoughtfully, "if these *are* amounts due, you all are going to have to talk to the mayor, I'm afraid. Didn't the city just award a major waste removal contract to some shady company? And he righteously claimed it was the cheapest bid?"

A slow smile spread across Patrick's face.

Mark looked at Philip. "Is she always this good at thinking of devious plots?"

Philip smiled proudly.

"She's good at it," Detective Brandon Something-or-other agreed. "And she's right, we will have to look into that. The question remains, though, how did these people get into the Benedetto family for this kind of money? I don't think it's payoffs or protection. The amounts are all different. Most crooks charge a set fee."

This guy was a font of knowledge. Excited to figure out the puzzle, she scanned the screen again. The workbook had a third sheet. She clicked on it.

"Bookie! It's a sports book's accounting!" Mark announced.

Brandon nodded. "You're right."

Grace was impressed. She looked at Mark. "How did you know?"

"There are dates, games, scores, spreads. I tried to make statistics class in college interesting by running a mock bookie outfit for a couple of weeks as a project, and this is exactly how you would track your winners and losers. The first page must be who owes money."

Patrick and Brandon agreed. Unfortunately, it didn't prove it was the Benedettos who wanted the drive back. Too bad the bad guys weren't dumb enough to put their names anywhere on the damn data.

At least, she thought as she carefully ejected the evidence, they were getting closer to having their answers.

Brandon offered that the guys on his team, or possibly the computer geeks, and even the Royal Bank of the Cayman Islands might be able to tell them more. He and Patrick took the drive, leaving the three of them tucked away with another uniform on the door, one in the lobby and two cars—one out front and another circling—on the building.

Grace still wished she felt safer.

Grace wasn't getting any homework done. She and the boys

had decided to try to pass the afternoon by distracting themselves. It wasn't working worth a damn. At least, her attempt at school work wasn't doing the trick.

To be honest, though, she was distracted. It wasn't her fault, either. It was Sunday afternoon and, in the rich tradition of autumn Sunday afternoons, her men were glued to the Red Sox game, arguing over every damn statistic and pitch. Their choice of distraction seemed to be working great for them.

Them, and every other couple of buddies in Boston.

Well, perhaps not *just* like every other. Philip's couch could seat five people, but they were practically on top of each other, right in the middle. And when they were arguing, one always seemed to have his hand on the other's thigh. And typical buds probably didn't sit around shirtless with the buttons on their jeans undone, which was really upping the distraction factor for her.

Philip hopped up to get another round of beers, bending down to kiss Mark before moving to the kitchen.

Looking back at her work, she tried to concentrate. After five minutes of reading the same sentence over and over, she gave up, tossed down her pen and packed up her papers. She'd done her assignments for class the next day and emailed those and her apologies for her absence to her professor. She could always catch up on her reading tomorrow.

In the meantime, she couldn't just stop thinking about what had happened. And if she was going to be trapped in the house with two ridiculously hot men whom she loved, she wanted to feel alive. To celebrate life. To affirm that her men were with her. Safe. Their strong hearts beating under her hands.

Philip and Mark cheered when someone hit a walk-off home run, ending the game without extra innings. *Thank god.* She didn't want to wait another minute.

Rising, she walked over to stand directly in front of the TV, her hands on her hips.

"You two recovered yet?"

Their discussion of what the general manager would say in

the post-game interview came to a halt. Without so much as a comment, Philip turned off the TV and tossed the remote over his shoulder.

Philip smiled up at her. "All better."

A delicious thrill ran down her back. She could see the hunger leap into his eyes. She looked at Mark. "And you?"

"Darling, you could revive a dead man."

She laughed, even as heat crept across her face. Ridiculous. There shouldn't have been much that could make her pink up at this point, but Mark's praise pleased her.

They stood, trapping her between their bodies. She wanted them. Now. They seemed more than happy to oblige.

Philip's lips caught hers in a drugging kiss, his fingers threading through her hair as Mark reached around to cup her breasts, already tender and heavy with arousal. She moaned into Philip's mouth when Mark's thumbs skated over the hard peaks, thrumming her nipples until they were firing electric jolts through her body.

She tore her lips from Philip's, sucking in enough air to speak. "Clothes off. Now."

Once again, they were happy to oblige, although Mark whispered something about a "bossy little witch". They discarded their clothing and hers, then sandwiched her between their glorious, hard bodies. She was enveloped in warmth.

Mark kissed her, his tongue thrusting in a carnal dance that mimicked the act to come. When he pulled his lips away, she reached for him, trying to tug him back. She frowned when he sat down on the couch, until he reached up and pulled her down with him.

That's better.

She straddled his lap on her knees, holding herself up and away from his bobbing erection as she turned to look back at Philip. His face was serious. Beautiful. Her heart fluttered in her chest, dancing with her love for him.

He sat on the coffee table and reached out with one hand,

drawing it down her back, causing each hair he touched to stand away from her body as an erotic thrill shivered through her. When he scooted forward, his hand slipping between her spread thighs from behind, she saw the bottle of lubricant and the condoms on the table behind him.

Where in hell had they been hiding that? She was about to ask if the supplies had ever been farther than arm's reach all day when Philip's wicked fingers slid through the crease of her ass, gently bumping over the nerve-rich knot of her anus before one thick finger slipped into her pussy.

She gasped, her head falling back on her shoulders, her hips working in time with his thrusts. Mark pushed her back, her body arching until her shoulders rested against Philip's chest. She was aroused beyond reason when Mark's thumbs spread her open and his tongue swiped across her swollen clit.

She rocked on Philip's hand, forcing his finger deeper as Mark tormented that magical bundle of nerves, biting and licking before pulling it between his lips and sucking hard. She ran her hand through Mark's silky hair and held him to her. She never wanted him to stop. She never wanted to let him go.

When Philip slid a second finger in, she went up and over. Fast and furious, her orgasm crashed through her, each one punctuated by the thrust of Philip's fingers or the lash of Mark's tongue.

She was still floating above the earth when Mark shifted, her slick thighs delighting in the tickle of coarse hair as he moved his butt to the edge of the couch, putting his cock beneath her. Philip pulled his fingers away.

Mark's entire body twitched, his face a mask of need and concentration as Philip's deft fingers quickly rolled latex down Mark's shaft. When he was done, Mark took a minute, his breathing ragged.

Once the tension cleared from Mark's face, he blinked and smiled up at her. Her heart fluttered again and she smiled back, knowing herself to be luckier than any woman had a right to be.

Running his hands up her thighs and over her hips, he

gripped her waist and urged her down on his long, hard shaft. The swollen head slipped through her folds and she closed her eyes, rejoicing in the stretch of her body widening to accept him, the thrilling shudder as the head popped into her. He controlled the speed of her descent, stopping when only the thick crown was buried. His smile widened when she looked at him and growled, spreading her knees so that the only thing keeping her from sinking all way down on him was his hold on her waist.

Suspended, she watched, waiting for some sign he would release her and offer some relief. He never gave even a hint before he let go.

His hands slid up her ribs, barely slowing her plunge as his cock slammed into her. She landed on his lap hard, grunting as his head bumped the entrance to her womb and her clit crashed against his pelvic bone. Stars burst behind her eyelids, her head spinning.

It was perfect. Grabbing the back of the couch for support, she eased back, running the length of his shaft along her sensitive inner walls until only the head of his cock remained inside her. Then she let herself drop again.

Philip's hands wrapped around her waist from behind, clasping over Mark's. Strong hands and arms helping her. Guiding her. Giving her speed and control she couldn't maintain on her own. More than one man alone could offer her. It was awesome. Mark was impossibly erect, as firm and long as he'd ever been as she impaled herself on him, striving for the climax that loomed in her mind and her quaking muscles.

Straining for a better grip on the back of the couch, she plunged and rose, ecstatic with the power they gave her, her orgasm coming on like a freight train. She lifted again but her back came up against Philip's chest, halting her mid-thrust.

She wanted to push him back, to force him to let her continue, but he wrapped his arms around her ribs and urged her down so that her chest pressed to Mark's, his cock fully seated.

"God, Grace, you're so close. I can tell." Philip's voice was rough. "I hate to make you wait, but I want to make it better."

She nodded, panting as she lay sprawled over Mark. When Mark's hands came up to palm her ass cheeks, spreading them wide for Philip, her heart tumbled in her chest. She felt drunk with nerves and excitement.

God, could she do this?

Her pulse thundered, her breath searing her lungs. She fought to relax and welcome Philip's entrance, even while the anticipation made her squirm, driving Mark deep inside her. She looked into Mark's wide blue eyes, so close to her own, and he smiled. She couldn't look away from those cobalt depths, couldn't stop the kick of her hips as she worked him deep inside herself. He had become a part of her, of them, just as Philip was. They each had a piece of her heart.

She was so lost to her thoughts, to the emotions racing through her, she jumped when the tip of Philip's finger pressed against her anus. It slipped inside, quickly, lubricant easing its way as it thrust and retreated. One finger was soon replaced by two. She arched her back enough to allow Mark to pull one stiff nipple into his mouth, distracting her as Philip's fingers began to scissor and stretch, preparing her. Waves of pleasure ricocheted through her body. She wanted to shout at Philip to hurry. To take her. But she knew he'd keep torturing her until he was sure she was open to him. Which, by god, she was.

His fingers spread wider still, an almost unbearable yielding of her flesh, then a cool flood of lubricant filled her ass.

Her fingers whitened, clutching the upholstery. Was this the same lover she'd once fretted would be dull? The thought made her want to laugh as he took her wider, burning her from the inside out. She'd thought she'd loved him then, but the memories of their lovemaking were pale shadows of what she felt now. Her love for Philip more brilliant now than it had ever been.

When Philip pulled his fingers away, anticipation warped seconds into hours until the wide, soft head of his cock pressed into her. She closed her eyes and relaxed every muscle she still had control of, offering herself to Philip. The stretch, the burn, was still there. But it was lost in the deluge of pleasure.

Philip's arms came around her ribs and clutched at Mark, pinning her between them. "Are you okay?" His voice in her ear sent shivers along her skin.

She nodded quickly, just trying to get enough air in her lungs. He was thicker than Mark. So big. She felt like she was coming unglued.

Mark groaned. "Push out, sweetheart. Like you're trying to push him back out."

She did, and, with a shout, Philip pressed all the way in.

Oh. Oh. Oh. Wow.

Holding herself perfectly still, she tried to absorb every feeling, every sensation swamping her body. She hadn't expected this.

Mark had taken her standing over the stool in his kitchen, Philip had fucked her while the butt plug had been locked in her ass, jammed into her with his every thrust. But nothing could have prepared her for *this*. Now she understood Mark's tears. And Philip's claim to have found heaven. There was nothing on Earth like this. Filled up and surrounded, enveloped by two people you love.

She was complete.

When Philip's hips gave a little pump, Mark gasped. "My god. I can feel you. I can feel your cock against mine."

Mark shoved his hips up, hard, forcing her even farther onto his shaft. Philip grunted. Mark wrapped a hand around Philip's neck. "Can you feel that?"

Philip moaned, nodding as his hips pumped again, sending electric shocks soaring through her. Whatever the men thought they were experiencing had to be only a fraction as good as it was for her. Nothing else could ever come close.

Philip braced his hands on the back of the couch next to hers and plunged deeper before pulling out again. This time, she lifted until Mark's cock neared the end of her passage, then she held still, allowing Philip to ease his shaft from her ass. She swore she could feel every vein, every ridge and bump that ran over the charged nerve endings of her anus. When Philip was almost free, she tightened, locking his head inside her.

Philip's muttered curse pleased her. She felt strong. Powerful. In control and totally out of control at the same time.

Then Mark thrust up.

She threw her head back and called out all the desire and love she had for these two incredible men, as if Mark's thrust had forced it up from her soul.

Philip and Mark fed on her frenzy. They didn't build up to it. Didn't ease their way. Within a stroke, both men were fucking her furiously.

Philip retreated and plunged, then Mark, then Philip. Within three thrusts they'd found a rhythm designed to make her frantic.

She felt every inch of their cocks as they stroked into her, their thick crowns bumping and rubbing through the thin membrane that separated them. She felt wanton. Free. Bearing down, she clenched around them, shaking with what was building inside her. Their groans turned to shouts and grunts as she wondered how she didn't fly into a million pieces.

And then she did.

With the first wave of her orgasm, her legs gave out and she drove Mark down into the couch and up into her, taking Philip with her until he slammed into her to the hilt, his weight pressing her tight between them. Her entire body shuddered as her climax rippled. Her ass muscles clenched unbearably, locking Philip inside her, his hips rocking like clockwork, driving her clit down on Mark's pelvic bone. When the hot wash of Philip's release filled her, a second, equally powerful orgasm ripped through her, leaving her panting, her eyes clenched shut against the barrage.

Tears slid down her face. Her body stretched to accommodate her lovers, the heat of their skin wrapped around hers, their arms binding her to them, between them. As the aftershocks of her climax continued to shake her body, she absorbed it all, and felt well and truly sated.

Grace didn't fully regain her senses until they were in bed, her body tucked between theirs in the dark room. They'd carried her, washing themselves and her before settling down.

Burrowing deeper under the covers, she pressed her face to Mark's chest, her back warmed by Philip's solid presence behind her. She was safe. Cherished.

When the sun rose in the morning, their extended weekend would be over. Somehow, she thought with a sigh of pure contentment, it just wasn't going to matter.

* * * * *

Again with that goddamn ringing, Grace thought as she burrowed under the covers to get away from the racket ruining her sleep. It wouldn't stop. It sounded like a freaking gong.

She tried to hide under Mark, figuring he might block the sound better than the duvet, but he only laughed and rolled away.

Traitor.

"She's a heavy sleeper, huh?" She could hear the smile in Mark's voice. Why was he talking at all? It was bedtime.

Philip's answering chuckle vibrated through her body. Then he left her, too. "She sleeps like a rock. Let's leave her be until we know who is at the door."

Crap. The door. The sound wasn't a phone ringing. It was the buzzer downstairs. Someone wanted to visit.

She sat up, pushing her hair from her face. "No way you two are answering the door in the middle of the night without me. Not after everything that's happened."

Philip's smile was gentle. "Baby, it's not the middle of the night. It's only nine thirty. We kind of fell asleep early after our adventure out on the couch." He looked at Mark. "We'll go see who it is. You stay here."

When they moved toward the door, she leapt from the bed and quickly pulled on Philip's flannel robe. She'd seen the look

198

that had passed between them. The *let's protect the little woman* look. Good god, she thought as she dashed into the living room, what had she done? She'd set herself up to have not one, but *two* men being overprotective of her.

She caught up with them at the front door.

Mark was nervous about this mysterious late-night visitor. Too much bad shit had happened already. He wanted to ask Philip to pretend they weren't home. Better yet, he wanted to steal Philip and Grace away and go somewhere the Benedettos could never find them.

Instead, they crowded around the little voice box by the front door.

"Yes?" Philip's voice was bland. Unconcerned. Not like it could be the gun-toting freak, right? Or the blow-torch dude? Then again, the building was crawling with cops, and the bad guys probably wouldn't use the doorbell.

"Philip? It's Patrick. Can I come up?"

Philip was about to press the door release, but Mark's hand stilled his. Call him paranoid, but he didn't want to take things at face value. "We don't know if it's really him."

"How can he prove it?"

"Badge number?" Grace suggested.

"Anyone could find that out," Mark responded. "I have an idea, though." He reached out to press the talk button, praying that if it was Patrick, he was alone.

"Patrick, it's Mark. I'm sorry to do this to you, but we need proof that it's you. Can you tell me what happened between you and your best friend last week?"

For a moment, this request was met with dead silence, then the speaker crackled and Patrick's laughter boomed over the intercom. "Shit, Mark, you're lucky I'm not standing here with a bunch of patrolmen. Or, better yet, my fucking captain!"

Yup. It was Patrick. Before he could press the door release

button, Patrick continued. "For what it's worth, my best friend, *who I kissed*, is Detective Brandon Barett from the Organized Crime Task Force and he's standing right next to me. You're damn lucky I don't have issues about that."

Mark could hear a voice in the background say, "I can't believe you told him."

Oops. Big cringe. He hit the button again. "Sorry about that. Come on up."

Patrick and a red-faced Brandon arrived at their door minutes later, and Philip led everyone into the living room. Patrick got right down to business. He plucked an eight-by-ten photo from a folder and passed it to Grace, indicating she should pass it around to the others.

"Do any of you recognize this guy?" Patrick asked.

"Oh my god!" Grace exclaimed. "It's the guy from booth thirty-five. The booth that was cut up! He and a woman about his age had dinner with us on…Wednesday night? Early. I think." She held the photo out for Mark to take. "I think he left before you came out of the kitchen for your meet-and-greet."

"Damn. It's also the guy that kicked my ass in my office. Philip, do you recognize him?"

Philip studied the picture over Mark's shoulder, shaking his head. "He looks familiar, but I can't place where I've seen him. I can't be sure if he's the one from the second break-in. I didn't get much of a look at his face. I just remember his build—he was a big guy."

Patrick read from some papers in his file. "How about six foot three inches, two hundred and thirty pounds, all muscle?"

Philip nodded. "That sounds right. Who is he?"

"Damian Benedetto."

Oh crap, Mark thought. That couldn't be good news.

Damian Benedetto. Philip's heart sank. That was why he'd been familiar. He looked like dear old dad, whose face often graced the evening news.

"Have you apprehended him?" Philip asked. He couldn't help but go into lawyer mode. He wanted answers. He wanted to know Mark and Grace were safe.

"Actually, he came to us," Patrick said, as if he hardly believed it himself. "Well, I should say he called us and we went to him. He's at Mass General, and he will be for some time. Turns out, when his father discovered what he'd been up to, one of his henchmen beat Damian within an inch of his life."

Grace gasped and, even though Philip wanted to pound this guy into the sand, he was forced to agree that it was horrifying that anyone's own father would do such a thing.

It was also a little disappointing. Philip couldn't very well go smack around an invalid, could he?

"What did he tell you?" Mark asked.

Brandon, Organized Crime Officer and, apparently, Patrick's new make-out partner, answered. "In the past we've known him to be a goon for his father's organization. Strictly muscle. Having met him, I can see why—not the brightest bulb in the chandelier, if you know what I mean. But his dad kept him busy and paid him well."

Patrick continued the tale when Brandon paused. "Only junior got greedy. He'd been doing collections for the sports book and thought he could really impress dad by bringing in more of the money owed. When his father's bookmaker turned his back, Damian downloaded the file onto the flash drive."

Philip nodded. He could see how this story would have ended, regardless of whatever fate had befallen the flash drive. He'd read some of the names on that list. The muscle-headed son would never have been privy to that information.

"But before he could begin his new collection effort," Patrick continued, "he took his girlfriend to Valentine's for a date, at which point the memory stick must have fallen out of his pocket. When he called, your bartender told him Grace had it, but when you didn't call him back, he panicked."

Brandon picked up the thread of the story. "From there on, you more or less know what happens. After the break-in when you two surprised him, he ran straight to Mario, expecting him to clean up the mess."

"Which, I suppose, he has been trying to do, but not how Damian intended. From what we can tell, his dad didn't care about the flash drive, per se, figuring it wouldn't be tied back to him even if someone did look at it. But then his son and spitting image was seen by you two and he thought you might have enough to put it all together if you did find the files," Patrick said.

"So, Mario sent some of his men to retrieve the flash drive, just to be sure. As you already gathered, the idea was to keep you two occupied while others took the drive from Grace. If that didn't work, then they'd use you as leverage to force her to hand it over, or vice versa," Brandon finished.

"And in the meantime, he had his son worked over to see that it never happened again," Patrick added.

Philip smiled. The two detectives kept finishing each other's sentences, completing each other's thoughts.

"When Damian woke up in the hospital, he got himself a good lawyer and called us. We took his statement and went right over to the Bella, Mario's restaurant, and arrested him."

Philip could see both detectives were trying hard not to smile. "What's it like to arrest the worst bad guy in town?" he asked.

Patrick's grin bloomed. "Well, it isn't protocol for most arresting officers, but Brandon and I found a way to celebrate once we got to my car."

Brandon's cheeks turned red once again and Philip laughed. Maybe there was something in the air these days.

Chapter Thirteen

The danger was over. Mark thanked god. With the flash drive out of their possession and Damian prepared to testify against his own father, the Benedetto family and their jailed leader would likely have little interest in the three of them.

Patrick and Brandon agreed, but told them to be careful and report anything. All three quickly assured them that they would.

As soon as the police detectives left, exhaustion, accompanied by an awful sadness, settled in Mark's chest. It was over. The mystery. The threat. The weekend. And, possibly, his time with Grace and Philip.

Philip smiled, also obviously tired. "Thank god that's over," he said, echoing Mark's earlier thoughts.

Mark tried to smile. He told himself to relax.

Grace leaned against Philip, her head resting on his chest. Mark watched them and loneliness returned, a deep black abyss opening up to swallow him whole.

Philip looked over at him but didn't reach out to pull him in. Mark's heart cracked just a little. "You must be relieved, Mark. I'm sure you want to get back into your apartment tomorrow and get things straightened up."

There was his answer.

He nodded jerkily. Philip was being gentle, but the message was clear. Mark was going home. Soon. Alone.

In an instant, hope died.

He tried to reassure himself that it wasn't over and that they could keep going on as they had been. That he was misunderstanding. He couldn't make himself believe it, though.

He looked at the couch where they'd made love just a few hours before. The memory of Philip's cock rubbing along his through Grace's body made his gut clench painfully. His eyes drifted to the floor, where Philip had finally accepted what was between them, given in to his desire, and kissed Mark like his life depended on it.

The moment he'd offered Philip his first taste of intimacy with a man, Mark had also given him his heart.

Like a lamb going to the slaughter, he followed them back to the bedroom and stripped down to his boxers. He couldn't tear his eyes away from them as they pulled off their clothes, desperately trying to memorize everything he could.

No one said much more than how tired they were and how good it would be to fall back into bed. A masochist to the end, he looked for clues in every word, some hint that Grace and Philip were going to ask him to stay, not just for the night, but for...for what? For a week? A month? Maybe the occasional sleepover? Someone to call when things got boring and they wanted some variety?

The thought made him feel physically ill. He turned his back to the bed and gulped air, trying to settle his stomach. They wouldn't treat him that way. They were his friends—had been before and would be after.

But then again, they had no way of knowing he was in love with them. They'd have no way of knowing how being their playmate would crush him.

He had to leave.

If it hurt this much now, what would it be like in the morning? Or the following afternoon? He wasn't such a great masochist after all. Even he had a limit.

Sliding back on the bed, he lay down. The moment his head hit the pillow, Philip reached over Grace and hauled him back against her chest, Philip's arm wrapped around them both. He was grateful when his voice sounded reasonably normal when they all said good night.

Then he just lay there. Awake.

The longest minutes of his life passed as he waited for Grace and Philip to fall asleep. At the end of the interminable wait, of what had felt like hours of agonizing thoughts and what-ifs, all he could remember was the grief.

Slipping from the bed, he pulled on his clothes, grabbed his bag from the office and left a note saying goodbye and thank you. It was the best he could do.

He'd told himself he'd never walk away from these beautiful people. He'd believed he would be willing to spend time with them any way he could, whenever he could. He'd been sure he could do that.

He'd only been right about one thing. He didn't walk away.

He ran.

The next morning, Grace bolted upright in bed the moment she woke. Something was wrong.

Where was Mark?

She listened for a moment but couldn't hear the shower running, or the sounds of breakfast being prepared from the kitchen. Climbing out of the bed, she padded through the apartment. When she found the note, she cried out.

"*No.* Philip, wake up!"

She snatched the note in her fist, ran back to the bedroom, and launched herself onto the bed. Philip caught her in his arms.

"Grace? What's wrong? Where's Mark?"

Her tears came in torrents, her voice hitching over sobs. "He's gone. He left, Philip. He left us. How could he do that? He can't just leave if we love him, can he? Didn't he care at all?"

Philip pulled the paper from her fingers and read it while she burrowed into his chest, grief rolling over her. She'd promised herself she'd let him go if he didn't want what she wanted, what they wanted, but now she knew she'd been a fool. A complete idiot.

She needed that piece of her heart with her. To feel. To love.

Philip tossed the note on the bedside table and wrapped her in his arms. He rocked her, whispering comforting words into her hair and holding her tight while she cried. His solid presence soothed her, but couldn't fill the hollow ache in her chest. It was a while until she eased away.

"Better?" he asked, concerned.

"No." She wasn't. She couldn't lie about it just to make Philip feel better.

"Me, either." Philip sounded angry.

Why was Philip mad?

Could it be he hadn't known she loved Mark?

If she'd thought her pain couldn't get any worse, she'd been mistaken. The loss of both her men, both her loves, would tear her apart. Pulling away from Philip, she knelt facing him, cupping his cheeks in her hands. She prayed he'd listen. That he'd remember and believe.

"I love you."

Philip's smile was fleeting, his gaze direct. "I know. I never doubted it."

Her relief was so great, she almost collapsed against him again.

He ran his hands up and down her bare arms, gave her a brief squeeze, and slid from the bed. "Now let's get the hell out of here."

She watched him walk toward the bathroom, confused. "Where are we going?"

"To find Mark and convince him to come back where he belongs. With us."

She sat back on her heels as relief and love poured through her. They were going to find Mark—and Philip looked awfully determined. She smiled a little.

Mark didn't stand a chance.

As tempting as it was to throw on the first clothes he could find and charge out of his house, Philip forced himself to slow down and shower. Not that he was funky, but there was something about the shower that helped him think. He needed to think.

Leaning against the cold tile wall, he watched Grace race

through her morning rituals before giving him a quick, albeit passionate kiss and charging from the room. She would be sitting and waiting for him by the time he was done showering. Then they would go to Mark.

And tell him what?

Standing under the hot spray, Philip tried to still his racing mind. He pictured Mark and Grace in the shower with him two nights earlier and smiled his first real smile of the morning. He needed to find a place with a bigger shower. Not that he minded how Grace and Mark's bodies slid along his, hips bumping, hands reaching out to steady each other as they made room to share or take turns under the spray of water. But seriously, one of them was going to slip and fall. And a bigger shower would hold so many...*possibilities.*

Possibilities. Funny how what wasn't possible once could suddenly become so. He wanted *two* people in his life. In his home. The fact that one of those people was a man, was Mark, had made it harder for him to admit, even to himself, but he'd known all along what the dull ache in his chest had been about. What the queasy feeling in his belly had really signified. It had been impossible a week ago, but a week was a lifetime, as far as he was concerned.

Staring down the barrel of a gun had clarified a few things. The man he'd been three days ago hadn't been so alive, so free, or been nearly so damn happy.

Or so scared. He'd been royally pissed off when he'd learned Mark had bolted, but the more he thought about it, the more his anger at Mark faded. Now he was mad at himself.

Grace had been ready to talk about what they were doing, what they were feeling, two days ago. He'd admitted he cared for Mark, hadn't he? When he thought back, he realized all he'd admitted was that it wasn't just sex, which wasn't much of an admission at all. If he'd been able to tell Grace the whole truth and had encouraged her to be equally honest, they might not have sent Mark fleeing in the middle of the night.

Then again, perhaps it wouldn't have made any difference. It could be Mark left because he needed space and wasn't interested in bunking with them. Maybe he thought it had all been a fun weekend diversion, a means for keeping safe and feeling good while they were at it.

Hell, it could hardly have been a more fucked-up weekend. Maybe extreme circumstances had led Mark to extreme decisions. Maybe now that it was over, Mark was seeing things more clearly.

Shit. That idea *really* pissed Philip off.

Mark was his. *His*, damn it. He'd seen the way Mark watched him. Watched Grace. He'd seen it long before Damian Benedetto had fucked up their lives. He couldn't have been imagining the looks. The longing. He'd seen it, had understood it because he was feeling it, too, even if he'd been too goddamn chickenshit to admit it. Maybe Mark was the one who was afraid now. Perhaps that's why he'd run.

Philip then remembered his off-handed remark the night before. The one about Mark returning to his apartment. He'd meant to clean up the mess. But what if Mark had thought he meant…

He shut off the water and dried himself quickly. The panic was back. Mark had run out into the night alone. He could be hurt. Or worse.

Philip had to find Mark. He had to tell him the truth.

Throwing on clothes, he raced from the bedroom, grabbed Grace's hand, and ran from the apartment. They arrived at Valentine's just as the glass company truck pulled away, leaving a pristine new window in the frame. They stopped their headlong charge to admire it but all Philip could see was Mark, hunched over a stack of papers in the booth they'd all cuddled up in two nights before. His hair stood straight on end, one hand running continuously through it. He still wore yesterday's clothes and, based on their condition, he'd either slept in them or never gone to bed at all. He looked awful, even from a distance. But at least he was safe.

Then he looked up, his stare glazed and unfocused, and

Philip saw his eyes were swollen and red rimmed.

He and Grace were through the door in an instant.

Mark had been staring at the same spreadsheet for an hour. After having run to Valentine's the night before, he'd stayed up and pulled together all the numbers for the insurance company. He hadn't slept a wink. Even now, when his brain was so fried with exhaustion and grief he couldn't see straight, he knew he couldn't sleep.

Because then he'd dream. About them.

Forcing the papers aside, he looked up, out over the bar, and tried to still his mind. He'd see Grace in a few hours when they prepped for dinner. He had to find a way to get through that, through the night in the kitchen, then maybe he could sleep the dreamless sleep of the truly exhausted.

"Mark!"

Turning his head slowly, he wondered if he was hallucinating. He'd thought of Grace and there she was, running toward him. Her beauty made him ache for her. And Philip, his huge frame filling the door, locking it behind him before he bore down on Mark like an enraged bull. He looked so damn good. So handsome and so...furious?

"What the hell is the matter with you?" Philip demanded.

Maybe he wasn't dreaming. His dreams wouldn't involve Philip yelling at him. No, his masochistic fantasies would take him back to each sweet moment he'd made love to these two incredible people.

"Philip." Grace touched Philip's arm, saying his name softly. Tears welled and, with a blink, coursed down her cheeks.

Mark's heart wrenched in his chest. Shit, it kept getting worse.

"Come here." Philip didn't wait to see if Mark would obey his command, but summarily hauled his ass out of the booth and onto his feet.

The moment his legs were steady, he stepped back. "What do

you want?" He'd meant to ask what it was he could do for them, but the question came out as a plea for mercy.

Philip closed the distance between them again. "You," he said. He sounded hurt. He said it as if he couldn't believe Mark didn't know. His fists curled into Mark's T-shirt and towed him forward until their chests bumped. "This."

The moment their lips touched, Mark lost the battle, thrusting his tongue past Philip's lips, his hands clasping the sides of Philip's head, holding him close. For that one moment, he didn't care if they only wanted him for play. He didn't care if they didn't love him.

Philip's strong arms wrapped around his waist, enveloping him in his warmth. His scent. It felt incredible. Real. But only because he wanted it to be.

Wrenching his mouth from Philip's, he pushed away and turned his back. "I can't," he said, his voice cracking. His heart breaking all over again. "I can't do this. I'm sorry."

His denial was met with silence.

When Grace spoke, her voice was soft. "Why not, Mark?"

He thought about lying. About telling them he didn't want anything more than a weekend. But the words stuck in his throat, bitter and vile. So he told the truth.

"I have to end it now. Before it hurts any more than it already does." He was grateful he had his back to them both. He'd thought he'd wrung himself dry, but the itch behind his eyes told him he might yet humiliate himself further.

He flinched when Grace pressed a warm hand to his back. He wished she wouldn't touch him, if only because he wanted her to so damn much.

"I don't know if it makes any difference, Mark, but this isn't about some weekend fling. This is about falling in love."

He turned around slowly, half convinced he'd misunderstood. Made it up. Imagined it.

"What?"

Grace stepped forward and took his hand. "I love you, Mark."

He stood still and silent. It took a moment to digest. Grace's thumb brushed over the back of his hand, giving him time to absorb what she'd told him.

Philip, however, was not as patient.

"Say something," he demanded, his voice fierce.

"I love you?" Mark said, his heart expanding in his chest. He'd never said those words aloud before to anyone.

Grace laughed and stepped into his arms.

"Is that a question?" Philip asked, clearly not so easily appeased.

"No, I'm pretty damn certain about it." He felt Grace's lips curve against his neck, watched how Philip's shoulders dropped before a smile teased the corners of his gorgeous mouth.

"Good," Philip sighed. He wrapped his arms around them both, pressing his cheek to Mark's. His solid warmth surrounded them and Mark was flooded with contentment. Relief. Love.

"Goddamn it, Mark, don't ever leave us like that again." Philip's stern voice tickled over Mark's skin, sending his blood south and his desire through the roof. There Philip went getting all possessive again. Mark wondered if he'd ever stop being turned on by that. By Philip. He doubted it.

"I won't," he promised.

"*Ever*," Philip said.

He leaned back to look into Grace's and Philip's expectant faces.

"Ever." He made the commitment gladly. Freely. They were his. He was theirs.

"And Mark?" Philip asked, his lips hovering over his, his eyes darkening.

"Yes?"

Philip's lips brushed his, "I love you, too."

It wasn't every day a man's wildest dreams came true, Mark thought as he drowned in Philip's kiss, but today was that day for him.

Check out a sneak peek and find out what happens when Patrick kisses his best friend...

Destiny Calls

Chapter One

He should have just stayed home.

Brandon swept his eyes over the crush of men around him, lingering on the more beautiful among them before turning to the man by his side. Brandon's already snug black leather pants grew even tighter as he studied Patrick's handsome face. Bright blue eyes fringed with sinful black lashes. Full, kissable lips. A rugged pink stain on pale cheeks. Dropping his gaze lower, Brandon admired the strong lines of Patrick's neck and the breadth of his shoulders. The way his thin sweater hugged the swell of his pectorals and accentuated the flat plane of his belly was sexy as hell. And those jeans. Jesus H. Christ, they looked like they'd been made to love Patrick's body, cupping his firm ass and hugging his long, thick thighs to perfection.

There wasn't much about Patrick that Brandon didn't find attractive. The man was gorgeous.

And it absolutely irritated the shit out of him.

He dragged his eyes forward again. Better to admire the men waiting in line around him than the one he'd arrived with. Better to admire just about anything other than Patrick.

Cursing his raging hormones and his now-regrettable choice in clothing, he shifted, trying to ease the ache in his cock where it was trapped behind hot, unforgiving leather. His tight white t-shirt was too short to hide much of anything, so instead he struggled to get his wandering thoughts and burgeoning erection back under control. The entire situation could have been funny, but after almost twenty years of reining in his attraction to Patrick, it had lost some of its humor.

He sighed, the sound lost to the noise of the crowd as they eased one step closer to the bouncer checking IDs and collecting the cover charge at the entrance to the Blue Door Tavern. Boston didn't have a lot of gay bars and the Blue Door only catered to this crowd one night a week. In hindsight, it was a complete mystery to Brandon how he had been talked into going out to see their friend's band play here, of all places, on a Saturday night, of all nights, with Patrick, of all the straight and beautiful people. He should have said no. He should have left town, claimed an illness, worked late, had a leg amputated—anything rather than end up surrounded by hot men he barely noticed because he was so hung up on the one standing right next to him. The one he couldn't have.

Stupid, stupid, stupid.

He looked again, trying not to flinch when Patrick dug his ID and money out of his pocket, pulling the soft denim tight across what Brandon knew to be a considerably sized cock. Not that he had ever gotten any up-close-and-personal time with said member, but having gone to high school, college, and the police academy together, he'd seen Patrick without his clothes on enough times to fuel a lifetime of fantasies.

Patrick glanced at him and he snapped his eyes back to safer places above his friend's neck. Shit. It wouldn't do to get caught staring.

With one last shuffle forward, they arrived at the door and paid the cover charge. Brandon was careful to keep his shield hidden as he pulled out his wallet and flashed his driver's license. They weren't here on business. They were just two old friends out to see another buddy's band.

Once inside, they had to fight their way to the bar. The place was a mad house. Charlie's band had a good following, but the real numbers came from the men who had so few options for a safe, fun night out on the town. Massachusetts may have been on the cutting edge of gay rights, but the nightclub scene remained seriously limited. Saturday night at the Blue Door was worth the hassle, if for no other reason than the sheer number of people forced a lot of bodies up against each other. If he'd been out with anyone but Patrick, Brandon might have worked his way around the room just to check out who was there. Instead, he slid onto the bar stool next to his best friend.

"Nice work snagging this space," Brandon said, pitching his voice to be heard over the house music. Charlie's band wasn't slated to take the stage for another half-hour.

Patrick smiled at him, laughter dancing in his eyes. "I can't take the credit. I got the impression that the young men who vacated these stools were headed to the bathroom for more intimate pursuits."

Brandon laughed and shook his head while Patrick ordered their beers. Anonymous bathroom sex—or any bathroom sex, for that matter—had always been a mystery to Brandon. He'd had his share of short-term flings in college, with both men and women, but he'd never been a one-night-stand person. In the decade or so since college, he'd been in two serious relationships—almost two years with Nina and a little more than a year with Derek. But since the thing with Derek had ended, he'd joined the Organized Crime Task Force of the Boston Police Department, which had eaten up a lot of his time. He loved his work, but right now it didn't allow for much in the way of a social life.

He'd once thought a man with the advantage of being equally attracted to both sexes would have little trouble finding someone with whom to connect, but that wasn't the case. He could, of course, try harder, make more time, but he found he was comfortable with his life as it was. And countless fantasies about Patrick helped him ease the ache when needed.

Which was abso-fucking-lutely pathetic.

He sighed again, feeling like the idiot he knew he was. He had to let go of his thing for Patrick. Patrick was straight. He was also completely aware of Brandon's bisexuality and had been since high school. If Patrick had ever entertained thoughts about trying a taste of the other half of humanity—the male half—he'd never so much as hinted at it to Brandon.

Which sucked. But on the bright side, thinking about how he'd never have Patrick was totally killing his erection.

Spinning on his stool, he leaned back against the bar. There were at least a hundred single, attractive men in the room, and a handful of women, too. He should find someone, brush off his somewhat rusty flirting skills, and see what could happen. It could be good. It could be great.

It could be that the king of unrequited love was giving himself pep-talks in his own head and still couldn't psych himself up enough to pick his ass up off his bar stool.

Damn it. The truth was that the prospect of meeting someone left him completely cold. Someone wasn't Patrick.

Once again, abso-fucking-lutely pathetic.

Determined not to be a complete loser, he renewed his efforts to find an interesting face in the crowd. He almost cringed when his eyes locked with those of a huge man dressed in full biker leather strutting directly toward him. Long strings of frizzy black hair hung over a beat-up leather vest, charmingly accented with nothing more than sallow, bare skin and lots of coarse chest hair curling over the neckline. Filthy jeans hung limp, presumably from a belt that was lost beneath the swaying bulge of his belly. And while the wardrobe was regrettable, it was nothing compared to the look on the man's face. Yikes. His beady eyes ate up Brandon like he was the all-you-can-eat roast-beef buffet at the Elk's Lodge.

Whirling back to face the bar, Brandon dove into the debate between Patrick and the pretty bartender about the Red Sox's chances at the pennant this year and prayed Big Ugly Biker Dude would go away.

When an enormous paw landed on his shoulder with a painful thump, Brandon barely resisted the urge to slump his head down onto the bar. Why him? He really wasn't in the mood to deal with this.

He briefly toyed with the fantasy of spinning around and telling the guy to take a hike, but he knew it wouldn't be wise. Instead he straightened, plastered a smile on his face and looked over his shoulder. "Yes? Can I help you?"

"I'm buying you a drink," Big Ugly Biker Dude informed him and at least twenty people in their immediate vicinity.

Brandon tried not to let his revulsion show. It wasn't easy. And it didn't help that, after casting a brief glance over his shoulder, Patrick stayed facing the bar. Some wingman he turned out to be. Brandon could see Patrick's smirk out of the corner of his eye, his delicious dimple winking. The jerk was laughing at him.

Brandon kept his focus on Big Ugly Biker Dude, his smile and his voice courteous. "No, thank you. I'm all set."

Completely ignoring him, Big Ugly Biker Dude looked at the bartender. "Get him another of whatever he's drinking."

Brandon turned to catch the bartender's eye. "No, thank you. I don't want that drink." He hated the look of sympathy she sent him. Patrick's hand came up to rub over his lips, obviously trying to suppress a grin. Brandon shot him a dark look.

Facing Big Ugly Biker Dude once more, he dropped his smile and spoke firmly. "Thank you for your offer, but I'm not interested." Praying that the guy would take the hint when it was smashed over his head, Brandon turned back to the bar and took a swig of his beer.

The bottle nearly fell from his hand when that huge, sweaty body pressed along the length of his spine, wet lips drizzling spittle as the Big Ugly Biker Dude spoke directly into his ear. "I'm buying you a drink, boy, and then I'm going to take you to the men's room, bend you over, and shove my entire fist up your ass."

Brandon's eyes automatically fell to the ham-sized hand clenching the edge of the bar. There was a black crust embedded under the jagged fingernails, and thick, nicotine-stained calluses, flaked white with dead skin, lined his fingers.

Brandon shuddered. Good god, the horror.

When the butt-ugliest man in the entire bar had made a beeline for Brandon, Patrick had almost busted a gut trying to hold in his laughter. Only Brandon. The poor guy hadn't gotten laid in months, and the first man to offer to remedy that was this giant mass of stink and grease. It was nothing short of hilarious.

He'd figured Brandon, who even Patrick had to admit was blessed with the face of an angel, had plenty of practice beating back unwanted advances. So rather than help, he'd left his friend to his own devices and sat back to enjoy the show. Only because of their long years of friendship had he been able to see the revulsion, and he'd admired how well Brandon hid it from his...err...gentleman suitor, keeping his green eyes wide, his smile polite. The guy hadn't backed down, though, and Patrick had gleefully anticipated Brandon dropping his nice-guy act and telling the guy to fuck off. When he was riled, Brandon was every bit as intimidating as the hardened criminals they worked to take off the streets.

To say the guy had then invaded Brandon's space was like saying the Pope was just a little bit Catholic. The man's body had pressed the length of Brandon's, his lips brushing against Brandon's blond curls. Patrick had actually started to get a little irritated by this guy. Hell, maybe more than a little. It had to be pushing Brandon to his limits.

But when the guy announced his intentions for their trip to the men's room, Patrick could do little more than sit with his mouth hanging open.

His whole fist? Seriously, that was just way over the line.

Standing, Patrick rose to his full six foot five inches, deliberately taking up as much space as possible by pulling his shoulders back and anchoring his hands on his hips. While Brandon's strength in tense situations was his ability to play it cool and smooth things over, Patrick knew his best asset was pure physical intimidation. He was a damn big guy and he didn't hesitate to use it to his advantage when needed. It went a long way toward encouraging assholes to leave him the fuck alone.

Looking down, he locked eyes with the creep trying to wrap himself around Brandon's rigid torso. He had an almost violent urge to shove the man away, to force his oily hands off Brandon's body. Suppressing that impulse tightened his chest and forced his voice down to a growl.

"You need to back off. Now."

Cold little brown eyes narrowed. "Why should I?"

Patrick didn't blink but his mind scrambled for a response. He needed a way to end this quickly and without creating a scene. The truth—my friend isn't interested in your nasty skank ass and you mauling him like that is really starting to piss me off—wouldn't do. He could just imagine the guys down at the station being called in to break up the fight at the gay bar and finding two of their fellow officers right in the middle of it. File that under "Not Pretty".

No, a fight, though sorely tempting, had to be avoided. Instead, he tried the other obvious way out. "He's with me, asshole, and I'm not in the mood to share."

If he hadn't been working so hard to look big and mean, he might have cracked a smile when he glanced at Brandon. It was hard to say who looked more incredulous—Brandon or his biker friend. Fortunately, Brandon's face was hidden from everyone except Patrick and the bartender.

Regardless, Brandon's new boyfriend wasn't buying it. "I've been watching you two. Your pretty boy here," he snarled, thumping a hand against Brandon's back, "has been scoping out the scene, while you've been more interested in your beer and the hot number behind the bar."

Well, crap. He had to give the creep high marks for powers of observation, but goddamn, he was not going to be caught out by this idiot. Reaching out, he manhandled Brandon from his stool and spun him around so they stood together, a united front. He looped his arm around Brandon's waist, clenching the soft black leather covering Brandon's hip and hauling him close.

It was a damn good thing Brandon was an expert at fronting a calm façade, since shock radiated from every inch of his body.

"Just because I like to flirt with the bartender doesn't mean he's not with me," Patrick said.

The big man laughed. "If you're gay, I'm the Queen of England."

"Nice to meet you, Liz. You look different in People magazine," Patrick shot back, his mouth outdistancing his brain for a moment. Damn it. He gave himself a mental kick in the pants and told himself to shut up. As often as Brandon's quick talking had gotten them out of a fix, Patrick's big mouth had gotten them into one. He needed this to not be one of those times.

Predictably, his wit was lost on their biker friend. "You're not funny. And you're not gay."

"I am so gay!" he declared vehemently, ignoring the stares from the people around them. They were starting to draw quite a crowd. Not good. He briefly wondered if anyone believed him. It didn't help that Brandon's entire body had convulsed with suppressed mirth when he'd declared his homosexuality. He shot his friend a dirty look.

"If you two are together, prove it," the biker challenged.

He turned back to the ugly man. "What?"

"Prove it," he said, gesturing to Brandon. "Kiss him."

Brandon's head snapped up, his eyes wide.

Damn. He should have seen that coming. One of Brandon's brows lifted and Patrick could practically hear Brandon's thoughts—What are you going to do now, you idiot? His mind raced, trying to answer that very question. Too bad he was coming up blank.

Fuck it. How bad could it be?

Turning, he speared his free hand into Brandon's thick, dark blond hair, the curls tickling his fingers as he cupped the side of Brandon's head. Brandon's eyes bulged, his mouth falling open. He didn't say a word out loud, but his face practically shouted, You wouldn't dare.

Patrick never could refuse a dare. After all these years, Brandon ought to know that.

Tightening the arm around his friend's waist, Patrick pulled Brandon's long, firm thighs up against his own, their hips bumping. The crowd around them fell silent, watching. Waiting. Holding their collective breath in anticipation.

Patrick wasn't going to disappoint. Dropping his head, he pressed his lips over Brandon's.

The first kiss was quick, a rubbing of mouths, Brandon's totally immobile beneath his. It was weird but not awful. Brandon's lips were firmer than any woman's had ever been. And actually, it was kind of interesting, since for the first time in his life, Patrick's big frame wasn't dwarfing the person in his arms. Brandon's tall, lean body fitted against him perfectly.

In the spirit of wanting to end the stand-off decisively—and knowing that one peck wasn't going to cut it—he dipped his head again, running his mouth along Brandon's, catching his lower lip before letting it go. The fine stubble tickling his chin and his palm where it cupped Brandon's jaw was distracting. Not bad, but...different. His heart started beating a little faster, the blood humming in his veins. He watched, fascinated, as Brandon's gaze lost focus and his eyelids dropped to half-mast. Not pushing him away, but not actually kissing him back either.

He was about to let Brandon go, hoping their new biker friend was suitably convinced, when a wave of motion rippled through the dense crowd, emanating from the stage and forcing their audience back toward the bar. Brandon's hand shot out, gripping the bar as he turned his back to the room, but the momentum of all those bodies crushed together was too much and the weight of the crowd pushed him forward. In an instant, Patrick's back was pressed against the bar as Brandon's lips, chest, hips, and legs were all crushed to his.

Sweet Lord, Patrick's libido had always had a short fuse, but never in his life had anything just flipped his switch.

Until now.

Brandon's erection ground against him, the heavy shaft straining against leather and through denim. It shouldn't have felt so good. But it did.

A very small part of Patrick's mind thought he should be horrified, but his own cock pressed back, surging with blood and desire to match the press of Brandon's rigid length. Another very small part of his mind thought he should resist no matter how good it felt. Brandon was his best friend, his pal. His bud.

The rest of his mind was thinking, fuck yes!

When Brandon's mouth opened beneath Patrick's lips, rational thought fled in the face of a tidal wave of desire.

Patrick's fingers came back up and threaded into Brandon's hair, holding his head at the angle he wanted it, needed it, while his tongue plunged into Brandon's mouth. Brandon met the assault head-on with one of his own. Their tongues met and clashed, warred and retreated. Patrick's muscles knotted, the need escalating, his cock so hard he could barely stand straight. He wrapped his arm around Brandon and pulled him closer, so that their hips collided again and again, the length of their cocks rubbing each time Brandon's hips twitched in response to the thrust of their tongues. Brandon's whimper rang through Patrick's head like a bell, drowning out the sound of their audience hooting and hollering their appreciation.

The kiss was wild. Carnal. Blood rushed from his head, flooding through his aching cock before tracing fire through his veins.

God, Brandon tasted good. Familiar and different. The strength of Brandon's arms, his sheer size, his flavor and texture. It was like Patrick's first kiss all over again. A world of discovery in one lip-locked moment. Heat poured through him, thrumming with rough need.

The big ugly guy was gone. The crowd was gone, the music, the bartender with whom he had, indeed, been flirting. He lost track of them all, no longer caring if they were near, if they watched, if they even existed. There was only Brandon.

Who is, Patrick thought with a last grasp at reason, my best friend. Should it feel this hot? Taste this good? He sank deeper into Brandon's mouth and into the kiss, even as his brain sent its last reasonable transmission.

This was probably not a good idea.

Also by Samantha Wayland

Destiny Calls
Fair Play (Hat Trick #1)
Two Man Advantage (Hat Trick #2)
End Game (Hat Trick #3)
Crashing the Net (Crashing #1)
Home & Away
Out of Her League
Checking It Twice (Crashing #2)
Take a Shot
A Merry Little (Hat Trick) Christmas (Hat Trick #4)
Breaking Out
Traded Out
Poetry in Motion
Changing the Rules (Crashing #3)

About the Author

Samantha Wayland has three great loves in life: her family, writing books, and hockey. She is often found apologizing to the first for how much time and attention is taken up by the latter two, but they forgive her because they are awesome and she clearly doesn't deserve them.

Sam lives with her family—of both the two and four-legged variety—outside of Boston. She is a wicked passionate New Englander (born and raised) who has been known to wax rhapsodic about the Maine Coast, the mountains of New Hampshire and Vermont, and the sensible way in which her local brethren don't see a need for directional signals (blinkahs!).

Her favorite things include dirty martinis, tiny Chihuahuas with big attitude problems, and the Oxford comma.

Sam loves to hear from readers. Email her at samantha@samanthawayland.com, visit her website at www.samanthawayland.com, or find her on Facebook (Samantha Wayland), Twitter (@samwayland), or Instagram (SamWayRomance). She also spends time in her reader group on Facebook, Sam's Wonderland.

Be sure to sign up for Sam's newsletter to hear about sales and new releases. You can sign up via her website!

Made in the USA
Monee, IL
01 March 2022